CW00969704

ALWAYS REMEMBER

CATHRYN GRANT

INKUBATOR
BOOKS

PROLOGUE

Frank leaned his head against the silken oak boards behind him, allowing the heat of the sauna to settle more deeply into his skin. The pleasure was indescribable, the first real pleasure he'd experienced since his double bypass.

He took a sip of whisky, grinning over the top of the shot glass. "Thanks for this. I know I shouldn't, but ..." He took another soothing swallow of the fiery liquid, the heat of the alcohol a perfect companion to the hot, dry air filling his lungs and the sweat oozing from his skin. Without turning, his gaze fixed on the rectangular container filled with large, smooth rocks, he said, "I appreciate you fixing me up like this." He raised his glass but didn't drink.

He could feel his brain settling down, easing away from the agitation of being so long away from work—eight weeks, and he was only three weeks into it. The surgery and recuperation were bad enough, but the forced abstinence from the pleasures of a nice whisky, or wine paired with a steak dinner, and the physical release of sex were almost too much. Still, better than the alternative.

Numbness was very welcome right now.

The voice beside him seemed to come out of nowhere, and he wasn't sure if he'd drifted to sleep for a moment, or his sense of time was distorted by the heat and the whiskey. A little too much whiskey at this point. "I need to—"

He straightened his back, tilted his head to release the tension in his neck, and laughed softly. "No worries. I'm fine by myself for a few minutes. It was inevitable you'd have to go after downing all that water. Like I told you, it doesn't really prevent dehydration if you piss it all away." He laughed. It felt good to let out a bellowing laugh.

The sauna door opened and closed. He was alone. He preferred it, actually. Now, his thoughts could wander without being pressed into conversation.

He took another sip of his drink, closed his eyes, and leaned his head back again. The complete muting of distant traffic sounds, shouting children, and the occasional noise of unwanted music drifting over backyard fences was one of the things he'd always loved about the sauna. He wasn't sure why he'd never built one of his own. Leave it to his son to try to one-up him with the creature comforts of a slick, high-tech home and a rather lavish pool and sauna.

He placed the empty shot glass on the bench beside him and shifted his position slightly. He was proud of Wyatt; he shouldn't view it as one-upping the old man. He should look at it as evidence of the kid's success, although he wasn't a kid by any stretch, heading fast toward his forties.

Frank moved his legs and readjusted the towel around his waist, the only thing between him and the oak bench. The sweat seemed to be pouring faster down his neck and spine, almost like someone stood behind him, splashing warm water over his back.

Straightening his posture didn't help. In fact, it was worse, because now he couldn't quite feel the floorboards against the bottoms of his feet. God Almighty, it was hotter than hell. He laughed, then stood. The sudden movement made him feel light-headed, and he pressed his hand against the wall to steady himself. He felt the towel slip, and he grabbed the end and tucked it in more securely.

He stumbled toward the door, feeling as if he wasn't breathing adequately. What was wrong with him? Was the room truly growing hotter, or was something going wrong with his body chemistry? The edges of his vision were fuzzy and slightly dark. A few shots of whiskey had never hit him like this before. And it wasn't as if he were a newbie to saunas. He expected the heat, welcomed it, but this was making him feel as if his blood vessels were pumping fire into every cell of his body. He wanted to scream, but he was so damn tired.

Falling against the door, he grabbed the handle and pressed down. The handle moved easily, but the door didn't open. He shoved his shoulder against the door and leaned harder on the handle. The door moved slightly, but then slipped back into place. He shoved harder. Pain shot through his arm as bone and muscle slammed into unyielding wood.

"Hey!" He rattled the handle. His hands were incredibly weak, and he wasn't sure his legs were going to support him much longer. The light-headedness was increasing. He threw himself against the door. He wrenched the handle up and down, hearing the latch click open and closed. It wasn't locked. Why wouldn't it open? Was he so weak he couldn't push open a wood door? Of course it was heavy—solid wood, well-sealed to create the perfect interior atmosphere, but he hadn't had any trouble pulling it open when he'd stepped inside.

He shoved his shoulder against it once more, but it felt like he barely tapped it. He was gasping for air. The heat was so intense he wanted to scream. He wasn't a child. He wasn't going to cry for someone to help him; he wasn't going to ... he coughed, the spasms becoming stronger, bile rising to his throat. He couldn't seem to get air into his lungs. Maybe there wasn't any oxygen left in this place.

He was delirious; of course there was oxygen. He just didn't have the strength to draw it into his lungs.

"Help! Please help me. I need to get out." He slammed his fists on the door, but it felt like he was slapping the wood with a dead fish. "Please. Please ... I need ..." He'd never experienced heat like this. He was being cooked alive—that dead fish tossed into a pan with a thin layer of sizzling oil on the bottom. He gasped again.

It seemed as if someone was holding the door closed. Was that possible? Did someone hate him so desperately they wanted him to suffocate inside a tiny room that was meant for pleasure, but had now revealed its potential to become a death chamber? The door wasn't locked, and it wasn't stuck, because it had moved in the frame. Someone was indeed holding it closed.

Before he could let out a cry of rage, his chest grew tight, his heart squeezed by an invisible force. He pressed his hands against his chest, frantic to keep the organ working. He heard something that sounded like a groan and a faint scream coming out of him. Then, it felt as if his heart exploded. He fell to the floor. Darkness filled his head, then nothing.

1

KELLY

The tray looked beautiful with a white plate in the center. The plate held whole wheat toast smeared with marmalade, scrambled egg whites, and three slices of cantaloupe. Beside it was a pale blue cloth napkin and a cup of tea.

I always placed a vase containing a single rose on the tray. Frank never thanked me for the rose, hadn't even mentioned it after the first day I'd brought breakfast to the room that used to be my home office. We'd temporarily converted the office into a bedroom so Frank didn't have to climb the stairs, giving him a bright, spacious place where he could recuperate from surgery. Although he said nothing, I still liked bringing him a rose each morning. I firmly believed that kindness went a long way, even with someone as off-putting as Frank.

My father-in-law was a difficult man in several ways, but I'd always tried to treat him with kindness, and I could tell—despite his lack of gratitude for the rose and even the breakfast delivered to his room every morning—that he appreciated the healthy meals and the space in our home. If we hadn't opened our house to my in-laws, they would have had to commute three hours from the north bay to Stanford Hospital for the follow-up appointments after his double bypass surgery.

I picked up the tray. Outside Frank's door, I set the tray on the narrow hall table and knocked. "Dad?" My tongue stumbled slightly as I spoke the uncomfortable and still unfamiliar word.

There was no answer. It was seven ten. I was late. Frank liked breakfast at seven on the dot, but I'd burned the first slice of toast and had forgotten to turn the kettle on for his tea. I knocked more firmly. "Dad? Frank? I have your breakfast."

There was no response. I knocked harder and turned the doorknob at the same time. The door swung open, revealing an empty room. I stepped inside, staring at the neatly made bed, the comforter I'd pulled tight the day before, when Frank had moved to the armchair in the corner where he spent quite a few of his daytime hours. It was obvious he hadn't slept in the bed after I'd made the bed and arranged the throw pillows along the headboard in the order I liked. The adjoining bathroom door stood open.

I backed out of the room. Where had he gone? He wasn't supposed to start going for outdoor walks until Monday, after his second post-op checkup. Had he gone upstairs and slept with Louise? It made sense that he'd miss being with his wife. At the same time, their marriage wasn't overly affectionate, from what I'd seen over the years. I stepped back into the room, looking at the shelf in the nightstand. His cell phone, wallet, and keys lay on the shelf.

Leaving the tray behind, I hurried down the hall and jogged up the stairs. Louise's bedroom door was closed, as was the door leading to the master bedroom. Because it was Sunday, Wyatt was sleeping late. Opening Louise's door was out of the question. My mother-in-law cherished her privacy and never neglected to tell me when I'd overstepped. I sighed. This was important. It could be considered an emergency. I turned the knob quietly and cracked open the door. Louise was lying with her back to the door, alone in the bed. I pulled the door closed. I had a mild sensation of being outside my body, watching my movements, as if I would need to recall them to report to Wyatt later.

It wasn't as if Frank were a prisoner and he'd escaped, but everyone knew he wasn't supposed to leave the house. He knew that. He'd been surprisingly good about accepting the limitations outlined by his doctor. He'd eaten the food I prepared and never once asked for something that wasn't on his meal plan. He'd been relatively content in his room— reading to his grandsons, playing online chess, and watching the news, getting up hourly to move around the first floor of the house and the garden, regaining his strength.

I hurried back down the stairs and walked through the rooms. They were all filled with dim morning light, drapes and blinds still closed, the rooms tidy and obviously unused. I stood in the kitchen, trying to think what I should do next. Even though his keys had been on the nightstand shelf, I looked out the front window to assure myself that Frank and Louise's Lexus sedan sat primly in the driveway.

I went out to the backyard, scanning the bench under the magnolia tree and letting my gaze wander over the still water of the swimming pool. The only sounds were the songbirds. I glanced across the pool at the tiny changing room and the sauna. Frank knew the sauna was off-limits for his damaged heart.

I walked slowly along the side of the pool, wondering if anyone was awake, watching me, wondering what I was doing walking so slowly past the pool at that hour of the morning. I grabbed the handle on the sauna door and pulled.

The oversized door moved toward me. A rush of hot air came from the darkened room. The last time Wyatt and I had used it was three days earlier. It shouldn't still be so hot. My gaze flickered toward the floor. As if my body already knew what I might find, the apple I'd eaten while I prepared Frank's breakfast spun inside my stomach. Then, apple and bile and the remains of last night's dinner rushed up my esophagus. I turned, letting the vomit spill onto the concrete outside the sauna.

Frank's body lay on the wood floor. He was on his side, his eyes staring directly at me, but not acknowledging me.

2

When I saw Frank's body, hideous and utterly without dignity, I screamed in a way I never had. I allowed near-hysterical sobs to pour out of me. "No. Oh, no, no, no! This can't ..." I stepped inside and knelt beside him. My impulse was to shake him, checking whether he was dead, but I recoiled from his pasty skin. All that skin. Except for a dark green bath towel that had come loose when he collapsed, he was completely naked. I couldn't look, didn't want to see, but I had to ... I stood suddenly. I needed to call 911. Now that my vision had cleared, I saw the skin of his face resembled the color of wet cement. I turned and stumbled out of the sauna, vomiting again, a thin stream of liquid that was so sour my throat clenched.

It was shocking to see a man who had been so sure of, almost pompous about, his perceived virility collapsed in a pile of bones and stiffening muscles that could only be described as grotesque.

Wearing only boxer shorts, Wyatt stood at the opposite end of the pool, just outside the family room door. I was struck by the healthy, living shade of his skin. "Why were you screaming? Are you okay?" He hurried toward me and put his arms around me. "You're shaking."

"Frank is ... your dad ..." The words were thick and strained; my throat raw. "He ..."

Wyatt stepped away from me. "What's wrong?" He glanced toward the door leading from the patio into Frank's room. "Why are you out here?"

I stared at him, feeling sick, but there was nothing left inside my gut. "He's not in his room. He ..."

"Then where—?"

"In the sauna." My whispered words came out slowly.

Wyatt started toward the open door of the sauna.

"No." I grabbed his arm. "Don't go in there. He's ..." I swallowed hard. "He's dead."

"He can't be. The surgery was—"

"He's on the floor. His eyes are open. Please don't go in there. It's awful. You don't want to see."

He pried my fingers off his arm. I grabbed him again, trying to pull him toward me. He yanked away and stepped inside the sauna.

"Oh, God." Wyatt's voice bellowed, filling the yard. "Dad!"

I didn't want to see Frank's body again. Not ever. I feared the image of his eyes, clear and unmoving, slightly filmy, that sickening color of his skin, the utter lack of movement would glue itself inside my head for years, maybe forever. But I couldn't leave Wyatt in there alone. I moved closer to the door.

"Mommy!"

I spun around. Sam and Nick stood in the doorway of the family room. "Where's Daddy? He said we can watch TV in your bed."

I ran toward our sons, my bare feet slapping the concrete. "Go inside."

"Where's Daddy?" Nick's voice was commanding. It

shocked me every time, hearing that sound of authority coming from a three-year-old. Sometimes—most of the time —it made me laugh. Not now. I reached the twins and put a hand on each of their shoulders. "You can stay in the family room and watch TV there. Is Nana awake?"

"Nana said to find you."

I pulled the boys close to my side. "Let's go inside. I'll get you a snack."

Once Sam and Nick were settled in front of the TV, a fleece blanket across their legs, cups of yogurt-covered raisins in their hands, I stepped back out to the yard, stopping just outside the doorway. I looked across the expanse of the pool.

As if she'd materialized out of nowhere, Louise now stood a few feet from the entrance to the sauna. She hadn't truly just appeared in that spot, obviously, but I hadn't been aware of her coming down the stairs, moving into the backyard to find out what the disturbance was. I'd been focused on making sure the twins weren't yet aware their grandfather had died. I didn't want them to realize something awful was unfolding in their backyard.

Louise leaned against Wyatt. He had his arms around her and appeared to be holding her up. I hadn't heard her cry out, and I wondered if Wyatt had stopped her from entering the sauna, as I'd tried to with him.

I took a deep breath and walked along the side of the pool, feeling my pace slow as I dreaded what might happen next. I still felt ill, my fingers numb, my bones like sticks of ice. My own parents had died when I was away at college. I'd never seen their bodies and had never considered what they might have looked like. In their case, death had created a feeling of nothingness, the debilitating awareness that people you loved were no longer occupying their space in the world.

This was different because Frank's corpse was right there, so ugly. Seeing the lifeless body had shaken me to the core.

For now, that image of his flesh in a melted heap on the ground, those vacant, frozen eyeballs, was so consuming there was little room for anything else.

I stopped a few feet from where Wyatt stood with his mother. Their bodies were so close, they looked like a single form. His hand gripped her hip, his fingers half-hidden within the folds of her pink bathrobe. Her feet were covered with the thick, fluffy socks she wore with her robe. Her hair, expertly colored in various shades of blonde to obliterate the gray, was limp from sleep. It clung to her skull.

The concrete seemed to grab at my feet, keeping me from moving closer, as if I weren't meant to interrupt mother and son facing the small building that held the body of husband and father. I wasn't sure if I should speak, if I should stand beside Louise and put my arm around her, or go to my husband. Louise and I had never been very affectionate toward each other, giving airy hugs and perfunctory kisses when she and Frank came to visit. Louise reserved her affection for her son and her grandchildren.

I sighed. There was no way of knowing whether Louise would shrug off any attempt at comfort. Finally, I moved closer. "I'm so sorry, Louise."

She didn't turn to acknowledge me. If anything, she snuggled closer into the circle of Wyatt's arms. She whimpered softly, while Wyatt remained stoic.

What was going through his mind? He'd had a difficult relationship with his father, especially after he'd learned that Frank had cheated on Louise, again, when Wyatt was away at college. The news, delivered by Louise in a late-night phone call to Wyatt, had split father and son apart. Wyatt didn't speak to his father for several months. After a while, taking the lead from his mother, who was determined to keep her marriage together, he'd developed a polite, sometimes friendly attitude toward his father. After an initial conversation with me, in which Wyatt condemned his father, his very personhood, he'd never wanted to discuss how he felt about the man. I wondered if his stoicism now came from shock more than actual grief. A shock that would eventually be overtaken by something unpredictable.

I moved closer until I was beside Louise. I patted her shoulder. We stood for several minutes, no one speaking. Finally, I cleared my throat. "We should call the paramedics."

Louise let out a short, bitter laugh. "Too late for that."

"I meant—"

Speaking over me, Louise said, "I suppose someone has to be called. Can you take care of that, Kelly?"

Wyatt turned his head to look at me. He gave a single nod.

Feeling as if I'd been dismissed, excluded from their private moment, I went into the kitchen and got my phone. I dialed 911 anyway because I had no idea what the process was for reporting a death. Then I went out front to wait for them to arrive, slowly and without sirens.

3

KELLY

The funeral for Frank Brooks, philandering husband, doting grandpa, successful businessman, oppressive father, and admired friend, had been attended by nearly three hundred people. Quite a number of them made the two-hour drive from Santa Rosa to our home in Palo Alto. There was a reception at the church with cookies and coffee. A smaller group of mourners had been invited to our place for a buffet supper.

Surveying the living room and looking out at the backyard, hearing voices from the family room, the group did not seem all that small. There were over fifty people wandering about, small plates of food and plastic wineglasses in their hands.

I was glad for the work. I'd ordered the food from a catering company, but keeping the platters replenished, making sure the wine bottles were opened, and picking up discarded napkins and utensils created a pleasant numbness in my body. I was able to move about quickly without engaging in lengthy conversations, still managing to make sure everyone felt welcome. I liked the way the tasks that needed taking care of prevented me from thinking too much.

The boys were kept occupied by a few older kids, children of Wyatt's childhood friends. Wyatt had asked Chris—Louise and Frank's attorney, who had become a family friend over the years—to stay by the pool to be sure the children stayed well away from the edges. It was easy, in a setting like this, for everyone to think someone else was looking out for the children. Too often that was the cause of tragic accidents.

I removed a fresh package of sliced turkey from the fridge, unwrapped the paper, and arranged it on the nearly empty platter. I carried it to the table and wiggled it into the empty space that was just big enough. I stepped away from the table and picked up the glass of white wine that I'd left on the breakfront while I put out food. I took a sip and let my gaze wander past the table, through the open doors into the living room.

Wyatt stood near the front window, talking with a brother and sister who had lived next door when he was growing up. At six two, Wyatt towered over them. His dark hair, which hadn't been trimmed in the midst of the chaos of the past few days, grew over his collar, curling at the ends. Seeing those curls made me want to cross the room and slide my fingers through his hair, but that wasn't appropriate funeral behavior, so I folded my arms and pressed them against my ribs to still the impulse. Every few minutes, he laughed, generously and loudly. Although I was too far away to see, I imagined his dark, almost black eyes glinting as they did when he laughed. The sound was reassuring. Since the moment Wyatt had seen his father's lifeless body, I hadn't heard him laugh once, not even when Sam or Nick did something silly or made one of their wise, adult-sounding pronouncements. He moved as if he were shrouded in thick fog, focused on making sure Louise received plenty of attention and support.

He and I had stayed up late that first night, talking about Frank. Wyatt kept repeating himself, a mantra every few minutes, as he paused between recalling memories—*He knew he shouldn't be in the sauna. Why would he go in there? Especially alone?* Then he returned to telling me about pieces of his childhood, staring blankly at the wall across from our bed as he talked. The sharp, sudden awareness of the finality of death—something that couldn't be felt viscerally until someone close to you was ripped out of your life—consumed him.

Still, despite pouring out an endless stream of stories from the past, he hadn't said much about his feelings about Frank's year-long affair with a woman he'd hired as a consultant for his marketing team all those years ago. He talked about how it nearly destroyed his mother, how he admired her ability to repair their relationship, how his father hadn't deserved his mother. All of his conversation centered around Louise's feelings and the impact to her life; nothing about his own emotions. I didn't push him. I'd wanted him to feel free to speak whatever was on his mind, not feel cornered by questions he didn't want to deal with yet, maybe ever.

I took another sip of wine and slipped out of the dining area. In the kitchen, I wiped a smear of potato salad off the counter, tossed a few dirty plates into the trash, and nibbled a chocolate chip cookie. My appetite had been weak, possibly suppressed by the steady flow of adrenaline over the past few days, the funeral arrangements, and preparing for so many people to come into our home.

I wandered out to the backyard. Louise and Chris sat beside each other in two Adirondack chairs facing the pool, Chris focused on his assigned duty despite being deep in conversation with Louise.

I stood a few feet behind them, aware it was creepy to eavesdrop, but not caring if any of the other guests noticed. I wanted to hear what Louise had to say when she wasn't filtering her words for my sake. With all the people milling around, Louise and Chris seemed to have lost any awareness that they weren't alone. Their voices were not softened, and they didn't appear to glance around to see whether anyone might be listening.

"It's still feels unreal," Chris said. "I've never heard of anyone dying in a sauna. It's almost hard to believe that's what happened." He stared at the pool, placing his hand along the top of his sunglasses to decrease the glare from the water, which he was studiously keeping his attention on. "I guess the heat was too much for his heart."

"We won't know anything until we get the autopsy report," Louise said.

Chris nodded. He ran his fingers through his hair, still dark except for a few streaks of gray on the sides, even though he was in his early sixties. From where I stood, I noticed more gray across the top. I'd never seen it before because at six three, the top of his head wasn't visible to most. "You wonder what that stubborn guy was doing in a sauna when he was recovering from a double bypass." He shook his head.

"Frank did whatever he wanted. He was always like that," Louise said. "From the day we met."

"There's doing whatever you want, and there's watching out for things that might kill you. Two different ideas."

Louise sighed. "Kelly was so strict with him." She gave a short laugh. "I think he was feeling like a prisoner. She treated him like a child. Maybe he needed to feel he still had some shred of control over his life."

"I thought he'd asked her to oversee his diet."

"Well, she took it a little too far. Not even a glass of wine allowed with his dinner? Forced to sleep on the first floor so he didn't need to climb the stairs?"

"That's all good," Chris said.

Louise giggled.

"What's so funny?"

"He was sneaky." Her giggle turned slightly bitter. "He had a drink the night before he died. A shot of whiskey, but he didn't tell her about it."

"How do you know? Were you his enabler?" His laugh started Louise laughing again.

It was jarring. I'd enjoyed hearing Wyatt laughing earlier, but laughing about the man who had died? Sure, laughing as you recalled pieces of his life was a good thing, healthy even. But laughing about the circumstances of his death? The man you were supposed to be mourning?

"It's good to hear you laugh," Chris said.

Louise stopped immediately. "I didn't mean to. It feels like there's something wrong in my brain. Laughing when I should be crying, forgetting things."

"It's all normal."

"Don't take it to mean I'm not broken by this."

"I know you are." Chris took his hand away from his forehead and placed it over hers, which was resting on her thigh.

She didn't push him away. She almost seemed to settle into him. It was a very subtle move, but it looked like her body oozed toward his. Or maybe I imagined it.

"And I'm here for you, whenever you want to talk. Or need to talk. You know that, don't you?"

She nodded.

"Day or night."

"Yes."

"Especially at night. A beautiful woman like you ..." He turned toward her, taking his eyes off the pool. "You won't be alone for long."

Louise stiffened. "My heart only belongs to one man," she said.

Chris nodded, keeping his gaze focused on the side of her face. She turned slightly to look at him.

"If something changes," he said, "you let me know. Okay?" He kissed her forehead, then dutifully turned his attention to the pool.

I took a few steps back. What was that about? Was he flirting with her? It was an extremely weird thing to do at a funeral. Especially with the widow of a man you'd supposedly been close friends with for years. At the same time, Chris was a charming, good-looking guy. And he had a certain style. Knowing him, his behavior toward her hadn't seemed as creepy as his words sounded.

What struck me even more was Louise's proclamation of her heart belonging to one man. It was dramatic. Maybe she'd just been trying to get Chris to back off, but I didn't think so. There was something flamboyant about the way she'd said it. Something phony. Although Louise had managed to make her marriage work, at least on the level of companionship and shared friendships and interests, Frank's affair had changed her. After it had happened, she was cold toward him. Not in a rude or punishing way, just cooler. Less passionate, no longer in love. She seemed more self-contained and less dependent upon him.

I knew I shouldn't have been so critical, but I also believed my opinion was correct. Louise's heart had not belonged to Frank for many years. And it was ridiculous of her to say it had, no matter how much his death had gutted her. Yes, she'd lost her life partner and the focal point of her home, the cornerstone of her social life, but it wasn't the end of a passionate, forty-year romance.

4

LOUISE

I've always believed that the best way to deal with tragedy, or even with major disappointments, with any unwanted situation, is to take the focus off yourself. Give yourself to others. Doing so frees you from self-pity. It fills your heart with warmth, and it has a way of softening the edges of pain. I've experienced this firsthand many times. Truthfully, it's the secret to a happy life.

The best way to get my mind off Frank was to focus on the family I had left.

I wouldn't indulge in self-pity because I was suddenly a single woman. My husband was gone, and although I was well-taken care of financially, I would have to figure out the rest of my life and where I fit in. Our marriage wasn't perfect, no marriage was, but we had each other for company. Now, though, because our social life had involved so many other couples, I'd become the fifth wheel.

I tried very hard not to indulge in those thoughts, although they did occasionally pass through my mind as I lay in my bed and felt the permanent state of sleeping alone.

Since I was always one for a challenge, I'd thought I

would start my journey forward by helping my daughter-in-law. She hadn't been the easiest person to get along with, although not for a lack of effort on my part. Since the first time I met her, I'd felt a coolness from her, bordering on dislike. I never had figured out what she didn't like about me. Over the years, watching Frank dote on her, almost flirtatious in the way he touched her shoulder or the comments he made, I wondered if that was what caused her chilly stiffness. Since Frank and I were a boxed set, she took out her annoyance with him on me. For a long time, it had been clear she didn't care much for either one of us, but she treated him with respect. I suppose because he was a man.

When I tried to ask her whether either of us had offended her in some way, she was vague. I'd finally accepted that was who she was—vague and standoffish. Cold. You can't change other people, so it's best to learn to live with what you're given. Another secret to life, I believe.

Kelly wanted what she wanted, and that made it difficult for me to like her sometimes, but I tried. And now, after she'd been accommodating enough to prepare the doctor-ordered meals required to keep Frank healthy, although it hadn't helped in the end. It's impossible to keep a man like Frank doing what he's supposed to. I had accepted that.

Kelly had not only cooked for him, she'd invited us into their home for the duration of the surgery and the prolonged recovery. I was quite sure that the impetus for that had come from my son, but Kelly had agreed, and I had to be grateful for that. I wanted to be a positive force in her life.

Near the end of the reception following my husband's funeral, I'd gone inside the house to get out of the sun. I was in the kitchen, cleaning up a bit, even though everyone told me I should just relax. It wasn't a party for me. I didn't feel right sitting around doing nothing, as if I were the guest of honor.

Kelly was in the dining area, a plastic glass of wine in her hand, as it had been for the entire afternoon, talking to a longtime friend of hers. This woman—Janelle—had been Kelly's roommate in college and was employed by the same organization where Kelly had worked before the twins were born.

Kelly was going on and on about how she missed her career. I'd thought she relished being a stay-at-home mother. In the few weeks Frank and I had been living there, and in the years before when we got together with the four of them for holiday dinners and birthday celebrations and occasional family vacations, she'd never said a word about it. I'd suspected she wasn't a born nurturer like I was, and she was proving me right. Still, I understood. She adored her children, but her career made her come alive.

Before the twins were born, Kelly had been a motivational speaker. She worked for a boutique—as she called it —organization that offered speakers with various styles and backgrounds, custom-fit to organizations looking for speakers at retreats, dinner meetings, and other events. Kelly gave inspirational talks about recovering from losing her parents at a young age. She also spoke about personal development and believing in your dreams. Or something like that. It all sounded a little fluffy to me, but she made quite a lot of money doing it, so maybe I was missing something.

"I do miss it," Kelly said. "I'm one of those women who wants it all."

"Lots of women feel the same way," Janelle said.

"I love every bit of being a mom. Nick and Sam make me laugh every single day. And their curiosity is almost thrilling, seeing how much they want to learn about the world. But I feel this pull. I want to be with them, but I want to be with other adults. I want to feel like I'm growing. I want that charge that comes with standing in front of a group, and the adrenaline of being in the office, sharing ideas, all of that."

"Maybe you can come back part-time. Especially since they'll be starting preschool soon."

"Maybe. I think about it a lot, but I can't seem to make a decision. It's only a few more years until they're in school most of the day, so ..."

"There's no rush."

I moved away from the door. I didn't want one of them to come into the kitchen and catch me listening. Kelly wouldn't take that well.

Hearing what Kelly had said made me see how I could do something for her. I could let her bounce her thoughts and confusion off me. I could share the wisdom that comes from being older. I could guide her if she would be open to it. And I had a few thoughts on balancing a career with motherhood as well.

A week or so had passed since the funeral. I was still disoriented and slightly hollow feeling, but our lives were settling into a routine. The timing seemed right. Our constant discussions about the terrible and strange way that Frank had died were finally fading as we all accepted reality. At least I'd accepted it. Possibly, previous scares with Frank's heart had readied me for the inevitable. It wasn't as if a single week had healed my heart, but simply that I felt a return to somewhat normal habits and thoughts.

I spoke to Kelly while she was fixing breakfast for Sam and Nick.

"Kelly, I was thinking, why don't you and I go out for lunch today?" It was a Saturday, and usually Wyatt and Kelly took the boys to the park or on some other outing, but Wyatt could easily do that by himself, giving Kelly and I some quality time together. That might have been part of the problem between us. We rarely spent time alone with each other.

"Sure. I guess." She looked at me with a slightly confused and possibly suspicious expression. She almost looked stoned—I was intimately familiar with that blank look from when Wyatt was a teenager. After a long pause, she said, "Where were you thinking?"

"Wherever you'd like. We could get dressed up."

"I'm not sure if I—"

"We could even go to San Francisco."

Kelly laughed. "I don't think so. How about Carpaccio's? The place we all went for Frank's sixty-sixth, remember?"

"Whatever you want."

She smiled at me and nodded, but didn't say thank you.

It was twelve thirty, the middle of the lunch rush, when we were seated at our table. I'd been lucky enough to reserve a table by the front window. Someone had canceled right before I called. It made me think this was meant to be, a tiny confirmation that I was doing the right thing—reaching out to my daughter-in-law, trying to build bridges, working to become closer to her, to try to be a more valued part of her life.

We each ordered a glass of red wine, since it was a treat to be out for a nice lunch—me in high heels and a dark green dress and Kelly wearing gladiator sandals with Capri pants and a long, silky white top. We looked quite nice. Seeing our reflections in the lobby mirror, I'd realized I didn't quite look old enough to be her mother-in-law, more like a mature friend. My daughter-in-law was a beautiful woman. She had black hair that was cut to her shoulders in wavy layers. Her blue eyes were stunning against her dark hair and pale coloring. She was taller than I was, about five seven, and she kept in good shape, doing laps in the pool every day, starting up again only two or three weeks after she'd given birth, and continuing in every season.

Kelly took a quick sip of water. She let a small cube of ice slide into her mouth and chewed it.

I folded my hands and placed them on the table. "I wanted to thank you for taking care of Frank. I know he was a difficult patient."

"Not at all. Knowing how he could be, I thought he was cooperative and easy to please."

I stared at her, wondering if she was telling the truth. She was not an easy person to please herself, so I couldn't imagine her thinking my husband was an easy man to care for. But why would she lie about that? I narrowed my eyes, trying to read her expression. It was impossible, but something about her felt off. Maybe she thought that was what I wanted to hear. Maybe she and Frank had come to an understanding. She might have been trying to be nice, not speaking ill of the dead and all that. Maybe there was something going on below the surface of her smooth, composed expression that I knew nothing about.

She talked more about Frank and his sudden, unexpected death. I was starting to think she was a little obsessed with how he'd died. While Wyatt and I mourned our loss in our own way, Kelly wanted to marvel over the gruesome details. Thankfully, our appetizers and wine arrived.

Once the waiter left us alone, I got right to the point. "I know eavesdropping is rude and a bit disgusting ..." I paused when her face changed from a pleasant smile to something rigid. I took a breath. I wasn't sure what that was about, but I pushed on. "Forgive me, will you?"

She nodded and picked up her wineglass. She took a sip and held it in front of her.

"I heard you telling Janelle how much you miss your career."

She gave me a weaker smile.

"I understand that."

"But you never had a career," she said. "Which is fine, I'm not criticizing you."

"I know." I took a bite of bruschetta and chewed it slowly. "That's why I think I have some wisdom here. It's wonderful to raise a child ... children, to be devoted to nurturing and shaping them. And you're doing a good job."

"Thank you."

Her words sounded clipped. It seemed as if she didn't believe me. I really did not understand why she was so suspicious of the simplest compliment. "Children grow up so fast, it makes your head spin."

"So I've heard," Kelly said.

"You have no idea. You're literally buried in toys and peanut butter sandwiches one day, and the next, they're asking for the car keys. It truly feels like that. And then, when they're gone, and the house is empty and silent, you realize you want a life of your own. If you've been too involved with them, you can miss out on that chance."

She laughed. "I'm not planning to stay home until they're in college."

"I know. It's just something to think about. Children are happy when their parents are happy."

"That's true." She took a sip of wine, then leaned back as our meals were placed in front of us. She gazed into the distance. After a few bites of her linguini with clams, she spoke. "We would need to hire a nanny, because we aren't planning on starting them in preschool for a while."

"Of course. But for now, I'm here. That would give you plenty of time to find the right person, someone who could remain part-time to pick them up after school."

She nodded.

We talked about other things: the boys, mostly, and a bit

about the guests at the funeral. She had deliberately changed the subject, and I didn't have another opportunity to encourage her further, but in the end, I realized I'd said enough.

That night during dinner, Kelly announced to Wyatt that she thought it was a good time for her to return to work. She actually had the grace to give me credit.

"Louise convinced me," she said. "And I really do miss it." She looked at the twins seated across from me, side by side in their booster chairs so they looked like tiny adults. "And of course I'd miss these guys, but before we know it, they'll be in school. And sports. Wanting to be with their friends, not Mom." Her eyes were watery as she smiled at them.

They looked slightly confused about this summary of their future, but they didn't say anything. They probably had no idea what she was talking about.

Wyatt placed his fork on the plate and looked at Kelly. "I think it's great timing. You don't want to get stale. They say kids thrive when they have a variety of caretakers. It makes them more flexible."

"And I'm here, for now," I said. "So you can take plenty of time to find the right nanny."

Wyatt grinned at me. He looked at Kelly as if he wanted to kiss her. He wasn't oblivious to the simmering tension between Kelly and me, tension that flared up from time to time, and it was heartwarming to see how he basked in knowing Kelly and I were getting along better. Maybe once she was satisfied in her career and had some balance in her life, the whole family would feel better. We could all move forward with our lives instead of reliving the lingering horror of seeing my husband's dead body on the floor of the sauna. I grabbed my wineglass and took a long swallow, hoping to blot out the image.

I glanced at Wyatt. He looked normal, happy almost, for

the first time since that awful morning. When I saw the pain in his expression, I wondered if he blamed Kelly for Frank's death. She'd volunteered to look after him, to ensure his return to health. Of course, she couldn't have known he would flout the rules and sit in a burning hot room, but still. It must have crossed Wyatt's mind that Kelly could have been more on top of things.

5

WYATT

Watching the change in Kelly as she began to ramp up her career gave me a good feeling. It made me feel like I had my wife back. It made me wonder if I shouldn't have been more perceptive, should have encouraged her more to create the life that would be most satisfying to her.

Kelly was an incredible mother, but twins are utterly exhausting and draining. They require nonstop attention in a way that parents of single children can't begin to comprehend. Not that those demands had cooled any in the five weeks she'd been back at work, or that they would any time soon, but not having to wrangle the boys all day long, seven days a week, made her calmer. When she was with them in the evenings and on the weekends, she was more attentive and patient and, best of all, more playful.

I had my mom to thank for that. We both did.

Dinnertime, when we all reconnected, was so much better. My mom cooked delicious meals, and Kelly and I could listen together as Sam and Nick interrupted each other, fighting for center stage to tell the stories of their day. On the weekends, Kelly and I took the kids to various parks, to the beach, and to the zoo as we always had, but now Kelly wasn't worn out from a week of caring for them on her own.

In those few short weeks, I'd also seen a change in the boys. They accepted that Mom wasn't their security blanket and pacifier and favorite stuffed toy all stitched up into one human being.

I was thrilled Kelly was doing this. After seeing my father yanked out of the world as he had been, I was focused, maybe too focused, on how short life was, how suddenly it ended. You move through your days thinking you have all the time in the world. It feels almost like eternity, there's so much time stretched out in front of you. It's incredibly easy to think you'll take care of things *later*. You and your wife will slip away for that exotic vacation, definitely next year. You'll sign up for a personal trainer to really get into shape, probably after your next birthday. You'll take the kids to one of a thousand fascinating places—to splash around and hunt for frogs in a mountain creek, to learn how much fun it is to hike, to ride on a pony. You'll get back to giving more in-depth time to your music, maybe take a private guitar lesson to refresh, and even advance your skills. I had no doubt I would do most, if not all of those things, but I'd never seen them as urgent. I'd thought they would happen organically. Now, I understood I had to make things happen.

Seeing my father defeated by his own body and his own arrogance—a man who had never let anything defeat him— had shaken me more than I would ever have imagined. It was difficult to believe he was gone. Sometimes, it felt as if someone had crept into our home and snatched him out of our lives while we slept. It was shocking to think about his business being consumed by his partners, money paid out to my mom, and the accounting firm moving on to acquire new clients that would never know him. Now, I understood the finality of death that everyone had talked about, as I realized I'd harbored an unrecognized hope that someday, my father might change, and our relationship could improve. Now, that potential was erased from my life.

During my morning commutes, when I was going for a run or a solo bike ride, when I was lying awake at two in the morning, wondering if I should just call it a night and get a head start on the glut of email that came from Europe and Asia every damn night while I was in bed, I wondered when my own life would end. How many years were left? Would I be one of those unlucky guys who dropped dead at fifty?

Did I feel any passion for my career? That was something I didn't even want to think about. But I knew Kelly loved hers, and I was thrilled that she was finding a way to enjoy our kids and live her own life at the same time.

It was a Friday afternoon, and Kelly was having dinner with her colleagues. She would be home after the twins were in bed. I'd left work early to mow the lawn and play with Sam and Nick before dinner, planning to catch up later on my laptop. At least, that was the plan.

I walked in the front door and found my mom standing in the entryway, a triumphant grin on her face. "I have a surprise for you."

"I was going to mow the lawn."

"That can wait. Come on." She grabbed my hand and began pulling me toward the double doors at the left side of the entryway, which led to my home office. I liked working there on the occasional Saturdays when I had to answer a few emails or work on reports. I could look out the picture window and watch the kids racing by on their scooters or balance bikes, admiring the way Kelly ran after them, egging them on, inspecting their bumps and scrapes when they fell, her low-key reaction forestalling tears.

I let my mother drag me toward the office. She let go of

my hand and flung open the doors, lifting her arm in a flourish. "Ta-dah!"

"What?"

"Look!"

I stepped inside the room. It was disorienting for a moment. I felt like I'd walked into someone else's house by mistake, or was in a dream. The desk and computer were gone. The credenza was gone. The framed photographs that Kelly and I had taken on our honeymoon to France and Italy were gone.

Mom had pulled my guitar out of its case in the closet. She'd bought a metal rack to hold it upright, and it now stood alone in the corner, the focal point of the room. There was a dark blue leather loveseat facing the front window, and a matching armchair to the right of the window that faced the side yard. Beside the guitar was a wooden chair that looked like it was sturdy and comfortable, allowing for hours of practice. There was a small table with brand-new notebooks and a container of fancy pens.

I continued to take in the changes—framed posters of popular musicians, mostly lead and solo guitarists. There were a few nicely arranged freestanding shelves attached to the wall that held old-looking sheet music in box frames and antique percussion instruments. "What is this?"

"Isn't it obvious?"

"Where's my desk?"

"You work enough in the office. You don't need to be working at home."

She was right about that. I turned to look at her. The grin was slipping to the side, a look of worry twisting the corners of her eyes. She spoke quickly, her words rushing at me. "You have a lot of talent, Wyatt. I think it's important to have a place dedicated to your music if you want it to have an important place in your life."

My mind raced back through the years, recalling how I'd loved playing my guitar, remembering the reams of notebooks I'd filled with chords and song lyrics. Remembering my father telling me that writing *poetry* was not something a guy should be spending his time on. The only benefit to a practice as delicate as poetry was to get girls. Sure, guys who played in bands got girls too, but a man should have a respectable career. A man needed work that earned him admiration from people who *mattered*, and allowed him to build a solid financial portfolio. Money was power. Trying to get there with a guitar was playing the lottery, and in fact, according to Frank Brooks, the odds in favor of success were even slimmer than those for winning the lottery.

"I miss hearing you play," she said.

"I still play."

"I haven't heard you since I've been here."

"There's been a lot ..." I felt my chest tighten as I thought about my father. My mind raced to a flash of paranoia that I was having a heart attack. Like him. He always wanted me to be like him, and maybe he'd willed his damaged cardiovascular system to me. I pushed the thought away, attributing it to the craziness, the near madness of loss. We didn't even know for sure yet whether his heart had killed him. It might have been something else.

She put her hand on my arm. "I hope this will inspire you to get back to it. You have a lot of talent."

"So you've said."

"Not just me. Others have said it too."

She was also right about that. My music teachers had said the same. The few people who had hired me to play background music at engagement and anniversary parties when I was fifteen and sixteen praised my ability. Kelly had often told me I was talented over the years we'd been together. I loved playing for myself and occasionally for Kelly. Mostly I fooled around to relax, and it worked like magic. But I didn't need an entire room for that.

At the same time, the look of the room was inspiring. It felt so much better than the office. It felt like the other parts of my life, beyond making and managing money, were important. I put my arms around her shoulders and gave her a hug. "Thanks. It looks really great. It makes me think about getting back to writing lyrics. Being creative would probably be good for my brain—stretch it a bit." What I didn't say was that it might be worthwhile to put my angry, despairing, confusing thoughts about my father to music.

"Yes." Her voice sounded like she was crowing. I wanted to laugh.

I stepped away from her, walked to the couch, and sat down. "Very nice. When did you do all this?"

"Oh, the boys love to go shopping. And some if it I picked out online. I have to do something when I'm alone in my room at night." She laughed softly. "It was fun. I hope it inspires you to bigger dreams."

"What do you mean?"

She crossed the room and sat beside me. She put her hand on my knee and turned slightly to look at me. "Wyatt, you are very, very talented. Everyone said that. Your father made sure to suffocate that in any way he could, so consumed with forcing you into his mold."

I nodded.

"Now that Kelly is working, it wouldn't hurt you to take some time off. Companies will give people a leave of absence." She looked at me, holding my gaze. "It's not like you have to walk away forever, but you need to give your music a chance. If you don't do it now, you never will." Her expression was solemn, waiting for my agreement.

When I didn't speak, she continued. "You'll have to discuss it with Kelly, obviously. But I can't imagine she wouldn't want this for you. I know she loves hearing you play."

"She told you that?"

She smiled and moved her head, although it wasn't clear if she was confirming what I'd said. "You're so caught up in your career, you've buried your creativity. You don't even notice what an impact your music has even on your own family."

She was making me feel things I hadn't experienced since I was a teenager, filled with hope, but hiding it all from my father. I hadn't wanted to hear him mock me. More clearly than I remembered many of my baseball wins, wins that were celebrated fiercely by my father, I remembered him finding one of my notebooks filled with lyrics. I remembered walking into the living room. I could still see it—the afternoon sun cutting across the room, making everything white, while he sat in a shimmer. The minute he saw me, he began reading the words I'd written, a song about whales and their quiet majesty. He read the words in a ridiculous, high-pitched voice, slaughtering the pronunciation, deliberately altering the rhythm of them so the song sounded awkward and childish and amateurish. Maybe it was. But I felt my skin burn and knew my face and neck were dark, vicious red, the heat spreading to my chest and shoulders. I'd grabbed the book out of his hands. I'd taken it out to the trash and stood beside the open bin, ripping out pages and tearing them into strips before I let them flutter into the depths of the container.

"Helloooo? Where is everyone?" Kelly's voice came from the kitchen. She'd come in through the side door in the garage and was walking through the family room.

I stood, realization striking me. "Where are Sam and Nick?"

"Watching TV."

"Where?"

"In my room."

"Don't get upset about the extra TV time. Please. I wanted to surprise you, and I knew they would be out of the way if I settled them there."

"What happened to your desk?" Kelly was standing in the doorway. "Where's the computer?" She looked around the room, shrugging off the little jacket that matched her pants, exposing her sleeveless top and her tanned, nicely toned arms.

I wanted to run my hands down her smooth skin. I shook off the thought. "Mom turned the office into a music room. Isn't it—"

"I can see that." Her voice was hard and clipped. She turned to my mother, the skin of her face blanched. "This isn't your house, Louise. You don't get to redecorate without consulting us."

"I didn't redecorate." My mother laughed shrilly. "I just—"

"You bought new furniture. You bought new artwork. You redecorated."

I stepped between them. "Okay. It's ... let's talk about it calmly."

Kelly spun toward me, speaking in a softer voice. "I'm talking calmly. Don't patronize me."

My mother got up and came toward me. She stood close so I could feel her shoulder against my arm. "Your husband is a very talented man."

"I'm aware," Kelly said.

"Now that you have an income, it's a great opportunity for him to take some time off to see where his music might take him."

"I don't disagree with that," Kelly said. "But you're

changing the subject. You shouldn't be rearranging and redecorating without talking to us about it."

"I can put it all back," Louise said. "I was trying to do something nice. You don't need two offices, and the room where Frank was sleeping will be put back the way it was, I assume."

"It's too late. Just leave it." Kelly turned and started toward the door. "Where are Nick and Sam?"

"In my room, watching—"

"You know I don't like them watching TV in the afternoon. And they absolutely shouldn't be doing it in your room." Kelly walked out, slamming the doors closed. I heard her jogging up the stairs.

Dinner was quiet, the silence between Kelly and I overridden by the chatter of our kids. My mother had said she wasn't hungry and would eat a piece of fruit in her room so we could have some time as a family. Kelly whispered to me that my mother was being dramatic. I cooked an easy stir-fry, and Kelly and I cleaned up together. We didn't say much, but she did quietly repeat what she'd suggested earlier—if I wanted to take some time off and work on my music, it was okay with her.

Later, in bed, she ranted for several minutes about my mother acting as if the house belonged to her, insisting she had no right to redecorate or change things around on a whim. "But maybe it doesn't really matter, because you need to find out when she's planning to leave."

I moved closer and placed my hand on the side of her head, pulling it toward my shoulder. "She's lost without my father. Give her some time."

"She doesn't seem all that lost to me. She had plenty of energy to redo our house."

"Come on, Kel. She didn't redo our house. She moved a few pieces of furniture and some artwork."

"It's the principle."

"Yes, she should have asked. But it was a pretty awesome surprise. And it's incredibly inspiring for me. Can you focus on that?"

"Maybe."

We slid down under the covers, and after a while, I started unbuttoning her nightshirt. She moved toward me, and her hands and mouth told me everything was more or less okay. I wasn't going to ask my mother when she was leaving. I knew she would return home when she was ready. It was cruel to push her.

6

The night after Kelly went crazy over the music room, I hardly slept despite my pills. I'd arranged it to encourage my son, to make him happy. It was heartbreaking to watch his joy slowly collapse as Kelly complained that I had no right to change a single thing in their house, as she chipped away at the anticipation I'd seen on his face just a few minutes before she walked into the room. It was so frustrating and, honestly, very hurtful that she always thought the worst about me. I kept trying to give her the benefit of the doubt, to be kind to her, but she still had such intense dislike for me.

Lying in bed, I stared into the darkness for over an hour, trying to decide whether it would be best to put the room back the way it had been. Wyatt had been so happy, so inspired, and she'd stolen that from him. I didn't see how he could get that feeling back. Now, every time he went in there, even if he was able to lose himself in his music, the experience would be tarnished by the knowledge that Kelly was upset about it.

Finally, I decided to leave it alone, for the simple reason

that I couldn't move furniture around in the middle of the night without waking the whole family. But I still couldn't sleep. I thought about taking a second sleeping tablet, but it was two in the morning, and that would make me drowsy during the day. I needed to be alert and full of energy for my grandsons.

In the morning, after Kelly and Wyatt had left for work, I buckled the boys into the child seats I'd purchased for my car and went to the grocery store. I was confident that making some of Kelly's favorite foods might help her stop focusing on the things I did that upset her. I loved cooking, and it was no trouble to grill salmon and make a delicious sauce for her. On the way home, I stopped at the bakery and bought tiny Bundt cakes for dessert—white chocolate with raspberry cream. She loved those little Bundt cakes.

Breaking another one of her rules, I let the boys watch three half-hour cartoon shows while I set a nice table and got everything ready. Once Wyatt arrived home and could look after the kids, I would prepare a fabulous meal.

Dinner was surprisingly pleasant. Kelly raved over my salmon. I'd known she would—I knew the secret for keeping it moist but flaky. And I'd sautéed the asparagus with garlic to spice it up, which she loved.

After we ate, Wyatt said he would clean up while Kelly and I took the boys to the park a block and a half from their house. She and I walked, hardly talking to each other, which is easy when you have two lively, curious three-year-old boys offering their observations of the world, talking almost without stopping, finishing each other's sentences. I loved that about the twins, how sometimes it felt as if they shared a single mind. I don't think Kelly found it as fascinating. She was big on making sure the boys were fully aware of their individuality. She never wanted to dress them in matching clothes, and she'd chosen names that didn't have any sense of belonging together, part of a set. I might have named them Nick and Nate, or Sam and Scott, but Kelly wanted them to know they existed apart from their sibling.

The boys were climbing on the webbed rope structure when Kelly's cell phone rang. She looked at the screen. "It's Janelle. I should take this. She wouldn't call in the evening if it weren't important."

I waved her away. "I have my eye on them. Go ahead and take care of whatever you need to."

She smiled at me, but her eyes were slightly vacant. I noticed that in her from time to time, a sudden blanking out as if she were somewhere else. But maybe she was simply thinking about the call. She started walking toward the picnic table area, and I turned my attention back to Nick and Sam. By now, they were close to the pinnacle of the structure. They waved down at me, grinning with the unfettered delight that makes childhood appear so magical to adults. I pulled my phone out of my pocket and snapped a picture of them together. Then I moved the camera to get individual shots, which Kelly would appreciate.

The boys climbed down and came over to the bench where I was sitting.

"Where's Mommy?" Nick asked.

"She had to take a phone call."

"Why?"

"It was someone at work. She thought it might be important."

"Why?" Sam crawled onto my lap.

I put my arms around him, feeling his hot, slightly sweaty body, the pleasure of it making my heart beat more deeply. I was so lucky to have these wonderful boys. They made me smile every time I saw them. They were so sweet and so devoted to me. I tried to remember to be grateful every single day.

"Is she going to work?" Nick asked.

"No. She just has to take this one call. It will only be a few minutes."

"Why?"

I laughed. The endless *whys* of preschoolers. They were entertaining, thought-provoking, and sometimes endlessly frustrating as each *why* built on the previous one, bringing me to the point where I couldn't answer the question. "Sometimes Mommy and Daddy have to work," I said. "That's how they get money for your house and beds and toys. Money for food and vacations."

"And for TV," said Nick.

"That's right. But no matter where they have to go, Nana will never leave. I'll always be right here, so you don't have to worry."

Sam wrapped his arms around my neck and kissed my jaw. I squeezed him tight, pulling Nick closer at the same time. "Other people come and go, but Nana will always be here for you. Don't ever forget that."

"Why did Poppa leave?" Sam asked.

"He's dead, remember?" Nick said.

"Where did he go?" Sam asked.

I thought for a moment. Kelly was firm that all questions should be answered, no punches pulled. She and Wyatt believed children absorbed what pieces they could, and it made them more aware to be given complete answers, the details filling in as their understanding grew. They did not want anything *downgraded to baby-speak*, as Wyatt called it.

"When someone dies, the person you love, their voice and the things they remember and everything they said and did —which is their soul—goes to heaven or hell. Their body turns back into the earth. That's what happens with animals and even plants." I pointed to a nearby tree with a branch that had fallen on the ground. "That branch died. And it will slowly crumble and become part of the ground, like the mulch in your mom's vegetable garden."

"What's heaven or hell?" Nick asked.

"Heaven is where you go if you're good. If you listen to grown-ups and are kind to your friends and do nice things and live a good life, you go to heaven. If you're bad, you go to hell. It's very hot there, with flames that burn your skin, and you always remember the bad things you did to deserve it."

"What are you *doing*?" Kelly's voice was almost a shriek behind me, piercing my ears and making me flinch.

She came around the bench and yanked Sam off my lap. As if she'd rescued him, he cried out, "Mommy!" He clung to her neck.

"I don't want you scaring them with beliefs that Wyatt and I don't share," Kelly said. "You know that."

"You and Wyatt told me I should answer their questions honestly." I stood and picked up Nick. He squirmed to get away, and I let him slide down my body until his feet touched the ground. He ran to the play structure.

"Nick! It's time to go," Kelly called after him.

He didn't always, but this time, Nick immediately turned and ran back to his mother. Maybe he'd taken to heart that he needed to be good if he wanted to avoid the flames of hell.

She put Sam on the ground, took their hands and began walking, leaving me to catch up, trailing behind as if I didn't belong. I followed them all the way to the house and into the entryway. Kelly hustled them up the stairs, talking cheerfully about their baths, leaving me behind without even a thank you for watching them while she took care of whatever issue had come up at work.

I wandered into the kitchen and filled the kettle with water. I turned it on and dropped a peppermint teabag into my favorite mug—the one with a beautifully painted angel on the side. Wyatt had given it to me for my birthday, years ago. I'd brought the mug and a few other favorite items when we'd come to stay with Wyatt and Kelly before Frank's surgery.

The tea was steeping, and the running water in the tub above the kitchen had stopped. I could hear faint shrieks from the boys. I lifted the teabag out of the water, drained it, and dropped it into the trash. I added a tiny splash of bourbon to assist the peppermint in calming my nerves. I turned off the light and started up the stairs just as Wyatt was coming down.

"Having your tea already? It's only seven."

I moved to the side so he could continue down the stairs before I started up. I didn't want to bump and jostle the tea. I moved the mug to my other hand. "I'm a little tired."

"Is everything okay?" He stopped on the bottom step and looked down at me, seeming enormous since he was already eight inches taller than me at six two. It filled me with awe when I looked at him and saw what a strong, confident, wonderful man he'd become.

I sighed. "I can't do anything right."

"What do you mean?" He leaned against the railing.

"Kelly is so upset that I fixed up your music room. And now—"

"It's okay. She's fine with it."

"That's part of the problem. The mood swings. She was furious; now she's fine. I'm told to speak to the boys one way, and when I do that, I'm criticized just the same. It's exhausting."

"We're all raw right now."

I looked at him, wondering if he really believed that was the problem. I was raw. Wyatt was raw. But Kelly? And yes, things were unsettled since Frank's horrible, puzzling death, but the issues with Kelly weren't new. She'd never liked me. She tolerated me. Most of the time. I took a deep breath. I would not focus on that. Wyatt was right. "I'm sorry. You're absolutely right. You know, I've wondered if she's dealing with a bit of trauma."

"Trauma?"

"Because she was the one to find Frank. The shock must have been awful. Seeing death when you didn't expect it. And it was so ugly. Like soldiers or crime victims." What I really was thinking was—did Wyatt ever pause to think about his father's death and wonder, even for a moment, whether Kelly had been negligent or worse? Had it ever crossed Wyatt's mind that Kelly might have been tired of caring for his flirty, aggressive father and decided to hurry him along to his grave? Did it occur to him how easy it would have been for her to lure him into the sauna?

"You mean PTSD?"

"Yes."

"That's a little extreme. We all saw his body. She wasn't any more traumatized than you or I."

"But she *found* him. You and I were slightly prepared because we heard her screaming, because she told us he was dead. It must have been so awful for her."

Wyatt stared at me for a moment. "Hunh. Maybe."

"Anyway, I'll try to do better, to show her more kindness. But right now, I need some sleep. I'm going to take my sleeping pill and drink my tea. I'll be as good as new in the morning."

Wyatt leaned down and kissed my forehead. I walked up the stairs, careful to keep my hand steady so the tea wouldn't splash out.

7

KELLY

Driving home from work was one of my favorite parts of the day. I suppose a better way to put it was that I didn't hate commuting like most people did. The traffic, even when it crawled, soothed me with its almost musical rhythm. I was in a cocoon where I could think about my day, settle my thoughts on that front, and then begin looking forward to the reunion with my family. It made every day a celebration—the welcoming hug and lingering kiss Wyatt and I had made one of our rituals since we'd been married felt even better when I greeted him and our children together.

Now, my mind was still back in my office, recalling the faces of my colleagues in our small conference room, the rise and fall of their voices in nearby offices, absorbing their energy.

It was one of the things I loved about my job—it never felt like work, even when I was thinking about it after hours or on the weekends. If my thoughts weren't focused on some of the upcoming speaking events that had been discussed that day, I found myself crafting my next talk, tweaking it so that the ideas were always fresh, even for me. Especially for me. If it was fresh for me, it would feel custom-designed for each member of the audience.

I loved standing at the front of a room filled with engaged, interested people, telling stories, feeling their interest and unfolding inspiration. I don't know what that said about me. Was I an attention whore? Needy? Arrogant? Harboring narcissistic tendencies? I certainly hoped not. But some degree of arrogance is required to be a motivational speaker. Any career where you forge your own path is the same. Wyatt required a certain amount of arrogance to believe he played the guitar well enough to dream of making money at it, or to write songs, believing he had things to communicate in a way no other person yet had.

Analyzing myself to this degree was never a good idea. It made me anxious. I just liked speaking in public. There was no need to overanalyze. I liked the way I'd fallen into it as if it were meant to be—working in HR for a large company right after college, and finding I was naturally drawn to any opportunity to stand in front of a group. The energy made me feel like I was transported out of my body.

The day had been hectic, as we'd gone over the calendar of new speaker requests. I hadn't yet gotten any of the plum jobs, the larger crowds, because they were usually longer conferences that required overnight stays. Wyatt and I hadn't discussed when I would start traveling. I hadn't brought it up because I knew I wasn't ready to be away from my precious children more than seven or eight hours at a time. I doubted I would be ready until they were in kindergarten, possibly older. But I had beat out Janelle in selling myself for a talk to a high school class of students planning to attend trade schools instead of college.

Janelle had argued she was the logical choice because she

hadn't graduated from college, and I had. But I ended up winning the debate when I said I would talk about my father and how he'd worked all his life in construction. He hadn't regretted it for a single moment, because being outdoors, using his hands, was what made him feel alive. It made him feel life had purpose and meaning.

I pulled into our curving driveway, maneuvering slowly past Louise's sedan. I eased my car into the garage and hit the button to close the door.

Inside, the house felt empty. I walked through the dining area to the family room and looked out at the backyard. To the right of the pool and sauna area was a small lawn, and alongside that was my vegetable garden. Louise knelt at the edge of the lawn. She wore yellow cotton capri pants, and her feet were bare, making her look young and carefree. Her hair was pulled back with a scrunchy, but a few strands had fallen over the side of her face. She was pulling weeds, which managed to make me feel neglectful of my garden, resentful of her intrusion, and grateful for her help all in a single wave of emotion.

Sam and Nick were at the end of the garden closest to the house. Small plastic watering cans sat beside them, and they clutched tiny spades in their hands. Packets of seeds were scattered on the dirt around them. As I paused to watch them, Nick grabbed a packet of seeds, tore it in half, and poured the contents onto the soil. Sam yelled and tried to grab the packet out of his brother's hand.

I kicked off my high heels and opened the glass door. I stepped out onto the patio. A stereo scream came from my sons' mouths as Sam lunged at his brother. "Sam. Nick!" I started toward them. By the time I reached the spot where they were now standing, grappling with each other, they were both screaming and crying.

"Shh. Shh. Stop shouting." I reached for the packet, but

Nick spun away from me, falling onto the dirt. He landed chin-first and managed to take in a mouthful of soil in the process. He opened his mouth wide and bellowed. I knelt in the garden and helped him up. I wiped his cheeks and lips, scooping my fingers into his mouth to remove the dirt and grit. While I tried to clean Nick's mouth, Sam fell against my back, sobbing.

"What's the problem here?" Louise said.

I felt her shadow fall over me, blocking the late afternoon sun from my face, which helped me see the remaining dirt in Nick's mouth. "Let's go inside and get you cleaned up," I said.

"It's a good thing we didn't cremate Frank and scatter his ashes here."

I gasped and looked up at her. What on earth had made her say that? We'd never even discussed cremation. Still, the image filled my mind, making me light-headed for a moment, my stomach wavering over the thought of his grandfather's cremated remains in my son's mouth.

"He took my seeds!" Sam's screech filled my ear. He shoved his head close to mine, grabbing my jaw as he tried to get my attention focused solely on him.

"Good grief," Louise said. "What *happened*? We were all gardening in peace and quiet, and Mommy comes home, and everything falls apart."

Both boys continued shouting, which helped me ignore Louise's comment, suggesting the fight was my fault. The boys had tussles like this all the time. It was normal. It was a coincidence that it happened just as I arrived on the scene.

"Come here, Sam." Louise lifted him away from me, picking him up and cradling him against her body as if he were an infant. He screamed louder. "My ... my ... car ..." He hiccupped. "My carrots are all gone," he wailed.

"They aren't gone, they're in the dirt," Louise said. "If we sprinkle another layer of dirt over them, they'll start growing."

"I want to plant them!"

"Here." She placed him on the ground and began scooping up the seeds, dropping them and the dirt that came with them into a green bucket that had been lying on its side a few feet away. "We can plant them again, spread them out a bit. The only problem was they were all in one spot, but we can fix it."

Sam stopped crying and took the handle of the bucket from her.

"All it takes is a little patience and figuring out how to fix the problem, right, Kelly?"

I said nothing. I stood and took Nick's hand, walking toward the house so I could get his face and mouth washed up.

Louise called after me: "Don't be so upset. Everything's fine."

The pleasant feelings from my satisfying day at work had leached out of me. The welcoming kiss and hugs from my husband and sons that I'd looked forward to now seemed like a figment of my imagination. I went into the house and tried to calm my thoughts while I cleaned the mud out of Nick's mouth.

That night in bed, I rested my head on Wyatt's pillow so my mouth was close to his ear.

"How was your day?" He spoke in a normal tone, and the fact he was just then asking the question summed up the chaotic dinner and bath and story time that had consumed us for the past few hours.

"It was great until I got home." I spoke in a whisper, my lips almost brushing his ear. The large guest room at the front of the house was across the landing from our bedroom. Both bedroom doors were closed, but I had a distinct fear that

Louise could hear me, that she heard every single thing that went on in our bedroom. More than once, I'd stepped into a hallway or around a corner and found her standing there, listening. She'd even admitted to her eavesdropping when we'd had lunch together, repeating verbatim my conversation with Janelle at Frank's funeral reception. Of course, I wasn't innocent of that shameful habit myself, but she was sneaky and seemed to go out of her way to find opportunities for listening to phone calls and private conversations between Wyatt and me.

"Why are you whispering?" Wyatt asked.

I knew he would dismiss my paranoia, so I raised my voice slightly, but barely. "Sam and Nick started fighting over their seeds the minute I got home."

"That sounds typical."

"Your mother acted like it was my fault."

"I doubt that."

"Which part? That it was my fault, or that she acted like it was?"

He stroked my cheek, as if to soften me for what he was about to say. "You've been a little oversensitive, adjusting to going back to work. Please don't read into what she says."

"I'm not sensitive. And I don't think I'm reading into it." Now my voice was in a normal tone. I moved away from him, closing my eyes for a moment, wanting to stay calm, feeling anything but that.

He slid his arm under me and pulled me toward him. "She's not used to three-year-olds. They fight. Especially twins."

"She should be used to them by now. She's been here for almost three months."

He began kissing me slowly, then with more intensity. I tried not to think he was trying to stop me from talking any more about his mother.

After a few minutes, I pulled away. "I didn't tell you what she said the other day."

He sighed.

"She was talking to the boys about hell. Telling them bad people go to hell."

"She's religious. Why was that a surprise?"

"I don't want her filling their heads with scary stories like that, trying to force good behavior with fear."

"She's not filling their heads. They don't hear it on a regular basis. They'll forget all about it."

"She needs to respect our views."

"She does."

She didn't, but I didn't want to argue. I just wanted him on my side. It was a childish desire, but as long as Wyatt and I were on the same page, I knew I could deal with her.

"We've had a lot of changes in a short time. You're back at work; you're still dealing with how awful it was to find my father's body and all of that. She's grieving. I'm grieving."

"She doesn't seem all that grief-stricken to me," I said.

"Kelly, please don't. We all grieve differently, you know that. Give her time. And cut her some slack."

"That's a mouthful of clichés." I laughed, hoping it sounded playful instead of critical. He didn't react, so I pushed on, even as I knew I'd regret it. "If she's so set on heaven and hell, maybe she thinks Frank is burning in the fires of hell for cheating on her. That doesn't seem like a very healthy way to grieve, if you ask me."

He tightened his grip on me, pressing his face into my neck. He didn't say anything.

"Do you think she's planning to go back home soon?"

"I don't know," he said.

"Did you ask her about it?"

"Not yet. Let's just appreciate what she's doing for us right now." He slid away from me and turned on his side. "Can we go to sleep? I'm tired."

I snuggled into his back, resting my head on the curve of his spine, hoping ... wishing he'd think about a timeline for her departure while he drifted to sleep.

8

WYATT

The moment my mother suggested I take a leave of absence from my job, I'd felt a surge of energy that I hadn't experienced in years. All the tedium and politics, bureaucratic oversight and long hours of my career as a product line director swelled to unbearable proportions. How had I allowed myself to end up working in a field that stimulated my mind, but left me feeling like my life's work was all about the money and pleasing other people and conforming to what was expected? That music room, the doors standing open, welcoming me every day, made me feel as if I'd been resurrected from the dead.

I liked part of my career—interacting with colleagues, building a team and working together. But part of the reason I liked it was because it was so damn consuming and full of pressure; the adrenaline kept me feeling alive. As I finally began to absorb the fact that my father was gone, everything began to shift, although I hadn't seen it right away.

When Kelly calmly said she wouldn't be opposed to me taking some time off, I felt like I'd tripped and fallen into an alternate reality, one where my life might take an entirely different, previously unimaginable path.

It was shocking how quickly I was able to put all the pieces into place. To demonstrate to Kelly that I was serious, I began playing my guitar for several hours every evening after we settled Nick and Sam in their beds. It wasn't that she needed proof, but I wanted her to know that I wasn't sinking into a depression over my father's death, unable to cope with work. I didn't want her to envision me sitting at home pretending to put in practice hours while I lost myself in a haze of video games and TV. I wanted her to know how free I felt, how excited that something I'd never anticipated being in the cards was suddenly possible.

In the middle of my life, I'd been given a second chance to chase my dreams. How many people were offered that opportunity? And Kelly was the reason. My mother could praise me and entice me with an inspirational setting. She could even remind me who I'd been before my father decided I needed to be a moneymaking machine—the definition of a man, in his view. In so many ways, in so many moments, my mother had rescued me from my father's oppressive attempt to mold me. She'd done that all my life. And I'd done the same for her.

But only Kelly could agree it was a good choice for our family. Only she could offer me the support with her income and her assurance that our lives wouldn't be hurt by this sudden change

Within a week, I'd requested a leave of absence. The wheels of the human resources department began to turn, opening the exit doors before me, telling me they would give me six months. That was the only part that struck fear like a punch to my solar plexus. I knew enough about the music industry to understand that you didn't become a self-supporting musician in six months. Six years was more realistic, and even then ... But for now, it was enough to see how things might unfold during that time.

The online world was filled with social media groups and forums where I could connect with other musicians. Before I knew it, I was experiencing a life that was profoundly different from the reality I'd been living just a few months earlier.

Now, I slept until the sky was growing light, instead of waking in the darkness to an insistent alarm. I went for a run and spent some time with the kids before walking into a room that made the entire house feel like it had undergone a massive shift. I practiced chords and bought reams of sheet music to start expanding my repertoire. I spent the early afternoons writing lyrics, the ideas and images pouring out of me as if they'd been lurking inside me for two decades and now had no time to waste.

Two afternoons a week, I went to the home of another guitarist I had connected with online, and we played together. Soon, a third guitarist, a guy who played bass, and a drummer joined us. We weren't an organized group by any stretch, but we lost ourselves in music, playing whatever stirred us on a particular day.

It was good to have more time with the kids, and it was good to feel my days racing by, not because they were over-loaded with meetings and deadlines and problem-solving tasks, but because I rarely even looked at a clock. I sang and played; I wrote and signed up for lessons to accelerate the refurbishing of my stagnant skills.

Quite a number of the new songs I wrote were about my father.

It wasn't an upbeat musical theme, something people might want to listen to while they ate a nice meal, or dance to if I crafted the right rhythm, but the words poured out of me, and I couldn't seem to stop them or turn my attention to any other subject. A lifetime of ignoring my instincts and interest, years of playing competitive sports when I preferred hiking or bike riding, and countless days spent listening to his unsolicited advice about choosing a college, selecting a course of study, finding the right entry job, considering the *right kind* of life partner, managing the upward climb of my career ... and on and on it went.

When I had an entire notebook filled with songs about my father, the need to capture those experiences finally began to subside. Maybe it was something that needed to be done in order to free my mind for other things that moved me.

Although I put those words about my father to music, I didn't feel like playing the songs much. Instead, I handed the notebook to Kelly when she asked me for the hundredth time how I was doing with my feelings of loss. She read the entire notebook while I sat beside her in bed, pillows propped behind us, each of us sipping a glass of red wine.

While she read, I occupied myself playing sudoku on my phone to avoid staring at her, trying to read her expressions.

My wineglass was empty when she closed the notebook. She placed it on the bed between us.

"That's a lot to take in," she said.

"I know there's too much repetition. Quite a few clichés." I laughed and shifted my position, placing my phone on the charging pad on the nightstand. I wondered if I'd turned instinctively so I didn't have to see her face. I felt suddenly exposed in a way I never had before.

"Did you show these to your mother?"

"No."

"Are you going to?"

"No."

She looked pleased. The look irritated me, but I didn't comment on it. There was no sense in pouring a tank of gasoline on that fire, one that appeared to have subsided for the time being.

"It sounds like you almost hated him."

"No. That wasn't what I was trying to say."

"Then what?"

"He consumed people. Me."

"That's true. But he did love you."

I let her words hang in the air. I had no idea what to say, no idea what she was trying to tell me. Was she implying that I wasn't as devastated as I should be? Was she saying I should be more forgiving? Let go of the past? Loving someone the way you want them to be, but is not who they truly are, isn't love at all. It's loving a caricature who doesn't exist outside of your own imagination.

"You can see that, can't you?" Kelly asked.

I stroked her leg, shifting my gaze to look out our window at a palm tree in the corner of our yard, backlit by the moon. "What I can see is that I have an amazing woman beside me who loves me enough to let me try something most people would consider irrational and irresponsible."

She placed her hand on the back of mine.

"And I also know that with him gone, I can finally live the life I want to. The feeling of freedom is indescribable."

She pulled her hand away. "I don't think you mean that the way it sounds. As if you—"

"I absolutely mean it."

The silence lingered for a few minutes; then she turned out the light. She slid beneath the covers, her back toward me. I sat there for a while longer, staring at that exotic palm tree.

9

KELLY

Wyatt's comment about feeling marvelously free now that his father was dead had chilled me. The cold creeping tentacles around my heart wouldn't loosen their grip. I understood that he was excited about his music, excited to step off the corporate track for a while, maybe for good, but I did not understand that comment. When I pushed him on it, he doubled down. Who says something like that? Did he not hear how it sounded?

His father had died in a very strange set of circumstances. For all we knew, the autopsy report might suggest someone had done something to contribute to his death. Currently, there were no answers. And my husband sounded as if he'd truly wanted his father out of his life. It had sounded, to me, as if Wyatt *wanted* Frank dead. I was disgusted by my own thoughts, but there's no controlling what materializes in one's mind.

I'd always known Wyatt had a difficult relationship with his father. And I'd known he felt like his father only permitted him to live a certain kind of life, but they'd seemed to get along despite that. I'd never sensed the level of anger I'd experienced in his recent lyrics, the kind of anger that would cause him to be *glad* his father had died! At least that was how it had sounded to me. I couldn't think of another way to interpret those words.

When my parents died, I felt like the floor had collapsed beneath me. Yes, I was younger. And yes, my parents adored me and cherished me for who I was. But Frank had grown up without a lot of money. He was raised for most of his life by his grandmother after his father took off and his mother checked out emotionally. It was easy to see why he'd become the man he was. Money mattered to him because he'd never had it. He wanted to create the secure family he'd never had.

Of course, he'd screwed that up by cheating on Louise. I understood the wounds he'd left in Wyatt, and even more so in Louise, but he'd broken off the relationship. He'd stayed with his family. I could understand if Louise never truly forgave him, but why couldn't Wyatt? If for no other reason than his own peace of mind. All the songs Wyatt had written centered around his own relationship to Frank. Only one had touched on his father's affair.

Wyatt's feelings were completely understandable; I'd just felt chilled by the tone in his voice when he'd said he felt free.

It seemed as if *both* Louise and Wyatt were almost glad that Frank had died. The thought was harsh, but I couldn't escape it. The only ones feeling sorrow seemed to be me and our sons. Nick and Sam asked about Poppa nearly every day. After having lived with us for several weeks, he'd become a much bigger part of their lives than he had in the years before when they'd only seen him every few weeks. Even with his restricted activity, Frank had given them a lot of attention, and they'd lapped it up like puppies.

The conversation with Wyatt had replayed itself in my

head all day. It kept me from progressing very far on the speech I was writing for a women's development day at a high-tech company based in San Francisco.

My husband was not a coldhearted individual. In fact, he was quite caring, even in his career. His kindness had made him a beloved manager. He was tender with our sons and treated me with extraordinary affection and consideration. Maybe that was why I'd found his words so jarring.

I drove home still thinking about the conversation. I'd planned to mentally work out the heart of what I wanted to say to women working in a male-dominated industry, despite the fact we were well into the twenty-first century.

At home, I found the house empty and silent. Louise had taken the boys to the park, and Wyatt was with his new musician friends. Being alone in the house was a strange feeling. It didn't happen often, and it always made me feel as if something was wrong. The quiet was too much, and the sense of emptiness gave me an irrational prick of fear that I might never get my family back. It was as if they didn't even exist outside of my awareness, so I felt that wash of dread.

Maybe the silence was the only time I could actually pause long enough to realize how lost I would be without them. The rest of the time, the constant hum of activity, the energy emanating from them even when they were asleep, kept those thoughts at bay. Chatter and the energy of small children, as well as the parts of our work life that spilled over into our home, had a way of keeping all kinds of unwanted thoughts locked in the attic of my mind.

I went into the kitchen and took veggies and spinach out of the fridge to start making a salad. As I turned toward the sink, I noticed a tray shoved against the wall in the corner. It contained two plates stacked on top of each other, the top one with a smear of tomato sauce and bits of pasta and meat from leftover spaghetti. There were two glasses containing the murky water that comes from melted ice and the remaining color of tea or a dark soda. Crumpled napkins were stuck to the spaghetti sauce. I rinsed the plates and stuck them in the dishwasher.

Mindlessly, I began washing spinach and pinching off the stems, tearing the larger pieces, and dropping the leaves into a serving bowl.

The rest of the veggies were already chopped when I heard the front door open. A moment later, Sam, Nick, and Louise were standing in the kitchen, heat coming off their bodies. My sons' faces glowed with perspiration, and their hair was damp at the roots.

"We want juice," Nick said.

"Nana said we could," Sam added.

I gave them hugs and pulled the pitcher of cranberry juice out of the fridge. After they'd sucked down half a cup each, they begged for a snack. I denied them because we were half an hour from dinner. They bolted out of the kitchen, and I heard them pounding up the stairs to their room.

"Can you keep an eye on them while I get dinner ready?" I asked.

Louise nodded. "Of course. Let me just grab something to take the edge off. I'm a lot more hungry in the afternoons when I'm watching them." She laughed. "They never stop." She selected an apple from the bowl and took a bite.

"What was that tray for?" I asked. The napkins and empty glasses were still sitting on it.

"Lunch."

"I prefer the kids eat lunch at the table."

"Oh, not for the boys. After they're down for their naps, I bring lunch to Wyatt."

"It would be nice if he took a break and ate with Nick and Sam."

"It interrupts his flow," she said.

I had no idea what she meant by that, but I nodded rather than arguing. "There were two plates."

"Of course. I'm not going to leave him to eat alone."

"You don't eat with Nick and Sam?"

"I sit with them, of course, but I don't eat. You should know, it's almost impossible to eat when you're supervising them anyway. I prefer to relax and chat with my son."

I wanted to roll my eyes, but it wouldn't help our relationship to make faces at her gushy comments about Wyatt. Still, I felt the muscles around my eyes twitching of their own accord. "I thought he couldn't be disturbed. Not interrupting the flow and all of that."

"This is different." She took a bite of her apple and chewed.

I knew I should drop it, but I can never seem to do that. I can't let things go. I know this about myself, and I know it gets on Wyatt's nerves, how I had to push everything to a conclusion, even if that conclusion did nothing to enhance a relationship. "He's taking his music seriously. This isn't a little mother-son bonding activity. You realize he's hoping to make a living with this at some point, right?"

"Absolutely. And that's why I eat with him. To offer encouragement. To hear how his day is going. He can bounce ideas and frustrations off me."

I set the oven to preheat and washed my hands again. It wasn't necessary, but I wanted to dawdle until she was out of the kitchen. I didn't like her looking over my shoulder when I cooked. I didn't like her looking over my shoulder at all, which it felt like she was doing constantly. "If you're almost done with that apple, the boys need checking on."

"I said I would." She nibbled closer to the core. She came around me and opened the cabinet under the sink, dropping the apple core into the trash. She washed her hands and stepped back. "Don't get upset about us eating lunch together."

"I'm not upset."

She smiled. "I'm his muse. So it's important that I'm there for him."

I laughed. "His muse?"

"It wasn't a joke. I inspire him."

"I don't think you're his *muse*. Besides, the idea of a muse is a fantasy."

"Don't mock him, Kelly. This is important. And he was absolutely serious."

"If you say so."

"Don't be so jealous. It's not attractive, and it just makes him uncomfortable."

"I'm not jealous. Far from it."

"You sound jealous."

"I'm not."

"It's natural that he considers me his muse."

I regretted pushing this, more than usual. But there was no stopping me. Before I could speak, she started up again.

"I encouraged him when he was young. In the face of a lot of obstacles," she said. "And that became part of him. He knows I'm behind him one hundred percent."

"So am I."

She gave me a condescending smile.

"Please don't mention this to him," she said. "He's feeling free from other people's expectations, and it won't be helpful if you're needy and make this about you."

"I'm not needy, and I'm not making anything about me."

"Wyatt has other people in his life, people who love and support him. Not just you. And that should please you, not stir up petty jealousies."

"I told you—I'm not jealous!" My voice rose sharply, making me wonder if I was quite jealous after all.

She smiled again. "I'd better check on the boys." She whirled almost as if she were dancing, and floated out of the room on a cloud of smugness.

10

WYATT

As I turned onto Cannery Row, headed toward the Monterey Bay Aquarium, I thought again about what a brilliant suggestion this had been. Touring the aquarium with Nick and Sam was going to be so much more enjoyable on a weekday morning. My mother had mentioned it when she brought a second cup of coffee into the music room.

"I know it's last minute, and maybe you already have your day planned, but it's going to be hot—in the mid-nineties. It's much too hot for the park, and obviously the boys can't spend the entire day in the pool."

I took the mug of coffee and gave it a trial sip. The temperature was perfect. She must have allowed it to cool slightly before bringing it to me.

"I was thinking it would be nice to take them to the aquarium."

"That's a great idea."

"Why don't you come with us?"

I put the mug on a coaster. The dedicated side of me whispered that successful endeavors don't result from slacking off every time a chance presents itself. But for the previous ten years, much of my life had narrowed to the hallways and conference rooms of an office complex. Expanding my awareness at an aquarium might be just what I needed. And the boys were still sad and very confused about the death of their grandfather. "Sure." I picked up my mug, took another sip, and stood. "Why don't you pack a lunch, and I'll get the boys ready."

She smiled as if she were a teenager responding to her first kiss, a faint pink glow spreading across her cheeks and forehead.

Two hours later, we were walking into the cavernous main room of the aquarium, the boys clutching brochures that included a map of the building. We started with the otter tank, where we spent nearly half an hour watching the furry creatures dive and twist and play in their tank. The twenty-foot depth of the tank was designed to allow visitors to watch the creatures underwater, then climb stairs to another platform where the otters could be observed floating on the surface or climbing out of the water onto the surrounding rock.

It thrilled me to see Nick and Sam were spellbound in front of the constantly moving otters. Aside from watching TV, or the books that grabbed their imaginations, I'd never seen them remain still for so long.

From there, we visited the dark hallway of the octopus's habitat and the kelp forest. The boys were least interested in the shorebirds, although still excited that they could walk along a human-constructed shoreline and see the birds without glass barriers. They played for a while in the tide pool that allowed children to touch some of the anemones.

Our last stop was the jellyfish. Sam couldn't get enough of the ethereal, silently undulating creatures. The usual flood of questions slowed as both boys gazed at the creatures that seemed almost as if they might have been transported from another planet, the jellies were so unfamiliar to anything they'd ever experienced. They loved the darkened rooms where we could turn on lights, allowing us to see how the creatures had been invisible in the dark water of deep ocean, then glowing under the lights.

We ate lunch on a balcony overlooking the bay, watching waves swell and crash against rocks, watching for the heads of sea lions poking out of the water and following the gulls drifting on the air currents. My mom talked about how the day had been her first day of feeling normal since my father died. The calming water and her easy voice, gently answering the boys' questions and making sure they ate their sandwiches, made me feel quite normal as well. It was good to know we were reshaping our extended family, showing the kids they could miss their grandpa but still find pleasure and love in the world.

Sam and Nick slept the entire way home, replacing their usual naps.

At home, my mom made tea, and we sat on the patio, watching the boys splash in the wading pool I'd set up beside our in-ground pool. While my mom and I talked, they raced plastic boats and flung water at each other.

It was quarter to six when I glanced up and saw Kelly standing in the doorway to the kitchen. I waved at her to join us. She gestured she would change her clothes first. A few minutes later, she came out and pulled the lounge close to my chair. "They look nice and cool," she said.

At the sound of her voice, Sam climbed out of the pool and ran toward her, plowing into her legs and flopping on top of her. As water dripped onto her bare legs and soaked the edges of her shorts, Sam began chattering about the aquarium, talking so fast it was hard to decipher what he was saying.

"And jellyfish don't have bones."

"That's right," she said.

"Some glow in the dark, and some have venom. What's venom, Nana?"

"It's something that can make you sick or sometimes kill you if their tentacles touch your skin," Louise said.

Kelly laughed as Sam began waving his arms to mimic a jellyfish. "Where did all this jellyfish knowledge come from?"

"The 'quarium."

"What?"

"The 'QUAR-ium."

Kelly looked at me.

"We went to the Monterey Aquarium."

Despite her dark glasses, I saw I look of near-despair sweep across her face. "You went to the aquarium? Today?"

"That's what he said." My mother's voice was sharp, and I wished she hadn't said anything, as I felt Kelly's obvious distress.

She hugged Sam, then lifted him off her lap. She kissed the top of his head. "Tell me all about it in a minute, sweetie. I'll be right back." She stood and walked quickly into the house. "Wyatt!" Her voice was loud enough that Nick stopped splashing in the pool and looked at her retreating figure. A minute later, the screen door scraped on the track as she wrenched it to the side. She left it standing open and disappeared into the house.

I stood and started after her.

"Don't go chasing after her," my mother said.

"She's upset."

"What else is new? I can't watch them in the water alone. What if something—"

"Boys! Time to get out and dry off. It's almost dinnertime." I handed the towels to my mother and followed Kelly into the house. For a few minutes, I thought she might have left. I couldn't find her anywhere in the kitchen or family room, and there was no answer when I called up the stairs. I finally found her in my music room.

"Close the door," she said.

I followed her command, starting to feel annoyed that she was ordering me around like this.

"How could you do that?"

"Do what?"

"You took them to the aquarium without me." Her eyes filled with tears, and a tiny, painful cry came out of her. "It was their first time. I wanted to go. You knew I wanted to go."

"I—"

"What made you do that?"

"My mom suggested—"

"I knew it! She did this deliberately. She's trying to ... I don't know what she's doing. But she stole that from me, and I'll never get it back." She pressed her hand against my chest. For a moment I thought she wanted to shove me, but that seemed a ridiculous thought. She would never hit me. She rarely even raised her voice at me until recently. Maybe my mother was right—she might be battling a mild form of PTSD. Although I'd seen my father's body, I'd known what was coming. Unlike Kelly, I hadn't walked in on a man lying dead, having expected to gently chastise him for taking a sauna. The shock must have been awful.

"She's not doing anything. We went to the aquarium. It was too hot to stay around here. That's all."

"That's not what this is about. She knew! She knew I wanted to take Nick and Sam. I wanted to have a family experience, and she stole that from me."

"She didn't do it to hurt you. She had an idea for an outing."

"No. I *told* her I wanted to take them."

"And we can. Just the four of us."

"It won't be their first time!" She backed away from me, collapsed onto the love seat, and put her face in her hands, sobbing as if she'd been given a horrible diagnosis, or been told that one of her children had gone missing. The hysteria was unbelievable. I had no idea how to comfort her. She wasn't thinking clearly or logically at all. The kids were three years old. If we took them to the aquarium when they were four, it was unlikely they would even remember this trip.

I moved toward her, unsure whether she would shove me away. I sat carefully on the corner of the love seat and put my hand on her knee. She twisted away from me, continuing to sob, her face covered by her hands, her fingers trembling slightly, her rings like a metal barricade that prevented me from seeing her eyes. "Kelly, please. Let's talk."

"She undermines me. She tries to make it like she's their mother. She edges me out of everything. I think she's trying to pull them away from me! Have you asked her when she's planning to go home? This is intolerable."

"She's watching Sam and Nick so you can work."

"We can get a nanny."

"Well, we don't have one now. And they love being with her."

She wrenched her hands away from her face. It was red from the heat and sopping wet, black streaks of makeup around her eyes. "Of course they do! That's the problem."

"Do you want them to be unhappy all day unless you're here? You wanted to go back to work."

"I know that, Wyatt. And of course I don't want them to be unhappy. *They* are not the problem. Your mother is."

I slumped back on the love seat. The kids and my mom and I had had a terrific time at the aquarium, and Kelly was spoiling it. If the kids saw her like this ... "You're acting like you're jealous of my mother."

"I'm not jealous. Stop saying that."

She made it sound as if I'd repeatedly accused her of jealousy, but it was the first time it had even crossed my mind. Until that moment, I'd never thought of Kelly as a jealous person. Was this another suggestion there was something going on in her mind that was twisting her perception? There was no way my mother was trying to undermine her or do anything to hurt her. She'd probably forgotten Kelly had mentioned the aquarium. Or Kelly hadn't actually said anything to her, she just thought she had. It happens to all of us, even under normal circumstances. We think about something and believe we've told another person, but the thought remained in our own heads.

"She isn't trying to hurt you. I'm sure she'd feel terrible if she knew how upset you were."

She made a sputtering sound of disgust and disagreement.

"You can't spoil the kids' day. They had a great time."

"I'm sure they did."

"Can't you let go of that and focus on what she's doing for us? Can't you be excited about the trip, for them?"

"Of course I'll do that. What kind of monster do you think I am?"

Right then, I had no idea. "My mom probably won't be here much longer. We should enjoy her while we can. Free childcare, not to mention premium childcare. She adores the boys more than a hired nanny ever could. She adores us."

Kelly said nothing.

"Please try to focus on that. Nick and Sam know you're their mother. Nothing will ever change that." I wanted to tell her she was being petty and childish and acting quite insecure. But I also wanted to be sensitive to her. Finding a man's lifeless body is not something that most people ever experience. Just as I wanted her to focus on what my mother was doing to help, I needed to keep reminding myself of what

Kelly had gone through. On top of that, as much as she loved her job and wanted to return to work, I was sure she felt torn at times, missing the kids, as I had when I was out of the house for most of the day.

It was an adjustment. We would all be fine. It was just a bit rocky right now. Soon, my mother would return home, we would hire a nanny, and before we knew it, the boys would be heading off to school. Kelly would be fine. Our family would thrive. I was sure of it.

11

KELLY

The boys were in bed. Wyatt, Louise, and I were watching a movie. A bowl of popcorn sat on the couch between Wyatt and me, and a smaller bowl was on the table beside the armchair Louise was occupying. It had come to feel like her chair. I hadn't sat in that comfortable, pale yellow armchair for months. Even when she wasn't sitting there, Louise had a book or magazine lying facedown, saving her place in more ways than one. Sometimes her knitting project was splayed across the seat and arms, the points of the needles seemingly at the ready to defend her space.

I ate a few pieces of popcorn. As I reached for my cup of tea, Louise suddenly turned toward Wyatt. "Can you pause it for a minute?"

"Sure." He picked up the remote and hit the pause button.

I took another sip of tea, settling back to wait while she used the bathroom or whatever she needed to do so urgently.

"I meant to tell you," Louise said. "The house sold. I know I didn't mention my plans, but I was very happy with the offer, so I accepted right away. All cash! And a short closing, so it's done. Escrow closed today."

"What?" I knew what she'd said, but I couldn't believe I'd heard correctly. My brain couldn't take it in. Surely she wasn't calmly telling us ... telling us, what?

"You sold your house?" Wyatt said, sounding as thick-headed and dull as I had.

"Yes." She smiled. "It's a seller's market, so I'm—"

"I know it's a seller's market," Wyatt said. "But why on earth ... why didn't you talk to us?"

"Where are you going to live?" I knew I sounded shrill, angry, and utterly unwelcoming, if she was planning to stay with us indefinitely. I knew with all my heart that was exactly what she was thinking.

Louise's eyes filled with tears. "You don't want me?"

"No one said that." Wyatt picked up the bowl of popcorn and set it on the table. He pressed his fingers into the corners of his eyes, as if he had a headache already.

"Without asking us?" I said. "You just decided you're living here permanently?"

"Not forever." Louise laughed. "You're hurting my feelings. I thought you—"

"I can't believe you sold your house," Wyatt said. "That was really rash. You should have discussed it with—"

"I'm not an idiot. I discussed it with Chris. He said it was a good time to sell."

"Maybe financially. But it's common knowledge that you shouldn't make major decisions immediately after the death of your spouse."

"It's not that big a decision. It was a good time to sell. I can't face going back to the house. Did you think about that?" She glared at me, as if I'd been the one challenging her mental capability. "That house is a shell without Frank. Everything there is about him, about our family. I can't go back. I just can't, and it's heartless of you to not realize that." Again, she looked directly at me.

"Mom, please calm down."

"I'm calm. It's the right decision. I have someone packing for me, so I don't have to face any of that. I can start fresh."

"In our house," I said.

"Taking care of your children, remember." She gave me a vicious smile.

"Okay. Let's not ..." Wyatt leaned forward, planting his elbows on his knees, as if his upper body might create a barrier between me and his mother. "I'm just ... we're shocked. We had no idea you were even thinking about this. It would have been good to discuss it with us."

"I never dreamed you didn't want me here," Louise said. "I thought you appreciated having me care for Nick and Sam. I thought you *appreciated* me cooking and helping around the house. It never crossed my mind you wouldn't even want me."

"No one said we don't want you." Wyatt's tone was deliberately gentle.

Their voices took on a buzzing quality backed by a high-pitched ringing in my head. I felt as if my brain were being assaulted by an electrical disturbance. This could not be happening. She could not possibly have sold a multimillion-dollar home without breathing a word about it to Wyatt or me.

"It was the best thing for me. You don't understand how it felt, thinking about going back there and touching all of those things that are emblems of our life together. It would have been torture."

"Other people do it," I said.

"It would have been torture, Kelly. And I'm not planning to stay here forever. When I feel ready, I'll find a smaller place. Closer to Wyatt and my grandchildren. And you." She smiled. "Besides, in case you didn't know, multigenerational families are stronger. Everyone knows that."

It was one of the phoniest smiles I'd ever witnessed. She

hadn't told us because she knew we would stop her. She knew I would object to her semipermanent status with us. How long would it take her to find a place of her own? When she was *ready*?

Selling a house is not a simple trade that takes a few hours. She must have worked overtime to figure out how to meet with a title company, to sign papers, and before that, to arrange inspections and open houses and all the hundreds of details that go into getting a house ready for sale without us ever realizing what was going on.

I didn't trust myself to speak anymore. I was so angry. I felt used. But if I said another word, I would come across like I was completely ungrateful and coldhearted. She was taking care of our children. And overall, doing a nice job of it. The kids were happy. She made dinner several nights a week. She did a lot of the grocery shopping. If it weren't for Louise, I wouldn't be thriving, enjoying my family and my career.

Complaining about how she was taking advantage of us, overstepping her boundaries in the most egregious way I could imagine, would make me look like a selfish bitch. And I wasn't. I truly appreciated her taking care of Sam and Nick. But this was too much.

Maybe she hadn't displaced me in my children's eyes yet, but if she stayed here for months, until they went to school, possibly beyond, that was a definite possibility. Was it my fault? I didn't think I'd made a mistake returning to work. And if I hadn't started earning a good income, Wyatt wouldn't have been able to follow his dream. I loved my work. And I loved being a mom. It was all writhing inside me, so that I felt like I'd fallen into a den of snakes who were now winding their way through my gut and my thoughts, making it hard to even know how I was feeling.

She'd manipulated us, and she knew exactly what she was doing, based on all the effort she'd put into not letting us know. "Why didn't you tell us your plans?" I asked, hoping my tone was even.

"It didn't seem important."

"Bullshit."

I spoke calmly, but Wyatt still reacted. "Kelly!"

A smile flickered across Louise's lips as Wyatt glared at me.

"As Wyatt said, it's a major life decision, and it's not a simple process to sell a home," I said. "You didn't want us to know because you knew we'd object."

"I did not know that. I thought you loved me ... I thought ..."

"We do love you, Mom," Wyatt said.

I refused to fall into the trap of reassuring her. She was trying to manipulate us into shutting up about it. I wanted to ask when she would be *ready* to find her own place, but I knew that had to come from Wyatt. She would answer me in a way that would alienate my husband and me as he worked overtime to make her feel wanted.

"Should we turn the movie back on?" Louise asked.

I stood. "I'm going to bed."

"I hope you'll still want me," Louise said. "I don't know who will look after the boys if I'm not here."

Wyatt picked up the remote and turned off the TV. "We can finish the movie tomorrow. I think we're all a little distracted right now."

"I didn't mean to spoil the evening," Louise said. "We were having such a nice time."

Louise had known her little bomb would destroy the evening. She knew everything—she knew the sale of her house would settle her indefinitely in our home, she knew I would feel smothered, and she knew Wyatt wouldn't want to give her a deadline for *finding a place of her own*. She'd been in our home for months already, studying how we lived. She was his mother. She knew how to push every little button and flip every tiny switch.

I wanted her out of my space. With a single sweep of a pen, she'd made me feel trapped in my own home.

"Also, while we're talking about changes," she said, "I've found a buyer for Frank's car."

"*Frank's* car? I thought it belonged to both of you," I said. "How will you get around? How will you ... what are you doing?"

"Buying that car was Frank's decision. I never liked it. I can drive Wyatt's now that he's not commuting."

"But sometimes I need to—"

She interrupted him. "You'll have priority for using it, of course. No question. I only need it for taking the boys on outings and doing our grocery shopping."

I walked out of the room, leaving my half-full cup of tea and the buttered popcorn behind. I no longer wanted any of it. I hoped Wyatt would follow immediately, but it was unlikely. Now that his mother had him to herself, she would keep him in the room, trying to get him on her side.

The sale of the car was almost as terrifying as the house. She was now utterly dependent on us for her physical needs. She'd trapped herself in our house as surely as she'd trapped me. The need to identify and buy another car would lengthen the time until her departure.

Upstairs in our bedroom, I lay on our bed, staring at the ceiling, waiting for Wyatt. It was another forty minutes before he opened the door and stepped into the room, saw me lying on top of the comforter, and sighed.

"Did you find out when she'll be *ready* to find her own place?" I asked.

"Not yet. I—"

"Please tell me you feel as shocked and used as I do."

"I don't feel used. I'm surprised, yes. Very surprised. But

I'm trying to focus on the good parts—we have family to care for Sam and Nick ..."

"You need to find out when she's planning to leave."

"Give her some time."

"We've already given her time."

"We need a nanny anyway, and until we hire—"

"I'm not hiring a nanny when we have no idea how much longer she'll be around. In fact, you should give *her* a date. One month to start looking."

"She's not a tenant we're evicting."

I stared at him. She sort of was a tenant, but I didn't say that. I went into the bathroom to get ready for bed.

As I stood in front of the mirror, staring at myself, I looked tired and angry and quite a bit older. Louise didn't need more time to grieve. She seemed content that Frank was gone so she could consume Wyatt's life, having him all to herself. I felt as if my house had been invaded by a presence that would slowly suffocate me.

A scream pierced my sleep. I knew immediately it wasn't part of whatever dream had been unspooling inside my mind. I threw back the covers, leaned on my elbow, and turned on the bedside light. Another scream echoed in the space outside our room. One of the boys. Before I could move any farther, Kelly was out of bed, tangled in the sheet for a moment, then scurrying to the door. I collapsed back on my pillow and lay there, listening to the continuing shrieks.

I expected the crying out to stop within a few seconds of Kelly arriving in their room, but it carried on as if one of my sons—I was pretty sure it was Sam—had woken to find his bed brimming with spiders.

A moment later, the crying still loud and frightened, I climbed out of bed and hurried across the landing to where they slept in a shared room, the adjoining bedroom serving as a playroom.

The light was on, and Kelly knelt beside Sam's bed, stroking his back, running her fingers through his hair. She was murmuring gently, but I couldn't catch what she was saying as Sam's cries drowned out her soothing voice.

A few minutes later, I felt my mother standing slightly behind me. "What's wrong?"

"Nightmare," I said. "But I don't think all three of us need to be here." I took a step back out of the doorway.

"Nana!" Sam screamed. "Where's Nana?!"

"Shh," Kelly said. "It's okay. I'm right here. It was just a dream."

"Poppa was scaring me," he sobbed. "He was all white, even his clothes. He said it was because he was a ghost now," Sam blubbered. "He didn't know why he was dead. He wanted to be alive, but he couldn't."

Nick sat up suddenly. "That's a dream, silly. He wasn't really here."

Sam glared at him, then began crying again. He whimpered at first; then the violence of his cries increased.

I stepped back into the room and moved toward the bed.

"It's okay, sweetie," Kelly said. "Nick's right. It was a dream. There's nothing to be scared of now. Poppa is in a good place—he's happy and—"

"Where's Na—na?" Sam's face was red and damp with tears.

Kelly wiped at his cheeks, but he batted her hand away. She tried to pull him close, half-dragging his tiny body out of the bed, wrapping her arms around him.

"Nana!"

"Kelly, why don't you let my mom give him a hug?"

She turned slightly, making sure her back was to both of us. "It's okay, Sam. Do you want to come into our bed for a little while?"

"Where's Nana? I want Nana."

"Kelly ..." I said.

She squeezed Sam harder. He writhed out of her arms

and flung himself to the side, knocking his head against the wall. He screamed louder.

My mother rushed into the room and sat near the foot of the bed. She pulled Sam onto her lap and rocked him gently. His cries slowly dissolved, and a moment later, his shoulders stopped heaving. "Why don't you let your mom give you a hug?" Louise said. "It will make her feel better."

A cry of rage and anguish came out of Kelly. I put my arms around her and pulled her close as she struggled against me.

"Come on, Sam. Come give Mommy a hug," Louise said.

Her tone was calm, without drama or any edge to it, but I knew that was not the way Kelly was taking it. I tried again to pull her close to my body, but she wrenched away so hard, she almost pulled us both to the floor.

"Mommy." Sam spoke in a whisper.

Kelly went to the bed, looking defeated, her hands wrapped around her upper arms as if she hoped to protect herself against the hurt of her son's rejection.

Sam put his arms around Kelly's neck as she knelt beside his bed. Even I could see that it wasn't the unrestrained devotion and assurance of safety with which he'd flung himself into my mother's arms. My mother didn't move off the end of the bed, which I guessed made Kelly more upset.

No one wants an audience when they're trying to calm their child. With the two of us watching, I imagined she felt a sharp stab of self-doubt. I was glad she hadn't refused to hug him, putting her own feelings in front of Sam's.

My mother finally stood. She kissed the back of Sam's head. She turned to Nick and gave him a hug and kiss, then walked slowly out of the room.

Kelly remained kneeling beside Sam's bed. I yawned. He was obviously okay. They both needed to get back to sleep.

The disturbance was likely to make them short-tempered the next day.

"Kelly?"

She ignored me. I kissed the boys in the same way my mother had—starting with the back of Sam's head. I moved toward the doorway. "I'm going to turn off the light, okay, Kelly?"

Again, she ignored me. "Kelly?"

She grunted, still holding Sam close.

I turned off the light switch. Sam was settled, the dream fading, sleep starting to creep up his spine. I wondered if Kelly needed comfort as much as he did. Not just for his seeming rejection of her, but because it was possible the dream mirrored her own dreams—dreadful thoughts about my father dying under her care, the memories of his lifeless face crowding out other, more pleasant images.

Finally, she stood and went to Nick's bed. She gave him a long tight hug. Like his brother, he tried to wriggle out of it, but she refused to let go until he made a whimpering sound.

Back in our room, she lay on her side, her back toward me. I put my hand on her spine, rubbing gently. "Don't take it personally."

She grunted. A moment later, she sat up. Moonlight fell across her face, contorting it even more than her tears had done. "She's said something to them."

"What?"

"I know she's trying to insert herself between me and my children, trying to make them love her more than me."

"No, she's not."

"She is. The trip to the aquarium. Acting like I was the cause of their fight in the garden. You think they don't pick up on that? They are so much more aware of everything than we give them credit for."

"They are, but—"

"Look at the story of his dream. They know their grandpa is dead, and they have some kind of idea what that means."

"I know. They're smart kids. And they also know their mom and dad love them desperately."

"She said something bad about me."

"She wouldn't do that."

"Then why did he want her instead of me?"

"He's a three-year-old kid. He isn't playing favorites."

"She's definitely not his favorite."

"But you just said she is."

"I did not say that. I said your mother is telling them negative things about me. She's trying to turn them against me."

I sat up and moved closer to her. I took her hand in mine. "It's okay."

"What's okay? That your mother is bad-mouthing me to my own children? Making them afraid of me?"

It wasn't what I'd meant to say. I was tired, and I meant that it would all be okay. I sighed. "He wasn't afraid of you. He's not afraid of you at all. You know that. He just ... he was half asleep, Kel. It didn't mean anything."

"It meant something to me." She pulled away. "Stop dismissing my feelings."

I tried to think about how to help her see she was being irrational. What exactly was PTSD, anyway? I knew the term, and I had a general idea what it referred to, but I didn't know what constituted the disorder. I didn't know if it applied to this situation at all. I was used to hearing it refer to victims of horrific crime, or former military who had served in war zones. Although it had struck me as valid when my mother suggested it, and I'd briefly considered it since, I didn't want to blow things out of proportion. And I didn't want to undermine the suffering of people who had experienced bona fide trauma. "I'm not dismissing your feelings. I just think it's not fair to accuse my mom of something so awful."

"There's a reason Sam was screaming for her. She must have said something. You know how easy it is to insert things into children's minds. They suck it all up and can't discern lies or manipulation or ... I just know she said something."

"You don't know that. He had a bad dream, and it was about my dad; maybe that's why he asked for my mom. Maybe he was worried something happened to her."

"No."

I squeezed her hand. "Kelly, please. Our kids love you completely. You know that. No one could say anything that would make them doubt that or pull away from you. It's not possible." It was hard not to tell her she was underestimating our son, suggesting he could be so easily turned away from her.

"So you agree she said something?"

"No." I sighed and moved away from her. "Let's try to get back to sleep."

She made a sound of anger and frustration but slid beneath the covers.

There was no reasoning with her right now. She needed to get some sleep. In the morning, or in a day or two, the memory and her interpretation of what had happened would fade. The sharp pain of that momentary rejection would soften. She would see how unfair she was being to my mother.

13

The day after Sam's nightmare, I took an unscheduled day off work. The nature of my job meant that I didn't have to be in the office during certain hours, as long as I was available for team meetings or one-on-ones with my manager. The work frequently involved weekends and evenings, although so far, I'd been able to grab speaking spots for midweek luncheons and breakfast meetings. I liked the regular hours as I eased my way into a new life, blending motherhood and my career. Once Sam and Nick were a little older, I would reassess. Once my mother-in-law was out of the house and Wyatt and I returned to normal, I would have a clearer idea of where I wanted to go.

However, I spent a fair amount of time wondering whether that was ever going to happen. Wyatt refused to push Louise into making plans, and she wasn't going to take any suggestions from me, so we were at a standoff.

I dressed in shorts and a tank top, brushed my hair into a ponytail, and packed a picnic lunch. I loaded the small nylon tent, a beach chair, towels, and sand toys into the back of the car. When I pulled my sons' swimsuits out of their dresser and announced we were going to the beach, I was rewarded with warm, gleeful hugs. The press of squirming little bodies should have erased the pain I'd felt at one o'clock in the morning, but it didn't. Not entirely. The dull ache that had lingered through the night remained.

After Sam chose his grandmother over me, I lay awake for a long time. When I finally drifted to sleep, I too dreamed of my father-in-law. My dream was not visited by a ghost, but by a decayed corpse, vivid images of Frank's slack face and body; memories of how he'd occasionally repulsed me when he was alive wavered at the edges of the dream. A vague sense of guilty despair over his shocking death had flooded my thoughts as I woke to the alarm a few hours later.

Pushing my father-in-law's cold, motionless body out of my head and recalling the upset from the night before, I knew I couldn't be away from my children all day. I needed time with my babies. I needed time without Louise breathing down my neck, watching, silently critiquing every move, causing confusion in my children with her not-too-subtle contradictions to nearly every word I said.

During dinner, I refused to give them a cookie until they tried the vegetables that had been served, but Louise often grabbed the offending pieces of green off one of their plates and popped the veggies into her own mouth, crowing—*Oh, look, it's all gone. Time for a treat.* She wouldn't listen even to Wyatt when he told her she needed to follow our lead. She whined that she was trying, but she forgot. Her mothering consisted of *strong, lifelong habits.* She couldn't help that she acted from *instinct.* The implication was—*I'm behaving correctly because it's based upon mothering instincts you lack, Kelly.*

Louise allowed the boys to watch TV at times I didn't agree with. She didn't encourage them to try new tasks that were difficult, and did a thousand other small things I disagreed with. Wyatt insisted I needed to let her care for the boys in her own way because you can't force someone to be a different person than they are. I thought she should follow our parenting style. It wasn't that difficult.

As I drove up the winding road into the Santa Cruz mountains, headed toward the coast, I answered the endless questions that flowed out of their busy, curious minds. We listened to some kids' songs for a while, and as we turned onto Highway One, drawing closer to the beach, we talked about what we would do there.

We hadn't been to the beach since the previous fall when Nick and Sam were two and a half. They seemed to recall the time we'd spent there, but I had the sense their memories were tiny scraps they were trying to piece together after a seeming lifetime of new experiences since then.

I pulled into a parking spot a few spaces down from a public restroom. I unloaded our supplies while the boys remained in their car seats. As I stacked tent and chair and cooler on the walkway, I wondered if I was out of my mind to think I could manage twin boys on the beach all by myself. Leaning into the car, I reminded them they had to do what I said or we would immediately leave for home. They nodded solemnly, in time with each other. I think they sensed the seriousness in my tone.

While I set up the half tent that would provide relief from the sun while we ate our picnic later, they sat inside the circle I'd drawn in the sand, digging with their shovels, scooping sand into the beds of their dump trucks. I arranged the cooler inside the tent, extra towels stacked on top. I set up my chair and smeared sunscreen over Nick's body, then Sam's, then my own. I plopped red baseball caps on their heads, and we walked down to the edge of the surf.

Time disappeared and accelerated at the same time as we splashed in the waves. I got almost as wet as they did, standing close beside them, making sure neither one ever ventured farther into the water than where I stood. We picked up pebbles and tossed them into the waves. We laughed and looked up at circling, diving pelicans. Everything was as it should be. I didn't sense a single moment in which either one pulled away from me.

When Sam had cried out for Nana, refusing my comfort, I'd felt as if someone had ripped my heart out of my chest. Millions of women carried on with their careers while maintaining tight bonds with their children. In my case, something was wrong. I'd seen it the night before, felt it throughout my body, and could look at it more calmly now. I knew children favored different adults at different times—sometimes Daddy, sometimes Mommy was preferred. And they were clever enough already to occasionally play one adult against the other. But this was different. At their age, they still wanted Mommy when they were scared or hurt. Sometimes Daddy, but more often, they cried for me. Sam had not wanted my comfort. And he hadn't asked for Wyatt.

As I'd knelt beside Sam's bed, I'd sensed Louise gloating, using my child to hurt me, using his suffering to make herself feel important. It wounded me, and it disgusted me. I wasn't going to allow it to continue.

Since I couldn't get Wyatt to agree to give Louise a deadline for moving out, I needed to find another way to reduce her influence over my children.

During the long drive home, I kept glancing in the rearview mirror at their faces—so precious to me I felt my heart swell when I saw them looking back at me. Part of me had hoped they would fall asleep in the car to make up for missing their naps, but another part of me didn't want them sleeping for a single moment while we had time alone together.

Feeling slightly ill, I decided to ask the question

tormenting me. "What does Nana talk about when she's alone with you?"

They stared at me in the mirror, eyes round and blank. The concept was too complex, the question too vague. I sighed, suddenly glad that they hadn't understood. It gave me a moment to pause and see what I was doing—walking down the treacherous path of putting my children in the middle of my conflict with Louise.

As we passed the summit of the Santa Cruz mountains, heading down toward sharp downhill curves, the answer came to me in such an easy way, it appeared stupidly obvious. I would hire a part-time nanny. I would find a college student who would accept part-time employment now, knowing it would be full-time at some unforeseeable point in the future. It would be challenging to find a person I liked and clicked with, who also fit those criteria, but it wasn't impossible.

Wyatt believed I was selfish for not appreciating his mother's care for the boys. He was wrong. I did appreciate it. I just didn't like the cost that came with it. Her care wasn't as free as he seemed to think. I hadn't wanted to hire a nanny because I didn't think it was right to dangle someone along with an unknown, ever-changing start date, waiting on Louise's plans. Offering a part-time position solved the problem.

At home, I made dinner. After the meal was finished, Wyatt and I supervised bike riding while Louise cleaned up the kitchen. She hadn't seemed as sulky as I'd expected, and the boys' evening and bedtime routine was actually pleasant. I hated that this fact surprised me. I didn't want my children growing up in a house with tension, sharp words always just beneath the surface. Some of that was normal in family life, but not the deepening pool of animosity our home had become.

In bed, I snuggled up to Wyatt.

"I'm glad you had a good day," he said.

"It was perfect."

"It seems like you're feeling better."

"I realized something. I think if your mother is going to be staying indefinitely, the boys will be too much for her."

"She hasn't said that."

"They're so active. You can't let down your guard for a second, and that can be exhausting. They're constantly fighting for attention, which is draining even for me. And she's almost thirty years older."

He grunted.

"I'm going to look for a part-time nanny. Someone who can give her a break. As much as she loves them, it's not fair to ask a sixty-seven-year-old woman to care for two small boys all day, every day. She needs time to herself. Time to recover from her loss. She needs time to look for a new place."

"That's a good idea," Wyatt said.

"She won't be staying here forever." I laughed, trying to make it sound light and casual. "It would be good to have someone to transition."

"She might argue that she can handle them," he said, "but in the end, I think she might be relieved."

I'd thought I might have to persuade him. I'd thought he would insist his mother was perfectly capable. Maybe he was vaguely aware of the same things I was; he just wasn't consciously aware, because he was so worried about Louise's feelings. I was helping my family by making this decision. We would all be much better off.

K elly had begun the selection process for nannies, spending an hour or so a day online at several nanny sites, looking at profiles, reading comments from previous clients, and making a list of her choices. I received three or four messages from her every day, asking me to check out a profile or give an opinion about how flexible we should be on hours. She was thrilled to have a plan, diligent about considering what our children needed.

Things between her and my mother had cooled down. This was good in one way, and not so good in another. They were no longer openly hostile to each other, but I could feel the distance between them growing. Their words to each other had reached a new level of formality. Their politeness and forced deference were almost embarrassing at times.

I was a little concerned the kids would pick up on it, that the tension of artificial behavior could be felt by them as easily as it was by me. I hoped once the nanny appeared on the scene, the dynamic would change. I still felt we were all dealing with a lot—the shift in roles between Kelly and me, the shock of losing my father, the ugliness of how it had happened. I think that awful discovery in the backyard sauna had affected all of us, although Kelly had definitely borne the brunt of it.

Sometimes, I found myself playing out the scene in my mind, imagining his final moments, wondering if he'd known what was happening. Kelly and I had spent hours in our sauna. We loved relaxing there after the kids were in bed, but now, I couldn't imagine stepping into that tiny room, anticipating a pleasant evening, ever again. It made no sense to me that he could die so easily. The surgery had repaired his heart, and the weird circumstances of his death seemed almost insulting. At least, that was how I guessed he would view it.

My mother was playing Candyland with Sam and Nick while Kelly and I cleaned up the kitchen. It had been another beastly hot day—over a hundred degrees. Now, it was finally cooling down to the high seventies. As soon as we finished with the dishes, Kelly and I would take the kids to the park to run off some energy before bath time. Only the four of us were going. My mother planned to have a quick swim and sequester herself in her room to allow us more family time.

It was sensitive of her to start making sure there was more time for our family. I was grateful, but Kelly had made a casual yet sharp comment that maybe my mother was leaving us alone simply because she was tired, confirming our decision to look for a nanny. Or, she'd added, *she thinks she'll be here permanently, and she's pacing herself.*

I didn't react, but I thought Kelly was being a little unfair. At the same time, I was starting to worry that Kelly might be right, that I was putting too much effort into defending my mother. I didn't mind having her around, and I felt I owed her after all she'd done for me, but eventually I wanted a return to regular family life. Once the shock of the house sale had worn off, I'd realized that had been a good decision on my mother's part. Living closer to us would make it easier for me to look after her, and make it easier for her to see the boys more often. Living closer would also make it more palatable for her to leave our home and start this new phase of her life —alone.

The doorbell chimed. I glanced at the clock—six twenty. It was an odd hour for someone to be ringing the bell. I wiped my hands and started toward the entryway. Before I reached the door, my mother appeared, stepping quickly around me and grabbing the door handle.

"Are you expecting someone?" I asked.

Kelly had joined us, a look of unease on her face as she saw my mother's obvious interest in whoever was standing on the other side of the door.

"It's a bit of a surprise." My mother laughed, the sound turning quickly to a nervous, excited giggle. She flung open the door. "Hi, Jason. I'm glad you could make it. Come in, and I'll introduce you."

Now, Sam and Nick had skittered into the entryway—a bona fide welcoming party for the young guy, barely past twenty-one, now standing in our entryway, looking eager for something that had yet to be explained.

"Jason!" Sam rushed at the guy, wrapping his arms around his legs.

Jason placed the canvas bag he was carrying on the floor and patted my son's back. "Good to see you, buddy." He nodded his head toward me, then looked past me, giving a big smile to Kelly.

"This is Jason Drewek," Louise said.

Jason shook my hand.

"Wyatt Brooks," I said.

"I saw how much time Kelly was spending trying to find a nanny who would be a good fit for the boys," Louise said.

Her words rushed at me with the force of an icy wind. I'd

already guessed what had happened before she spoke, and I felt an unsettling fear over how Kelly was going to respond. All of that in the flicker of a thought, before I had the full story.

"Jason was able to meet the boys at the park a few days ago, and they absolutely fell in love with him," my mother said.

Now Nick was hanging on Jason's leg, and Sam was digging through the canvas bag filled with rugged and colorful cars and trucks built for traveling over sand and grass.

"What?" Kelly said.

I turned. Her face was blank, her eyes wide and staring, the surface of them appearing flat in the dim evening light of the entryway. I turned back toward our visitor.

Jason wore dark blue board shorts and flip-flops, a white tank top that showed off well-developed shoulder muscles and biceps. His skin was lightly tanned, and his reddish brown hair was long, pulled into a ponytail, the tip of which brushed his spine between his shoulder blades. He was clean-shaven and had dark blue eyes. He had the air of someone who was easy to like, yet I felt a subtle flicker of resentment. Not because my mother had obviously gone behind our backs in an effort to help, but because he was young and fit and very good-looking. His mere presence made me hyperaware of the thickness above the waist of my jeans, the barely noticeable slackening in my muscles.

"Jason plays the drums," Louise said. "He's in a band, and he's going to school, so he was looking for a part-time position. He's studying music. I thought you and he would have a lot to talk about." She gave me a beatific smile.

"A nanny?" Kelly said, still trying to get her head around what was unfolding before us, momentum forward that had taken place entirely outside of our awareness.

"Yes. A nanny. He and I clicked immediately. And clearly the twins love him," Louise said. Her smile held no hint of guile, but I had no doubt that was the *only* thing Kelly was seeing.

"Why would Wyatt need something to talk about with a nanny? We need someone to look after Nick and Sam, not someone for him to jam with."

Jason smiled awkwardly.

It was a strange thing to say, and I sensed Kelly's frustration building, starting to erupt in brief, somewhat random statements like the one she'd just made. I did not want to have a family fight in front of a stranger. Especially in front of a stranger who could have been me nearly twenty years ago, if I'd had the guts to follow my own path instead of letting the man who fathered me terrorize me into becoming a replica of himself.

"Why don't you all go into the family room. I'll make tea," Louise said. She gestured past the stairs and the short hallway that led to the family room. She turned and walked ahead of us.

We followed obediently, Kelly going last, stabbing me in the shoulder blade with her fingertip. I ignored her. I wasn't going to do anything but show respect to this kid until she and I could be alone, later. I didn't like public drama of any kind, and despite my shameful feelings of envy or competition or whatever weird thing was nagging at me, Jason might turn out to be a good fit for our kids. The goal in hiring someone was to give my mother a break, to return to normal family life. Starting a fight in front of a guy who might very well do an excellent job caring for my sons, who clearly liked him, was not a good way to begin a working relationship.

In the family room, Jason sat cross-legged on the floor and began pulling toys out of his bag. At the bottom of the bag was a box filled with tiny cars and construction vehicles.

This was obviously what Nick had been after. He tried to open the clasp, but couldn't manage it. He handed the box to Jason, leaning across Jason's leg, smiling and almost vibrating with anticipation. My sons' affection for this stranger made me wonder how much time they'd spent with him. They were utterly comfortable in his presence.

"Jason has a stunning resumé," Louise said. "I'll show it to you later. Right now, let me get that tea going." She scurried out of the room to the kitchen. A moment later, I heard water gushing into the kettle.

"This is awkward, Jason," Kelly said.

"How so?" Jason asked.

"My husband and I are conducting a search for a nanny. My mother-in-law isn't involved."

Jason looked startled. "Oh. Well ..." He laughed. "Here I am. Just like Mary Poppins. The children's hearts called out their desires, and I appeared."

He was nothing like Mary Poppins, but I was glad Kelly didn't feel the need to argue that point.

Jason embodied the stereotype of a laid-back musician, someone who had played in one of the surfer bands from the 1960s. His clothes, hair, and suntan created an aura of a guy who was untroubled by our awkwardness, who didn't seem to feel the need to conform to expectations.

"Let me know if you have any questions," he said. "I've been working with little kids since I was fifteen. I was a counselor at a music camp and a few sports camps—baseball and soccer. I was actually babysitting my younger cousins when I was twelve." He laughed. "I have a huge family, so there are quite a lot of them. Like Ms. Brooks said—"

"I'm Ms. Brooks," Kelly said, her voice sharp and overly loud.

Jason laughed as if it was the funniest thing he'd heard in

days, but his laughter didn't sound false or overdone. "Of course you are. The senior Ms. Brooks."

Even those words came out smoothly, without the cloying flattery they might have carried from someone else's lips. Mine, for example.

"I've taken some early childhood education classes along with my music classes, since I need to round things out with electives anyway. And I have great references."

"Sam and Nick obviously feel comfortable with you," I said.

"Wyatt." Again, Kelly's voice was loud and sharp, like metal pellets hitting the sliding glass doors behind us.

I avoided making eye contact, knowing what I would find there.

A moment later, my mother came into the room. "Jason, what kind of tea do you like? I have peppermint—"

"Louise, this has caught us by surprise, and I don't think it's a good time to have tea," Kelly said.

Louise gave Kelly a tight smile. "Let's not be rude."

Kelly knelt beside Nick and Sam. "You know what, guys? It's bath time. If you say good-bye to Jason and hurry upstairs, we can read two extra stories tonight."

Neither boy moved, captivated by the trucks.

I felt the knot in my stomach swell to the size of a fist. This could spiral out of control very quickly, and I didn't think my mother or Kelly was going to do much to keep that from happening. "Hey, Jason. Kelly's right. It's almost time for their baths. We should plan to get together another time." I scooped up a few small trucks and cars and dropped them into the box.

"No worries," Jason said. "We can set something up for the weekend. Or we can meet for coffee, so you can ask me whatever you want." He gave us an agreeable, easy smile. "I brought the toys because they loved them, but I didn't really think that through." He laughed. "Nick, Sam, let's see if we can get all this picked up before your mom gets to the top of the stairs."

"No," Nick said.

Jason began singing a song about picking up toys, and as if they'd been hypnotized, Nick and Sam began following his lead, singing and dropping trucks into the canvas bag.

When Jason was gone, Kelly hurried the boys upstairs.

"That was unbelievably rude," my mother said. "I hope Jason didn't sense the tension in this house and decide it's not a good fit. He's absolutely perfect. And as you saw, the boys love him."

I said nothing. My mother returned to the kitchen to make a cup of tea for herself, and I climbed the stairs, walking slowly toward the bathroom and the sound of splashing water and Kelly's calming voice.

The moment the boys were tucked into their beds, Kelly marched down the stairs without talking to me. I trailed behind, wishing I could be nestled in bed like my sons, drifting peacefully to sleep.

Kelly found my mother in the living room, sipping tea and flipping through a magazine.

"What was that all about?" Kelly asked.

"I'm trying to help you out, Kelly. Wyatt said you wanted to hire a nanny, and I have a lot more free time than you do. I thought you'd appreciate it. Clearly, I was wrong. Again."

"I'll decide who looks after my sons. Not you."

My mother's eyes filled with tears. They began to dribble down her cheeks. She took off her glasses and placed them on top of her magazine. She put her hands over her face and began crying without restraint. I went to the chair and knelt beside her. "Please don't cry."

"I'm trying!" She sobbed harder.

"I know. But you have to communicate. Like when you

sold your house. You can't spring a nanny on us without any input."

"Well, I'm so sorry for trying to take some pressure off the two of you." She stood suddenly. She grabbed her glasses and teacup and left the room.

I looked at Kelly. At least she appeared upset that this had brought my mother to tears. "I will decide, you and I will decide *together*, who takes care of Sam and Nick. Not your mother."

"She was trying to help. She was clumsy about it. She loves the boys. You know that. And I'm sure she chose someone who will connect with them, who has stellar references. He seems like a pretty good guy." I swallowed, forcing my thoughts to the needs of my kids and wife, away from my petty envy of a guy who seemed to be doing a better job at living the life he wanted than I ever had. "Let's give him a chance. We can interview him outside of the house, like he suggested. If you don't think he'll work, we can continue the search."

She said nothing. In fact, she didn't say another word to me that night.

15

LOUISE

It didn't take long for Kelly to realize that she was on the verge of cutting off her nose to spite her face. She finally agreed that hiring Jason was a good idea, although she didn't say a word of thanks to me for taking the burden of finding the perfect nanny off her shoulders. Her failure to acknowledge what I'd done for them didn't upset me for more than a day or two. I'd come to terms with her ingratitude. She wanted, *needed*, to be in control, and every time she saw her grip slip even a little bit, she came unglued.

I would have loved to have been a fly on the wall in my son's bedroom, to hear how Wyatt had managed to make her see that she was being selfish. It was certainly something I was never able to do, but my son was good with words. He was a peacemaker, and I knew it mattered a lot to him that Kelly and I got along. It should have also mattered to her. It certainly did to me.

The boys adored me, and even though Kelly claimed to always put their needs first, the steady flow of power struggles that she tried to drag me into were hurtful to them. And to Wyatt. No one feels good when two of the people they love the most in the world are at war with each other.

I'd learned in life that people are who they are, and you can either accept them as is, or you can isolate yourself from other human beings. I'd chosen to do the former. I'd done the same with my husband. I truly wanted to get along with my daughter-in-law. Despite everything, I was optimistic that could still happen. I believed that living in their home gave us a perfect opportunity to form a closer bond with each other.

Once Kelly got past the trauma of finding Frank's body, and once she adapted to her new life as a working mom, I was sure we could find a way to be closer to each other. I had no doubts at all that, eventually, she would want that as much as I did, if only to make her husband happy, and to provide her children with a tranquil home. I was patient. And once again, I vowed to work harder at being kind to her.

It was possible that with Jason added to the mix, all of our relationships might change. A new person added to the family, in a sense, can change how everyone else sees each other. She might not feel so threatened by me. She seemed to like Jason, and he was the kind of guy who liked everyone. In fact, he'd said that during our interview—*I've never met anyone who I couldn't find something about them to like.*

His philosophy was admirable. I wondered if he'd been born that way or had an unusual upbringing.

As perfect as Jason was, I worried I'd made a slight mistake in hiring him. I'd thought he and Wyatt might connect over their dreams to be successful in the music industry. But so far, Wyatt was keeping Jason at arm's length. He almost seemed threatened by him, as if he had to prove himself. Not to Jason, but to himself. I planned to talk to him about that at some point, depending on how things went. Maybe it would work itself out.

So far, things with the boys couldn't have been better.

They adored Jason, as I'd known they would from the moment they met. I liked him too. He was a handsome, charming young man. He made me feel noticed, which was a new experience for me. He made me feel younger and calmer. To be honest, I did sometimes get very tired chasing after the boys. Now, Jason did all the active care on the playground while I sat on a bench, knitting and enjoying the sunshine and the pure joy of being near my grandchildren.

To show my appreciation and make him feel welcome, I made Jason a cappuccino every morning, so it was ready when he arrived at the house. He'd mentioned he was saving up to buy an espresso machine because he was *addicted* to cappuccinos. His gratitude for the drinks was almost embarrassing, he gushed so much over that small pleasure.

After he'd been with us for a few days, I borrowed Wyatt's car one evening after dinner and drove to Stanford Shopping Center, where there were all kinds of cute little shops scattered among the larger department stores and home decor chain stores. The one I had in mind was a place that sold teapots and cups and premium teas.

Jason had told me how he loved to drink a few cups of tea in the afternoons while the kids were napping. I hated making him tea with the bags that Kelly purchased online. It seemed so pedestrian. I bought him a small cast-iron teapot with the infuser built in, and two glass cups with porcelain saucers. I bought three flavors of tea.

The next morning, the box, wrapped in shiny red paper with a professionally tied white satin bow, was sitting on the table beside his cappuccino.

He sat down and took a sip of his coffee drink, ignoring the gift.

"That package is for you, Jason." I sat across from him and took a sip of tea.

"Whatever for?"

"To thank you for all the care you give to the boys."

"I'm paid for that." His laugh was kind, removing the potentially crass tone from his words.

"I know. But I want you to realize how important you are to this family. To me."

"Thanks, Ms. B ... Louise." He pulled the end of the ribbon, and it glided out of its bow, falling around the box like a graceful dancer collapsing into a ground-sweeping curtsey. He removed the paper and took the lid off the box. "Nice. Thanks."

"I'm glad you like it."

"It looks expensive."

"I'm happy to do it for you. I know you live on a tight budget—working part time, going to school, even playing for free with your band sometimes ... that's a lot." I patted his arm. "Besides, I love buying gifts. Don't think about the cost."

"I'll use this a lot. It's very cool. Thanks."

"You're welcome. You can leave it here during the week if you want to make nicer tea than what we have to offer."

He didn't respond, but later, I found the teapot and cups on the pantry shelf.

A few days passed. Jason continued to prove himself worth every penny, even helping clean up the kitchen after breakfasts and lunches. It wasn't something we'd asked him to do, and when I tried to stop him, he said he was happy to help. He liked being useful.

That afternoon while the boys napped and Wyatt practiced chords, Jason and I sat by the pool, sipping tea and talking about his musical aspirations. I looked at the smooth surface of the pool and tried to keep my attention turned away from the sauna where my husband had taken his last breath. I closed my eyes for a moment to block it out completely.

"You look content," Jason said.

"Looks can be deceiving."

"True. Missing your husband?"

I sighed.

"It must be hard, after a lifetime together. I can't imagine," he said.

I nodded slightly. My eyes were still closed. I wanted another sip of tea, but didn't feel like opening my eyes. I was enjoying the deprivation that comes from blotting out sight. I yawned, covering my mouth, letting the yawn stretch out as long as it wanted.

"Are you having a hard time sleeping?"

"Sometimes. I have a prescription, though."

"That can be dangerous."

"I've taken it for years. Sleep has never come easily for me."

"I'm sorry to hear that."

"Do you have trouble sleeping?" I laughed softly. "I think men in general tend to sleep better than women. Women are worriers."

"I don't know about that."

"In my experience, it's true. Which is limited, I suppose."

He laughed. "When concerns pile up, everyone has trouble sleeping. I usually smoke a little weed; that helps." He spoke quickly, his words running together in his rush to assure me he only did that on the weekends. "Don't worry, though. I would never, ever smoke it when I was going to be around children."

"It's fine. It's not any different from drinking a glass of wine or a cocktail in the evening."

"Okay, cool."

"I think most people your age tend more toward mari-juana than alcohol. And maybe that's a good thing. It doesn't seem to cause as many problems. It doesn't seem to make people violent, like alcohol sometimes does."

"That could be true. I never thought about it."

The conversation moved to other things.

A few days later, I decided it was time for another gift. A gift to reassure him about his lifestyle and our acceptance. I made a phone call to Chris and asked him if he knew how to get his hands on some good quality marijuana. Chris had always been a godsend to me when I had unusual requests. In addition to being a great lawyer, he seemed to know just about everything a person might want to know about the world. And as I'd guessed, he knew about this as well. He said he could buy some for me, and he'd bring it by the house.

He laughed. "Are you taking up smoking?"

"It's a gift."

He didn't ask any more about it, which was another thing I loved about that man. No questions to put you on the spot, forcing you to tell white lies. He had utter discretion.

Sitting on my bed at night, the bedroom door closed, I opened my laptop and searched recipes for cannabis-laced brownies. They were easy enough to find. On Friday, when Wyatt was out playing music with his new friends and Jason had taken the boys to the park, I whipped up a batch of brownies. I was half-tempted to put one aside to try myself that evening, but decided that at my point in life, I'd better stick with what I knew—a nice glass of wine with dinner, a shot of brandy in my tea before bed. No fooling around with new chemicals.

I cut the brownies into small squares and placed them in a cookie tin that had a design of musical notes on the lid. I'd bought it specially for Jason. When I told him what was inside, he laughed. "You're kidding, right?"

"You seemed worried that using pot might change our

opinion of you. I want you to know that's not the case. Enjoy your weekend. Besides, eating a brownie is much healthier than inhaling smoke."

"Cool." He took the tin and shoved it into the canvas bag he always carried with him, a constantly rotating selection of toys and art projects inside.

I walked out to his car with him. "Maybe it's best not to mention this to Kelly or Wyatt, now that I think about it. They're fine with it, but they might think I'm encouraging you." I laughed.

"I don't know ... I don't want to ..."

I put my hand on his forearm. "It's okay. They aren't opposed to it. And it's legal, so people expect it now."

"Yeah."

"Anyway. We really do appreciate all you're doing. You're so great with the kids."

"I love kids. I love watching them figure out how the world works. It's a trip."

I smiled. "You're a born nurturer."

"Yeah, I guess so."

"Kelly is not a born nurturer." I laughed at the obviousness of the statement. "I suppose that's why she needs the boys' grandmother and a nanny on top of that."

"She loves her kids," Jason said. "And she has a great connection with them."

"Oh, of course. Yes. She adores them. But she can be moody."

Jason shrugged.

"I don't mean to criticize her. I'm just saying ... she's volatile. And she's had a lot of change in her life lately. So just be patient with her. I have to walk on eggshells with her, that's all I'm saying."

"Not a problem. I get it."

"Drive safely," I said.

He closed the door to his tiny Honda and started the car. I stepped back and watched his car move slowly around the curve of the driveway. At the end, he put on his turn signal even though we lived on a quiet residential street. I wondered if the turn signal was for my benefit.

16

KELLY

A fter only a week or so helping my mother-in-law
care for our children, Jason was becoming close
friends with Louise. When I came home from
work, they were often sitting beside each other, watching the
boys, and talking with their heads close to each other as if
sharing secrets.

It was an odd relationship; I couldn't make up my mind
whether Louise saw him as the second son she'd never given
birth to, or a companion to fill the void left by her husband.
Either way, it was weird. If they hadn't been caring for my
children, it wouldn't have bothered me, but their closeness
made me feel like I'd accomplished nothing in disrupting her
ability to feed Nick and Sam whatever nonsense crossed her
mind. It was as if she now had an ally in shaping their brains
to her view of the world.

I hated thinking about the care of my children as a battle,
but that was what she'd decided to make it. The only way to
resolve it was for her to leave, but no one was talking about
when that might happen. If I brought it up again with Wyatt,

he'd simply dig in his heels and tell me to be nicer, reminding me she was grieving.

I wanted to be grateful for what she did for us. I wanted to focus on the positive aspects of the situation. Nick and Sam had attentive, caring adults looking out for them. I felt terrible complaining about it, even in my own thoughts. Still, I didn't like that I still felt as if I were being edged to the periphery of my boys' lives.

Finally, it occurred to me that maybe part of this was my own doing. Jason might be feeling awkward around me, still wondering if I resented the way he'd come into our lives, and was keeping my eye on him because I hadn't been the one to choose him. I needed to erase all of that. I also needed to make sure he realized that all guidance for my children's care should come only from me or their father.

The perfect opportunity arose when I came home from work early one day after he'd been there for several days. I'd given a lunchtime talk to a group of artists. When it was over, I went directly home instead of back to the office, which was twenty minutes in the opposite direction, closer to forty as the afternoon traffic began to get thicker.

Jason and the boys were playing Candyland on the family room floor.

"Where's Louise?" I asked.

"She had a headache," Jason said. "She's lying down."

I went upstairs and changed my clothes. I filled a glass with cold water and returned to the family room. "I'll join the next game," I said, settling beside them on the floor.

"We're going to water," Nick said. "Our carrots need water."

Jason looked up at me. "You can take my place in the game." He moved away from the board.

I took a sip of water and placed the glass on the coffee table. Sam drew a card that sent his playing piece back almost to the starting point. He accepted it easily enough, which I suppose was because neither of them had yet fully grasped the concepts of winning and losing.

We finished the game and went outside to survey the garden. Jason had already seen the garden, but still, I was overcome with pride as he surveyed the healthy vegetables starting to appear on the plants. While I chatted about my approach to gardening and the absolute pleasure of truly fresh vegetables, he was a devoted listener. He asked questions and praised my careful attention to nurturing my patch of living things. He managed to make me feel as if I were the most gifted gardener he'd ever encountered. Maybe I was. Maybe he hadn't met many people who loved raising their own vegetables. At the same time, he was one of those people who possess that almost magical aura that makes you want to tell them everything on your mind.

Talking about plants, we walked down the rows, inspecting green beans and zucchini, pumpkin vines that just the week before had sprouted tiny green pumpkins the size of Ping-Pong balls. I'd grown pumpkins before, and I knew they would be the size of basketballs by the time Halloween rolled around. I looked forward to carving jack-o'-lanterns with Nick and Sam. The previous year, they'd just begun to get caught up in holiday traditions. I knew this year would be absolutely precious.

"You seem really interested," I said. "Do you do a lot of gardening?"

"I live in a studio apartment. But I could see myself getting into it at some point, when I have a yard."

"It's very centering. It makes me feel connected to the earth."

While we talked, Sam and Nick continuously refilled their watering cans at the hose, sprinkling their carrots and two cherry tomato plants. Most of the water ended up on the lawn surrounding the garden, but slowly the plants were getting some moisture.

"It sounds like your family has had a lot of changes."

"Louise told you?"

"You found your father-in-law's body? That must have been ..." He shuddered and glanced toward the sauna. "Have you used it since then?"

"No. Neither of us has even suggested it. We might end up tearing it down."

"That's too bad. It's a cool thing to have. Not very many people do, at least around here."

"I do love it, or I did. I had a friend who was really into the health benefits, and she got me all excited about it." I laughed —somewhat bitterly, I thought, and maybe I *was* bitter. "I feel like it's a curse. If we'd never built it, maybe ..."

"You probably shouldn't think like that. Shit happens."

"I know."

"Do you have nightmares? About finding the corpse?"

I wasn't going to share my dreams with this kid, nightmare or otherwise, no matter how interested he appeared to be. "It was pretty shocking. But we're all coming to terms with it. Slowly."

"That's cool."

He looked at me, his eyes easy and calm, waiting to hear more. And despite my sense that I didn't want to share anything too personal with him, I started talking. "I still can't believe it happened like that. It seems so ... I don't know, like, how did that *happen*? I ask myself that all the time. It's unbelievable. He was doing really well. And he knew the sauna was off-limits. I don't understand why he decided to risk his health like that."

"Are you feeling like you could have stopped him from dying? That's not good. You can't blame yourself."

I shrugged. I didn't feel at all guilty. His death was just so outside of our normal experience, or the experience of anyone we knew. It felt like it could have been prevented, but by whom? And maybe Frank was simply destined to have another heart attack, no matter what.

"Do you think about moving, to get away from the memory of it?"

"No. We love this house."

"Still, it must be a bummer, looking out the window and seeing the thing that sort of killed him. Remembering him lying there."

He was starting to veer toward the morbid, and I wasn't sure why. It made me realize that although Wyatt and I had had an extensive interview with him, without Louise, there were thousands of things about him I didn't know. Things that would affect my children. Both significant and trivial things. I should have thought, during our interview process, to ask for links to his social media accounts. It wouldn't tell me everything, but it would provide clues.

I changed the subject, although not very artfully. "I apologize if I was a little rude to you when we first met."

"No worries."

"I really want this to work—having you as our nanny. Nick and Sam are very taken with you."

"I told Louise, kids seem to like me. I guess I act like a kid myself, and they like that." He laughed.

"You've been great for them. All I wanted to say is, I was caught off guard. It was difficult having my mother-in-law taking control of finding a nanny. She likes to be in charge. And she has a hard time with boundaries. She forgets we're the boys' parents." I laughed in what I hoped was a kind manner. "She ..."

After a moment in which I struggled to find the right words without making it sound as if I was bashing Louise, Jason filled the gap between us. "You don't need to explain. I get it. I've been a nanny for a while. I get the overbearing grandma thing."

I laughed. "It's a thing?"

"Pretty common. They want a do-over."

"A do-over?"

"A do-over raising kids," he said.

"I never thought about that."

"Anyway, no worries."

The hose was dribbling water onto the pavement, not turned completely off by tiny hands that were more excited to feed their sprouts than to worry about faucets. Jason walked over to the spigot and turned it off. He came back and squatted beside Sam, asking him which sprouts were doing the best.

After several minutes of detailed information from Sam and Nick about the condition of their plants and their hopes for huge carrots—*bigger than Jason, so big, THIS big*—with arms stretched high to suggest the carrot plants might reach the roofline, Jason stood and returned to where I was standing.

"Didn't mean to walk away in the middle of things," he said. "Anyway ... you have great kids. They're smart, and they seem really confident."

"Thank you," I said.

"They'll be fine with me. I'm a born nurturer. Not everyone is, but that's cool. We're all different, right? Each of us is on our own path."

I smiled. "Well, as I said, we're thrilled to have you here. The boys are thriving." I pulled my phone out of my pocket. "I was thinking, if you don't mind, can you give me the name for your social media accounts?"

"Checking up on me?" He laughed, but didn't seem offended, just amused.

"Just curious."

"No worries. I don't have anything to hide." He named the details for finding him on various platforms.

"What about Facebook?"

"Um, I don't really use Facebook."

"Only for the middle-aged, right?"

He laughed. "I have an account. But only because I need it to allow me to have a public page for the band. I never post anything personal—just updates about the group. I can send you an invite. It would be awesome if you liked my page. The more likes ... you know how it is." He grinned.

"Thanks. And of course I'll like your page." I planned to look through all the things he'd posted, just to get a better sense of who he was. If I knew more about him than Louise, I would feel as if I had a little more control. It would ease the lingering sense that she had a closer connection to the person caring for our children than I did.

A few minutes later, we went inside the house, and he packed up his things. After wildly extravagant hugs from Sam and Nick, he left. From the living room window, I watched him load his bag into the trunk of his car and drive away.

Louise was cooking dinner—making tiny meatballs to drop into the homemade lasagna sauce that had been simmering all afternoon. On another burner was a large pot ready to cook the wide, wavy noodles. I was looking forward to the comforting dinner of cheese and pasta and sauce.

Now that I knew Jason was on my side, I felt slightly more charitable toward Louise. Jason and I had an understanding, and I was confident he would recognize now that he should go to me first with any issues. I wondered if I should have said that more directly, but I hadn't wanted to make it sound as if I was competing with Louise. She was caring for the boys. She *was* part of my family.

"Smells delicious," I said.

"Nick and Sam love lasagna. Just like their daddy."

"So do I."

She smiled and pinched another wad of meat out of the bowl. She began rolling the meat between her palms.

"Can we help?" Nick asked.

"Why don't we go for a swim and cool off?" I said.

"I want to help Nana," Nick said.

"We want to help Nana," Sam echoed.

"Is there anything they can do?"

Louise ignored me. My charitable thoughts began to crumble. Now I felt smug, knowing that anything she tried to do to disrupt my relationship with my children, Jason would see through it. Any snide comments she made, hoping to twist their little minds, as soft and squishy as the raw meat she was rolling into perfect balls, would be witnessed by Jason. I felt much more relaxed and more confident. But I was also tired.

When was this going to end? It wasn't the way I'd planned to raise my children, and I was tired of the manipulation and the tension, the sheer presence of another person who wasn't part of our family unit. Right then, all I wanted was a glass of wine.

I noticed a glass of red standing on the counter, ready to fortify Louise while she cooked. I repressed my own desire for wine. "Nana's almost done. You can help another time. Let's go jump in the pool."

Obediently, they followed me out of the room and upstairs to get their swimsuits. It was not a satisfying journey, because I knew Louise would make a big deal out of her solitary meal prep once we sat down for dinner.

Upstairs, neither one of the boys wanted to put on his swimsuit. Instead, Nick ran out of the room. "I'm hiding!"

Sam chased after him.

"Count, Mommy."

I closed my eyes and counted to ten. There was nothing

that changed their moods faster than hide-and-seek. They'd been playing it since they'd moved out of the peekaboo stage, hiding under blankets when Wyatt came home from work, hiding behind furniture when the other parent came into the room, hiding behind trees and poles at the playground, and ducking down to hide behind shrubs in the garden.

Sometimes, they pushed too far, wanting to play the game when we were in a store or going for evening walks around the neighborhood. It scared me, their utter lack of understanding regarding the moment of panic when I turned and they'd ducked out of sight, assuming I would know to look for them. I tried to keep the fear out of my voice when I called. Wyatt and I were aligned on that—he hated their devotion to the game even more than I did. Unlike most other children their age, they stoically stayed in their hiding places. Having a sibling by your side made it easier to stay hidden. It was cute at home, but so nerve-racking in the wrong place. I'd assured Wyatt they would grow out of it. I didn't want to push them out of this phase because it was adorable, most of the time. But Wyatt and I had trouble balancing their total fascination with finding increasingly clever hiding places, and our worry, sometimes bordering on terror, that they would take the game too far someday.

17

On Saturday afternoon, Kelly and I went for a bike ride. It was my idea.

A day or so earlier, I'd come out of the music room and seen Kelly in the backyard with our new *nanny*. It felt strange calling a guy a nanny, but I suppose that exposes some dark corners of my mind that echo my father's voice.

They'd been standing at the edge of the vegetable garden, talking and laughing like they were best friends ... or more. I wasn't sure why I'd thought that. An instant, uninvited comment from my gut. Kelly looked more relaxed than I'd seen her in weeks, smiling and staring at Jason like he was a luscious dessert. Of course, that probably wasn't the case. You can't tell how someone is feeling by how they look at another person. All you can do is project your own state of mind onto them, and my state of mind was that this guy was too good-looking to be real. He came across like he had life all figured out. Being around him made me wonder if I had some emotional deficiency that had kept me living like a lemming until I was almost forty years old.

In her sunglasses, with her hair down and her feet bare,

Kelly looked almost as young as Jason. It made me physically ill, watching them. And then it made me ill that I'd felt ill. It wasn't as if they were touching each other or flirting, although I couldn't know that for sure, because I couldn't hear what they were saying.

Whatever it was, they both seemed really into the conversation. I didn't think they would be talking that passionately about vegetables and garden pests.

Worse, Kelly hadn't mentioned the conversation to me. I'd hinted around, asking what time she'd come home from work that day, asking her how Jason was adapting, and she'd said he was doing *fine*—a term I hate. It means nothing. She hadn't told me she'd been chatting with him in the garden. She hadn't told me any details about him, and he'd certainly been doing his fair share of the talking, so she must have learned something that was worth passing on to me.

It bothered me so continuously that I'd briefly considered asking my mother if she'd been aware of them chatting and laughing at other times. Thankfully, I managed to get a grip. I was being an idiot for even entertaining these thoughts. There was probably no better way for me to upset my wife than to offer my mother a peek into the private world of our marriage. I would have to wait.

But I thought some time alone as a couple was in order. We hadn't had any date nights since my father died. Our conversations took place in bed, the sole time we could be alone and not overheard. It made me realize my mother was having an impact on our family that went beyond Kelly feeling imposed upon. Still, I also needed to be patient with my mom. I needed to leave it to her to decide when she was ready to be out on her own. After more than forty years with my father, it was going to take some time. My mother had never lived alone. She'd moved directly from her parents' house to her husband's. I hoped I could continue the overly delicate balancing act of acknowledging both their feelings without feeding their conflict.

Kelly and I pedaled out of the neighborhood, headed toward the Stanford campus where there were lots of quiet roads perfect for cycling. We rode for several miles before stopping at a café and ordering smoothies. The patio was dotted with round tables shaded by red umbrellas. At three in the afternoon, most of the tables were unoccupied. We sat down and sipped water before digging into the smoothies.

"This was a great idea," Kelly said.

I felt a surge of pleasure that she'd missed having time doing something fun together as much as I had.

"It's good to do something besides swimming for exercise. And really nice to get away from your mother." She smiled. "I don't mean that to sound as bad as it did."

"Are you sure?"

She laughed.

"Are things better with her now that Jason's helping out?"

She shrugged. "She's probably not bad-mouthing me to the boys as much now that she has a witness."

"I hope you didn't give him the idea that part of his job is watching Mom. That will make her feel—"

"Of course not."

"Are things between you and her better at all?"

"I'm not sure they can ever be better. She thinks she's Sam and Nick's mother. And she hovers around you so that I can't even get near you. Sometimes, she talks to you in such a quiet voice, I can't hear her. It pisses me off, because I think she likes it that way."

"That's not true."

She shrugged and took a long sip of her drink, the skin of her cheeks clutching her bones as she worked to get the thick liquid through the straw. She paused. "To be honest, I think she wants to replace Frank with you."

"It's natural that she's leaning on me more now that he's gone."

"This isn't new. She's always been too attached to you. She's just worse now."

I took a sip of my smoothie. I didn't want to screw up the afternoon with a fight. "She can be overbearing."

"Your father was overbearing. This is so much more."

I reached for her hand. She didn't meet me halfway, so I ended up holding her fingertips. "I know she's been underfoot a lot. But it's been good for Sam and Nick. And good for us. It would have been hard, almost impossible for you to start back to work and help the boys adjust to a nanny at the same time. This is perfect, the way we're slowly transitioning. And the chance for me to take time off, to dig into my music, to reassess my life ... do you know how much that means to me? That you're behind me in this?"

She nodded, but looked as if she hadn't absorbed what I'd said. "Selling her house was like staking her claim. I don't think she's planning to leave at all."

"Yes, she is."

"How do you know that? Did she say something about it?"

"No ..." I glanced around me. A few tables were now occupied. The people sitting nearby looked so peaceful, as if they didn't have a single troubling thought, as if their lives flowed smoothly and they were casually talking about all the fun they were having with life and their quickly advancing careers. They basked in the sunshine, and not a single one looked to be on the verge of a fight with the person they loved most in the world, about the fundamental structure of their family. Before I could compose my thoughts, she spoke.

"It's not a good situation."

"I don't want to hurt her feelings." It wasn't what I'd wanted to say, but I realized it was a large part of my reluctance to ask my mother to move out. She'd been hurt and disappointed most of her life. I was the one good thing in her world, the only person who truly loved her, aside from her grandchildren. I couldn't tell her I didn't want her around. Besides, lots of families had grandparents living with them, and they were thriving. Still, I knew it wasn't ideal for our family. Kelly was right, my mother wanted the version of me she'd had thirty years ago, the relationship she and I had shared then. She'd always been critical of Kelly in small, irritating ways. But she was a recent widow! You don't throw a widow out onto the street unless you're a horrible human being.

"I wish my feelings mattered to you more than hers," Kelly said.

"They do."

She didn't meet my gaze. "We have a nanny now. Louise needs to start looking for her own place. It could take months before she finds something and makes an offer, not to mention the time to close escrow."

"I'll talk to her."

"Talk to her, or tell her we're giving her a deadline?"

I sighed, defeated and tired. My bike stood beside me, taunting me with the illusion of freedom. Not only had riding it around the campus lost its appeal, it now felt like the simple act of cycling home would require strength I didn't have. "I'll talk to her and find out where her head is at."

She slurped her drink loudly, stood, and began buckling on her helmet.

"I'm not finished with my smoothie."

"Oh." She sat down, but didn't remove her helmet. She pried the lid off her cup and dropped her napkin inside. It immediately began to change shape as the dregs of the pulverized fruit and juice soaked into it.

"You and Jason seem to be getting along well," I said. "Are you glad my mother hired him after all?"

"He's good with the kids."

Had she deliberately misunderstood my meaning, or was I too subtle? I couldn't tell. Her face gave away nothing. I wanted to know that things were okay between us. Jason was a kid, but I considered Kelly hot, even as we neared forty, even after giving birth to two kids. And she couldn't help but notice Jason's appeal. I'd never distrusted her, and I wasn't at that moment, but I found myself craving some reassurance. This was the first time I'd been on my bike in months. I was softer around the middle than I had been even six months earlier. And I suddenly felt a little foolish—trying to launch a music career at my age.

What had I been thinking? It was the definition of a pipe dream. Jason was at the stage in life when it was appropriate to launch a risky career in the arts. I was so far past that point it wasn't funny. Even though Kelly was completely behind my decision, I now worried she was simply humoring me. What did she *really* think of this venture? Did she think I was going through an early midlife crisis and it would soon pass? Was she wondering what it would be like to have a crisis of her own and enjoy a fling with a twenty-year-old? The thought made my skin cold, and with the icy smoothie chilling the inside of me, I thought I might start to shake from the cold.

"What's wrong?" Kelly asked.

I shrugged.

"Don't sulk."

"I'm not. So you're okay with my mom hiring him now that you've seen him around the kids and talked to him more?"

"I'm not okay with your mom hiring him. I'm okay with his qualifications, that's all."

I nodded.

"And you click with him?"

"I suppose. I think he's good for Nick and Sam."

I couldn't decide whether she was deflecting, or she didn't pick up on the anxiety beneath my questions. I certainly wasn't going to spell it out for her. If there was a way to feel even more foolish, that was it.

We rode our bikes home, and all I could think about was that good-looking guy with all the free time and connections in the world to start a musical career. That, and the conversation I did not want to have with my mother. A day that began full of promise and optimism had left me feeling as if I'd been kicked in the stomach by someone wearing steel-toed boots.

18

LOUISE

The twins were napping when Wyatt and Kelly returned from their bike ride. They did not look like a couple who had just been on a lovely Saturday afternoon date. Kelly immediately went upstairs to their bedroom. A moment later, I heard the shower running.

Wyatt went into the kitchen and refilled his water bottle from the spigot in the fridge. I could hear the stream of water rattling against the interior of the metal container. I waited in the living room, plumping the throw pillow I'd used for a short nap. The afternoon had contained a rare silence, defined by the peacefulness of my sleeping grandchildren, the absence of their contentious mother, and the vacuum left by my son.

I heard Wyatt open the patio door. I went into the family room, following him outside. "How was your bike ride?"

"Nice."

I kissed his cheek.

"Don't. I'm all sweaty."

"Doesn't bother me." I kissed his other cheek and laughed

as he tried to duck away. "I was going to have some nuts and a cup of tea. Do you want anything?"

"No tea, but nuts sound good."

"I'll be right back."

"Maybe you should ask Kelly if she wants ..." His voice trailed off, telling me that he'd realized it wouldn't be a good idea for me to knock on their bedroom door, offering Kelly a cup of tea.

A few minutes later, I was out on the patio, carrying a tray. I placed the bowl of nuts on the small table, my teacup beside it. We each pulled one of the lounge chairs closer to the table. I settled in and took a sip of tea. I'd splashed a bit of bourbon into it, knowing Wyatt wouldn't notice. He was rarely close enough to smell my breath. Besides, it was a tiny splash. I needed a little something to fortify me, because I knew something was coming that wasn't good. It was traced through all the lines in his face.

It pained me to see him so worried, so crushed by stress. He was living the career of his dreams. I was absolutely confident that any day, things would take off for him. Talent can't be kept down. His expression should be eager and filled with enthusiasm. Instead, Kelly had done something to stir him up. I was quite sure it had to do with me.

"So ..." He gobbled a few nuts, then spoke too quickly, his mouth half-full. "What are your plans for looking at condos?"

"I have none."

"None?"

"Are you trying to kick me out? Again?" My voice trembled, although I tried to stop it. "Why are you doing this to me, sweetheart? I've given my whole life to you and to your family, and all you want to talk about is when I'm leaving."

"That's not true."

I sighed and took another calming sip of tea. I ate a few

cashews and waited for him to continue this latest attack on my peace of mind.

"It was a shock when you told us you'd sold your house."

It was a very faint sound, but I heard the door on the balcony outside the master bedroom slide open. Of course. Kelly had put him up to this, and now she was up there, listening. Probably letting him know ahead of time that she planned to eavesdrop, adding pressure to something he already didn't want to do, something that wasn't in his heart.

"I don't know what's so shocking about a widow wanting to leave behind painful memories."

As if he hadn't heard me, he kept talking—"But I realized it's not so strange. You can find a place a little closer to us and—"

"A lot closer."

"Okay. Well, it will be good for us to see each other more often. And for the kids, too."

"What is this about, Wyatt?" I sipped my tea, wishing he would get to the point, knowing already what that point was likely to be.

"I'm just wondering what your timeline is."

"So you don't want me here."

"Of course I do."

"But she doesn't."

"She has a name, Mom."

"Is it so horribly intrusive for me to want to be near my son when I'm all alone in the world? Look at how much I'm doing for your family. For her. You two have everything you want, thanks to me. I don't mean to sound boastful, but I think I contribute quite a lot, and it's very hurtful that you don't appreciate that or seem to want me around at all."

"I'm not saying we don't want you around. I'm just interested in your plans."

"I don't have any plans, Wyatt. I find comfort these days being around my son and my grandsons."

"But you also want your own life, your own friends and interests. What about finding a new book club and golf partners, a new church? Aren't you missing all those things? And Kelly and I want to have some people over for dinner. We want—"

"Feel free. I can stay in my room. I'm not interfering with anything you want to do."

"It's not just that. We want to take day trips on the weekends, hang out with our friends, do stuff with other families."

"And I'm in the way."

"Please don't interpret it that way. What about your own life? Do you want to spend the years you have left taking care of children? And even if you do, that's a very small window. In a few years, they'll be in school."

"I love taking care of my grandchildren."

"Okay. Let's back up here. I'm just asking what your thoughts are. Maybe *plans* is too strong a word. Do you ever think about your own place, about living according to your own schedule? Don't you want to have a social life again at some point? I know not right away, but ... it would just be helpful to know your thoughts about the future."

"Helpful to whom? I have *no* thoughts about the future. I'm trying to live in the present moment, as everyone says I must, for the best mental health." I sounded dramatic, but he didn't complain. I could tell he felt he needed to be careful about what he said. Children don't realize how deeply mothers can see into their minds, their hearts, how we're fully aware of their little games and white lies. "I have nowhere to *go*. Have you thought about that?"

He took five or six nuts out of the bowl and placed the first one in his mouth, holding the others on his palm, shaking it slightly so they shifted position. When he finished chewing, he placed the second nut in his mouth.

I wondered if he wanted to give me a deadline for moving out. It wouldn't have surprised me if Kelly had insisted they mark it on the family calendar, draw a big red circle around it, plan a celebration after my departure. That poor, insecure girl was determined to tear me away from my son.

Encouraging Kelly to return to the career she loved had gotten me nowhere. I'd thought my insight and suggestion would create more of a bond between us. I'd thought she would appreciate me. I'd thought she would settle down a bit and look past herself and her own needs for just a moment, to see that I needed Wyatt.

Still, I was tough. A lot of people had tried to hurt me in my life—my mother, who told me I shouldn't be so choosy about men because I didn't have the *je ne sais quoi* required to attract the cream of the male crop. And my father, who said college wasn't for girls, handicapping me for life, forcing me to be almost completely dependent upon my husband. There were those girls in high school who barked like dogs when they saw me, making the boys laugh, because the girls were adopting the boys' disgusting behavior. I bet I looked better than ninety percent of them now, but the wound remained.

There were all those women at church who judged me for complaining about my husband cheating on me. They said he wouldn't have cheated if I'd kept him satisfied.

When people are cruel to you all your life, when they try to hurt your chance of happiness in the world, a very hard shell forms around your heart, enclosing all the tender parts of your soul. I had that shell. It was cast iron. Kelly could keep trying to throw me out on the street, but it wasn't going to crush me and make me leave on my own, just to save my pride or avoid further hurt. Some people would ask—*Why stay where you're not wanted?* My response was—*I know what's best for me. And I also know that my son adores me.*

It was all her.

I never did give Wyatt a date for moving out. I didn't have one. I knew he believed he'd failed. I was sure his directive from Kelly had been clear, but I wasn't going to allow him to be her mouthpiece. If she wanted a date for my departure, she could ask me herself.

After a few minutes, he made a cup of his hand and poured half the remaining nuts into it. He went inside, and I closed my eyes, sipping my tea until the cup was empty, smiling the entire time, imagining Kelly's fury. I was also curious about what she would do next to cut me out of my son's life.

THE NEXT DAY, Jason and I were standing on the sidewalk in front of the house. Nick and Sam were riding scooters and push bikes around the deserted street. On weekdays, once everyone left for work, there were rarely any cars passing by on the quiet secluded street buried deep within the suburban neighborhood.

"It amazes me how they can race around when it's this hot." I took a few steps away from Jason so that I was in the shade of the enormous fruitless mulberry in the front yard. The shade was constantly inching away from me, as if it too wanted to torment me. I was hot and distracted and feeling cornered. There were times when that tough shell got some hairline cracks.

If Kelly wanted me out of there so badly, maybe her life was just too easy. If the only thing she could think about was kicking her children's beloved Nana, her son's cherished mother, the primary caretaker of her family, out into the cold, maybe she needed to face a few challenges of her own.

"Come stand in the shade," I said.

Jason complied, sidling toward me, keeping his focus on the boys. "Ahh." He lifted his face to the branches above. "The breeze feels so good over here."

In some ways, I marveled at Jason as much as I marveled over the boys each time they made a new discovery about the world. Jason was still very much like a large child, with so much to learn. He was filled with optimism, viewing the world through a haze of acceptance and love.

"I don't know if you've noticed ..." I paused for several seconds.

He turned to face me. "What's that?"

"Kelly is very ... drawn to you."

"What do you mean?"

"I've seen her looking at you. When she thinks no one is looking."

He laughed. "She's my employer. I would never think of her that way, if that's what you're implying."

"She seems to think of you that way."

"That's effed up. She and Wyatt have a great marriage. You're imagining it."

"I don't think I am."

"I really wish you hadn't said that." He hesitated, his gaze shifting to a point beyond me. "I guess she was kinda intense about connecting with me on social media. But I thought she just wanted to check out whether I had a dark side." He laughed for a moment too long.

"I know I'm right. I think deep inside, you know it too."

He shook his head. "I don't want to think about it. I can't believe that's what it is."

I let his words hang there, giving him time to realize he

did believe it. "Well, I thought you should know." I laughed. "Maybe you should feel flattered."

"Please don't say that."

I gently squeezed his upper arm, feeling the hard muscle and the smoothness of young skin. He moved away from me, back into direct sunlight. Then he walked into the street and began talking to Sam, showing him a trick for maneuvering the scooter more efficiently.

I watched, thinking about my daughter-in-law, wondering what Jason would do with this information. He would probably find it impossible not to think about it, and without meaning to, or wanting to, he would try to catch her in the act of looking at him.

19

Normally, I didn't talk about my marriage, or at least any challenges in my marriage, to anyone. Not to close friends, not to strangers, not to colleagues who didn't even know Wyatt. It seemed a betrayal. But Louise's seemingly permanent installation in our house was making me irritable and angry and frustrated. I felt absolutely powerless over my own family, my home, and as a result, my entire life.

My job was to empower people, to show them how to control the parts of their lives they could, to help them build self-confidence and belief in themselves. I tried to think about what I might say to a group of women who were facing the issue that had consumed me. My mind came up blank, which had the added downward effect of making me feel unqualified for my job. I comforted myself that I was too close to the situation. Once I was past this, I would have a lot of insightful stories and suggestions. But now ...

Celia was a woman I'd worked closely with before I took a few years off to stay with my children. We'd known each other for two or three years before that, and although we didn't socialize outside of work, I considered her a friend. I think she felt the same—we talked about nearly everything. It was a benefit that she'd never met Wyatt. It made me feel less like I was bad-mouthing him. And really, I wasn't. It was Louise. It only felt like I was hurting Wyatt because his refusal to insist Louise pack her bags and move to her own home made him seem weak. He was anything but weak. Even with all this, I'd never thought that about him. I knew he was being kind and sensitive to his mother. I knew he felt closer to her than to his father, protected by her. But I also thought he had a mistaken view of who she really was.

As Celia and I placed folders containing sheets of questionnaires and the pens with our company's logo at each place in the conference room, she asked how our new nanny was working out. I couldn't have asked for a better opening, and it made me glad that I'd told her about the unusual, but ultimately perfect step of hiring a male nanny, and how lucky we were to have someone that the kids really liked. Sam and Nick never seemed to feel they were being babysat, although I'm not sure how I would know that. Still, it was my impression. They viewed Jason as a member of the family—a fun older cousin. "Good. He's really great with the kids."

"So you keep saying."

"Because I mean it. Now if my mother-in-law would just take the hint and stop trying to take over our home ..."

Celia laughed. She went to the front of the room and adjusted the position of the podium. I moved to one of the large boxes sitting on the floor near the back and pulled out another armful of folders and a fistful of pens.

"I didn't realize she was still there."

"She sold her house. Without even mentioning it to us."

"Wow. That's impulsive ... among other things."

"Yes. And now she has nowhere to go."

Celia laughed. "Of course she doesn't."

"I feel terrible complaining about it. She cooks amazing meals. She does some of the cleaning and laundry. She was the one who nudged me toward going back to work, and I have to be grateful for that. The boys love her ..."

"But?"

I stopped weaving my way up and down the rows of conference tables. I hugged the folders to my chest as if I needed them for comfort. "She's so ... she's so attached to Wyatt. It's like all the years of him living on his own have been wiped out. She's always going on about how she makes Wyatt's favorite food, as if she's only cooking for him. She follows him around, trying to get him alone so she can have private conversations with him. And I told you about the music room. It was sweet, but it's like I don't exist. Everything is for him. And our kids, but even that seems to be focused on him, if that makes any sense. It's hard to explain."

"It sounds like she wants Wyatt to replace her husband."

"I understand how that might be a normal reaction. But something about this feels very abnormal. It feels like she's being sneaky, sometimes, trying to get him away from me." I laughed. "I sound like a nutcase."

"Not really. Just honest. And highly frustrated."

"It's almost as if she hasn't accepted that Frank's gone. She's living in some weird bubble of ... I've never seen her cry."

"Maybe she wasn't that shocked. He'd already had one heart attack. And his surgery was so serious; at least, that's how it sounded when you were talking about it right after you came back."

I held the folders even more tightly, feeling as if I were frozen to the spot, stuck in more ways than one.

"I almost wonder if she blocked it out, because of the shock of seeing his body. Wyatt tried to keep her from seeing him crumpled on the floor. It was pretty awful, so I can see why he did that. I think she barely caught a glimpse of him."

"So maybe she doesn't truly believe he's gone."

As I talked, listening to myself and to Celia, I wasn't sure what that had to do with her behavior toward Wyatt. It was the opposite of what was happening. "Except she sold her house."

"Oh, right."

"It's just weird, how she is around Wyatt. Sometimes it almost feels like she's in love with him. Romantically." I shuddered. It was shocking to hear the words come out of my lips, to feel them waft across the soft cooling air coming from the AC vents. If it were true, it was so disgusting and disturbing I couldn't even think about it. Why had I said that? It seemed to have come out of some dark place inside I hadn't realized was there. But that was exactly how it felt—as if it were some weird Oedipal mix-up and Louise had fallen in love with her son. I think she would have been perfectly happy if I walked away from Wyatt, as long as I left my sons behind. I shivered with more force, the tremors causing my whole body to shake. Apparently that was an internal sensation, because Celia didn't seem to notice.

"It's entirely possible," she said.

I laughed, my voice shrill and piercing. The folders started to slide out of my arms. "I don't know why I said that."

"It's your gut talking. Instinct. You know that—we feel things and don't realize the instinctive knowledge we have, even when something isn't verbalized or consciously thought about."

I did know this. But the idea was so repulsive. I felt guilty for even thinking it. Memories of Frank leering at me behind Louise's back, subtly trying to touch me when he caught me alone in a room ...

"When you think about how he died ... alone in the sauna

like that, a heart attack—maybe. But since you don't know for sure yet, and like you said the other day, it's taking an awfully long time to get the autopsy report. Maybe he didn't have a heart attack. It almost sounds like someone wanted your father-in-law out of the way. Someone who wanted her son all to herself." She laughed, going on for several seconds longer than she should have, edging toward hysteria. I guess the idea made her as uncomfortable as it did me.

I hurried to place the folders on the table. Putting them down with hard slaps, moving too quickly, so some of the papers inside slid out of place, exposed at the upper edge of the folders. I didn't care. I needed to get out of there. I needed to think. I only had two hours before the seminar was scheduled to start, and I couldn't speak with this thing flaming inside my head, burning up my brain cells.

It had been a terrible mistake to talk to Celia about this. I'd said things I didn't even know I'd thought, wanting to ease my mind. Instead, I was more disturbed than ever. And I felt ashamed that Celia was thinking about our family in this creepy way—seeing incest and murder bubbling up in our backyard like we had thick, gooey tar pits out there concealing all kinds of sins.

The afternoon passed in a blur. I was never so glad to get into my car, locking myself away from the world. How had I turned a situation with an unwelcome guest, an interfering mother-in-law, into this dark, Shakespearean story? What was wrong with me? Maybe I hadn't really grieved either. It was just hard to grieve for a man you didn't really respect.

I drove home slowly, wanting to stay in my state of isolation. Yet in some weird jujitsu twist, I arrived home several minutes earlier than usual. Maybe I should try driving at a snail's pace all the time.

Inside the house, I heard the faint sounds of Wyatt's guitar seeping through the closed door of his music room.

Jason, Nick, and Sam were watching *Sesame Street*. Jason had cut a giant R out of cardboard and helped the boys paint it red, to further drive home the puppets' letter of the day.

I kissed my children, who weren't eager to turn away from the TV, even for the brush of my lips on their warm, petal-soft skin. I exchanged a few words with Jason before I started moving toward the front hall. I climbed the stairs. When I saw Louise's open bedroom door and the neatly made bed, I realized Jason hadn't mentioned her. She couldn't have gone out, because Wyatt's car had been parked in the garage when I pulled in. She might have taken a walk, but it wasn't her usual time of day for that. I checked the boys' room. It was empty, the open window drawing a cool breeze into the room, causing the pale green curtains to billow.

My own bedroom door was closed, which was strange. I opened it and stepped inside. The blinds were closed, leaving the room quite dark. I pressed the light switch for the lamp on the dresser and started toward the sliding glass doors to open the blinds and the door. The room was stuffy and hot and gloomy. With the light on, something drew my attention to the bed.

Sprawled across Wyatt's side of the bed, the comforter partially pulled down and draped over her bare legs, was Louise. Her back was toward the door, her blonde- and brown-streaked hair splayed across his pillow. The color of her hair made her appear younger than her sixty-seven years. Much younger. She was slim, and the curve of her hip was accentuated by the loose top she wore that clung to her body. Her arms were wrapped around the pillow, hugging it to her.

Before I could speak, momentarily gagged by the sight, she sighed softly and moved as if she were burrowing into the blankets.

"Louise!"

Instead of jerking awake as I'd expected, she moaned softly, her body writhing like a snake's.

"Get out of our bed. Right now!"

I yanked the cord to raise the blinds and flung open the sliding glass door. Sunlight poured into the room. I lunged toward the bed.

Louise had raised herself slightly, leaning on her elbow, turning her head at an awkward angle to look at me, giving her face a distorted, almost monstrous appearance. That, too, was a shock against her silky, youthful-looking hair. Her makeup was smudged, turning her eyes to dark holes.

I went around the bed and tossed the covers to the side, exposing her legs and bare feet with their burgundy toenails.

"Shh," Louise said. "You're giving me a headache." She shivered. "My feet are cold."

"Get out of my bed. Now. Or I'll make you."

She laughed. "You'll *make* me? Calm down, Kelly. I'm just taking a nap."

"You have no right to come into our bedroom, much less help yourself to our bed." This room was our sanctuary, but I wasn't going to say that to her. Speaking it out loud would make me feel I'd been even further invaded.

"Don't be so dramatic. I can hear the TV in my room, and I needed a nap. The whole point of having Jason here is to give me a bit of a break, isn't it? Or do you begrudge me my rest now, too?"

I grabbed her wrist and pulled.

"You're hurting me."

"Get out."

"That's what you really want, isn't it. You want me out of your house. You probably want me out of your life entirely. Out of my son's life ... my grandchildren's. You'd dance on my grave."

"You don't belong in our bedroom."

She was sitting up now, her legs over the edge of the bed. She ran her fingers through her hair and wiped the corners of her eyes with her pinky fingers. "Relax. I'm sorry to be *so very* burdensome by taking a little nap to give me the energy I need to care for your children and cook your dinner and be always available so you can pursue your career."

"That's not what this is about."

"I think it is." She stood. She nudged me out of the way and walked slowly—seductively, if I wasn't mistaken—toward the bedroom door. A moment later, she was gone.

I ripped the blankets and sheets off the bed. I peeled away the fitted mattress cover and heaved the entire bundle onto the bathroom floor until I could get the laundry basket. I opened the bathroom linen closet and took out a fresh set of sheets, foregoing the mattress cover for now.

Wyatt found me tucking in the top sheet and blanket. He hit the switch to turn off the light now that the room was bathed with sunshine. "What happened?"

"What did she tell you?"

"She said you flipped out. You attacked her."

I laughed. "That is not what happened. She was sleeping in our bed."

"That's not cool."

I didn't have the guts to tell him how finding her there had looked to me, especially following my conversation with Celia. He wouldn't see it as I did. I was absolutely sure of that. "It's creepy and way out of line. Don't you see how weird this is?"

"I'm sure it won't happen again."

"Damn right."

"Kelly, please."

"Our bed belongs to us. No one else sleeps in it. Ever. Definitely not your mother."

"I agree, but—"

"Good. Make sure she gets that."

"She does. You scared her."

"Good."

He came closer and put his arms around me. My first thought was to shove him away, but I resisted the impulse. This was about his mother, not Wyatt. I loved him. I just wanted him to feel what I felt, but I wasn't sure that was possible.

After Kelly freaked out about my mom napping in our bed, I told my mom that she was not allowed in our room. She assured me she wouldn't try to nap there again, but followed that with a lengthy lecture about Kelly's territorial behavior and how it would surely undermine our marriage, and wouldn't serve our children well, whatever that meant. I didn't ask. I repeated my demand, and she said nothing more.

Within two hours of that explosion, the conflict completely evaporated from my thoughts. Brad, one of the guys I'd been practicing chord transitions and trying new stuff with a few days a week, texted me to let me know about an opportunity to play backup with a local band. Lovestruck had a regular gig at a restaurant that served fancy burgers, microbrews, and local wines. They needed a second guitarist. Their guy was taking a three-month trek through parts of Asia. A brief audition was required, but if they liked my style, the gig was mine—playing Wednesday through Saturday nights, eight to eleven.

I looked in the mirror, staring deeply into my eyes, as if I wanted to read my thoughts from the outside. Staring back at me was a fourteen-year-old kid with enormous dreams.

When I told Kelly about the offer, I didn't try to describe how I felt—as if I were floating through the atmosphere, as if my blood had been replaced with a carbonated substance and I felt nothing but a steady, gentle popping of tiny bubbles, fizzing with pleasure as they pinged against my heart.

It was almost too good to be true, which drove me to keep rereading the text message exchange, assuring myself it was real. This thing I'd loved all my life was now, quite suddenly, a part-time job. They would be paying me! It wasn't anywhere near what I'd made in my high-tech career, obviously, but it was real money, enough money to take a vacation, enough money to work toward paying off the car loan early if it turned into something more permanent. It was the first step.

The moment I told her about the offer, Kelly seemed to forget all about her rage toward my mother. She hugged me like I was one of the kids, as giddy as I was, demanding to know when she could come hear me play, making plans about how we should adjust our family schedule to accommodate time together and my budding musical career.

That night, she made dinner—grilled steak and corn on the cob. She ran to the store for potato salad and a watermelon and returned also carrying a very nice bottle of red wine. We ate on the back patio. It was the first time we'd eaten out there since my father's death, the sauna directly across the pool from where we sat. Without making a big deal out of it, Kelly adjusted the table and chairs so that none of us were looking directly at that beautiful oak door. Once we started eating, the threatening presence of the sauna faded to the back of my mind. I hoped it was the same for Kelly and my mother.

Things went so well the first night I played that I told Kelly I would love for her to come hear us on Thursday.

The band played all original music, written collaboratively by the lead guitarist and their sax player. I'd done three days of heavy rehearsal to get quickly up to speed, since the guitarist had dropped his extensive travel plans on them without warning.

When I looked out at the solid crowd of people munching fries and sipping beer and saw Kelly's face glowing angelically in the midst of them, I felt like the luckiest guy on the planet. I could have sworn the sense of her presence made my fingers more adept, the emotion I put into the chords becoming something that was a tangible addition to the group's sound. For nearly half an hour, I played with my eyes focused only on Kelly's face.

After our break, I once again located Kelly in the crowd, loving how she'd put on heavier, more exotic makeup for the occasion, along with a fancier, low-cut top. She'd clipped her hair loosely on top of her head, so that strands of it fell around her cheeks. My glance shifted, and I noticed my mother was sitting beside Kelly. Both of them were smiling. They were sharing a small table that had two glasses of champagne on it. They were celebrating my success. All the tension of the past weeks slid off my back, and I lost myself in the music and the adoring love of my wife, the pride of my mother. Of course Kelly and my mother could get along, if only to make me and our kids happy. We'd all struggled to make sense of my father's death, and now we were slowly moving toward healing.

After we finished playing, I packed up my guitar, spent a few minutes talking to my fellow band members, then made my way to the table where Kelly and my mother were seated. The champagne glasses were empty. Kelly and my mother were flushed with the heat of so many people in one room, along with the alcohol they'd consumed.

As I drew close to the table, my earlier elation turned in the opposite direction. Kelly's jaw was tight, her smile forced. She'd turned slightly so that my mother was behind her, looking lost and very alone. Kelly put her arms around me and hugged me close, leaning her head against my chest. "That was awesome, Wyatt. I love their music! I love your music! Seeing you up there makes me so happy." She kissed my neck and snuggled closer, pressing her body hard against mine. She whispered into my ear, "I'm so disappointed. I wanted this to be a date night for us, but your mother showed up uninvited. Now do you get why it's so difficult with her? I told her this was a date night, and she said she would watch Nick and Sam. Instead, the minute I left the house, she called Jason to take care of them and took an Uber here."

I squeezed her more tightly, wanting the initial feeling of her hug and the things she'd said about the music to stay with me, hoping irrationally that I could pretend she hadn't mentioned my mother. I felt my mother beside me, stroking my arm.

"My turn!" My mother laughed and tugged on my sleeve.

How, in the space of a few seconds and a few words had this night gone from blissful and satisfying to another turf war? And I was the turf. I started to release Kelly, but she clung to me with more force. I rubbed her back.

"That's enough, Kelly," my mother said, raising her voice slightly to be sure there was no chance of Kelly not hearing her with the roar of other conversations around us. "Carrying on in public like this is low class."

Kelly ignored her.

I tried again to release Kelly. She moved her arms down from my neck and turned, snaking her arm around my waist and holding tight. "I told you it's a date night, Louise. A few kisses are normal. No one is bothered by it except you."

"It's not a *date night*. Wyatt is working. You should be here supporting his career and making sure he has a chance to network, not hanging all over him like a drunk teenager."

Kelly laughed.

My mother moved closer. She reached up with both hands and took my face, pulling my head lower. She kissed my cheek, pressed her head against mine, then let go. "You were incredible, Wyatt. I always knew you were. From day one."

Another member of the band came over. Kelly moved away and started talking to him. My mother gripped my hand and leaned against me for a moment. "You have no idea how gratifying this is for me," she said softly.

I nodded.

After some socializing and a beer for all of us, Kelly stood. "Tomorrow is already here. I'd better get some sleep. Home soon?" She kissed my forehead.

"Yeah. In about twenty minutes," I said.

"Come on, Louise. No sense spending money on another Uber," Kelly said.

"I'll ride home with Wyatt."

Kelly glared at me.

I held her gaze. "Go ahead with Kelly, Mom. I have stuff to do."

"I don't mind waiting at all. I spent half my life waiting for you to get out of sports activities and school clubs." She laughed.

Kelly turned away. She started toward the door without glancing at me again.

Later, when my mother was settled beside me in the car, I started the engine, then turned it off again.

"What's wrong?"

"Did Kelly tell you this was a date night?"

"That's ridiculous. It's your job, not a date."

"You showed up when you said you'd watch the boys? She trusted you."

"That's nonsense. Jason is perfectly capable. Or doesn't she trust him?"

"That's not the point, Mom." I started the car again and pulled out of the parking lot.

"This is your career. I don't see you showing up at one of Kelly's talks and calling it a date. The idea of it being a date hardly deserves a comment, it's so ridiculous. If you two need a date night, let me know, and I'll be there to manage the boys' bedtime routine."

It was a jarring comment, because she was always there. I didn't think she realized how phony she sounded.

"After tonight, I'm even more concerned about Kelly," she said. "You must realize she's not doing well. She's moody. Explosive."

"She's feeling a little pressure, that's all."

"Pressure?" My mother laughed. "She has her mother-in-law caring for her children and running the house, *and* a part-time nanny. What is she pressured about?"

"Please don't. Kelly and I are running our household, not you."

She made a grunting sound, then remained silent for several minutes. We were almost home when she started up again. "I really think she's feeling more guilt than we realized about your father's death."

"Why would she feel guilty?"

"She was taking care of him. It was her job to keep him alive."

"It most certainly was not her job to keep him alive. It was his job."

"Guilt can be funny. It isn't always rational. Kelly was

responsible for his meal plan, overseeing what he was served and what he ate. She even monitored his medication. I suppose she didn't think I could do it right."

"She isn't a nurse. She was just caring for her family."

"I understand. But she might feel guilty that he died despite all her hard work. I'm not criticizing her. I'm telling you, she invested a lot in caring for him, and it's natural she would feel guilty."

"I don't think she does."

"But do you know for certain? Maybe she can't bring herself to talk about it. Some guilt is so deeply rooted it feels like you're exposing yourself if you bring it into the open."

"Kelly and I tell each other everything."

She laughed. "That's not possible. Everyone has a private life they share with no one."

I turned onto our street, slowing as we neared our house.

"We need to be kind to her," my mother said.

A surge of anger rushed through me. Was my mother telling me how to treat my wife? I was always kind to Kelly, because I wanted to treat her well. I loved her.

"We need to treat her with respect," she continued, "but at the same time, not be indulgent with her out-of-control feelings."

"Mom. Stop. Don't tell me how to treat my wife, and don't talk about this as if it's you and I trying to coddle her or manage her. It's degrading." I pulled into the driveway and hit the remote.

She continued talking with such a steady tone, I wondered if she'd heard me. "If she doesn't improve, you might need to insist she attend therapy. To make sure she gets help and doesn't cause any damage to Nick or Sam."

"She doesn't need therapy."

"Just keep in mind what I've said. There's no rush. I just think—"

"That's enough." I turned off the engine and got out of the car. I went into the house, leaving her alone in the harsh overhead light of the garage, the light that was timed to go out shortly, so I hoped she wouldn't end up tripping around in the dark if she sat there for too long. I didn't wait around to find out. I went upstairs to check on the boys. I kissed their sleeping faces and went into our room. Kelly and I talked more about the show. As our conversation wound down, I got up and locked the bedroom door. Then I made love to her.

21

KELLY

I pulled into the garage after work. Still sitting in the car, I checked my email, as I always did before going into the house, just in case there were any simple requests I could take care of easily rather than waiting until after my sons were asleep and I was close to brain-dead.

There was nothing from work, but there were three new messages in my personal email. One was from a friend who was coming to the Bay Area for the holidays and wanted to know if we were already completely booked. The other was a shipment update for sunscreen I'd ordered, and the third was from the county coroner. Attached to the email was the autopsy report for Frank Brooks.

I tapped to open it and began reading the summary.

The report confirmed that Frank had died of a heart attack. This conclusion was followed by a bunch of medical terms and explanations I didn't fully understand. I scrolled down, but was quickly overwhelmed by more technical details. I tapped back up and was about to close the email when a number caught my eye.

Blood alcohol—0.091%.

I stared. I wasn't sure how I knew, maybe we've all heard about it enough on the news that it just sank into the random facts container retained in the brain, but I knew the legal limit was 0.08%. Why was his alcohol level so high? He hadn't been drinking. The paramedic who removed his body had mentioned smelling alcohol, but I hadn't thought too much about it. I'd assumed he might have snuck a glass of wine, even though he wasn't supposed to drink at all with his medication.

But that number said it was a whole lot more than a few sips of Chardonnay.

He'd been drunk, at least that was what a highway patrol officer would say. Had drinking caused his heart attack? Maybe not directly, but with his medication, his already weakened condition ... I scrolled through the report, but again, it was too difficult to digest, especially on a small screen, sitting in a dark garage.

This was not something I wanted to talk to Wyatt about when Louise was anywhere within earshot. It struck me that this was my first thought, an almost instinctive decision. I assumed Wyatt and Louise had also received copies of the report. I wondered if Louise would mention it, if she would want to talk about it or have the details explained.

I could hear Louise and the boys in the backyard, playing in the sandbox. I found Jason in the kitchen, slicing grapes in half and putting them in tiny plastic cups that contained small cubes of cheese.

He glanced toward me. "Hey, Kelly. How was your day?"

"Good." I put my bag on the counter. "It's a little late for a snack. I'm about to start dinner."

"I know, but they weren't interested in snacks after their naps, and now they're *starving*." He laughed.

"That's strange. Usually they ask for food the minute they come downstairs."

"Well, they did have a few potato chips, so that might be why."

I sighed. I'd been pretty direct with both Louise and Jason about what I wanted my children to snack on, and at what times. I didn't believe in free-range grazing. I would have dinner ready within an hour, and now the boys would pick at their food because they'd be stuffed with fruit and cheese. If I told Jason to skip the snack, they'd get cranky and still might not eat their dinner with any enthusiasm, because they were so wound up.

I asked Jason what the boys had been up to all day. He dove into a detailed itinerary, embellishing it with cute things they'd said on their way to the park, over lunch, while they glued seeds onto cardboard, and while they were digging in the sandbox. I loved that about Jason—he had a great memory for the moments of entertaining conversations and amusing observations of a child. It made me feel as if I wasn't missing as much of their lives as I did when Louise gave vague reports that they'd read stories and kicked their over-sized ball around the yard.

"How's your band doing?" I asked.

"Really good. We're booked every weekend in this month. Mostly birthday parties, but it's a solid way to build a following."

"That's great."

"It's a little weird when people talk while we're playing at a party, but we need to hit the next level before people pay just to listen, right?"

"I'm sure you'll get there."

He laughed. "You sound awfully confident."

"When people focus and work hard and stay consistent, things usually work out for them."

"Yeah. I definitely have the consistent part nailed." He laughed. "Maybe that's why I'm a good nanny."

"Some people think consistency is the most important part of life."

"Sounds boring as ..."

I laughed. "I know. What kind of life is that? Do you want to lie on your deathbed and say, 'I had a satisfying and fulfilling life because I was consistent'?"

He laughed with me. He picked up the small tray with the snack cups and two boxes of juice. "Later."

I was relieved he was gone. Chatting about snacks and his band had felt like there was a thick layer covering my brain, performing necessary tasks, while the rest of me was screaming—*He was avoiding alcohol. How could he be drunk and I didn't know? What happened between the time I went to bed and the moment when I found his body the next morning?*

For dinner, I made pan-fried trout with wild rice and a salad. As usual, Nick picked out every piece of the salad and lined the veggies around the edge of his plate, preparing to negotiate each bite. Sam drank all his milk in a few swallows, then informed us he wasn't hungry.

While Wyatt handled the food negotiations, I stared at him, trying to think what I wanted to say when we were finally alone. What was bothering me that I couldn't express even to myself? Why did it seem so disturbing to think Frank had been drinking behind our backs?

After the dinner antics, stories, and bedtime chats, I declined to watch a movie with Louise and Wyatt. I think Wyatt knew how I'd feel about him spending another evening watching a movie his mother had chosen—one of her favorites, a decades-old version of *Romeo and Juliet*—while I read a book in our bedroom. A few minutes after I'd settled into bed with my tablet, the bedroom door opened, and he stepped inside.

When he was seated beside me in bed, his own tablet opened to a game of chess, I closed the cover on mine.

"Before you get into that ... I wanted to ask you—did you get a copy of the autopsy report?"

"Yup."

"What did you think of it?"

"What did I *think* of it? Nothing. It was a heart attack, which we already assumed."

"You didn't read it?"

"No."

"His blood alcohol was really high."

"I don't want to talk about all of that. I didn't read it, and I don't want your summary of it."

"Aren't you interested in how—?"

"No. It's morbid. I don't even know why they sent it to us."

"Well, they—"

"He's gone. The details aren't important," Wyatt said.

"I think they are."

"Whatever, but don't talk to me about it."

"You aren't curious? Or concerned?"

He laughed. He put his hand on my thigh and squeezed it. "What is there to be concerned about? He's dead."

"I just ... that's a lot of alcohol. He wasn't supposed to drink with his medication. You know that."

"Well, then it sounds like he wasn't following the rules like we thought he was, but never managed to do in any situation. So I guess we blame him for killing himself?"

"I'm not blaming anyone for anything. I'm just bothered by it."

"I said I'm not interested. Why are we still talking about it?"

"Is that my fault?" I asked.

He picked up his tablet and studied it. He slid his finger to move a chess piece.

"I really think you—"

"I told you how I feel about it. I'm not reading it, and I

don't want to hear about it." He turned to look at me. "I came up here to be with you, to spend some time together, not to talk about my dead father."

"Okay." I leaned over and kissed him lightly. I returned to my book. My mind refused to cooperate. I read the same paragraph four times. I closed my eyes, trying to refocus my mind. My earlier thought about Frank consuming a lot more than a few sips of wine on the sly returned with a nagging pressure. Louise's giggle flitted through my mind. I recalled her voice at the funeral, the giggle, then her sharp comment to Chris about my father-in-law—*He was sneaky. He had a shot of whiskey. He didn't want her to know.*

I'd known then—*she* referred to me. Frank had been sneaking things he didn't want me to know about. Or was that Louise's spin on it? She'd said *a shot of whiskey.* I remembered it so clearly now it was almost like hearing her voice in our room. Why would she spell it out like that? And why did she downplay it when he'd obviously had at least two or three shots, possibly more?

I opened my eyes and started reading. Wyatt was right, Frank was gone. The details were nothing but trivia at this point.

F rank's activity during his final hours nagged at me all weekend. I couldn't imagine why he would have been so stupid. He knew the danger of alcohol for his condition. The quantity he'd consumed made no sense. Not to mention going into the sauna, which he was well informed about as well. Did he pause to realize the deadly combination of the two?

Why had Louise made that slightly insistent comment about him having *one* drink? At the time, it had washed over me, but now I wondered what had gone on between them the evening before Frank died. If she knew about the drink, she was with him for part of the night. As far as I'd known when I'd gone to sleep that night, Louise had checked on him before going upstairs. Yet when I brought his breakfast to his room that morning, Frank's bed had clearly not been slept in.

I tried a few more times to get Wyatt interested in what the coroner had to say, but he shut me down just as firmly each time. By Monday, it was all I could think about.

Instead of heading north to Menlo Park where our offices were located, I headed south to the concrete and high-rise office buildings in downtown San Jose. Just before I'd fallen asleep the night before, I'd checked the report for the name and address of the medical examiner who had written it. I'd thought about calling her, but I decided it was one of those conversations that demanded face-to-face interaction. It was a risk, thinking this swamped county official would have time to chat with me, but I've always been good at connecting with people. I figured whatever gatekeeper was in place, I could win their support and charm them into being an ally.

An hour later, I was seated in the cafeteria where Dr. Blankenship was eating eggs and whole wheat toast, sipping from an enormous mug of coffee.

"Thanks so much for talking to me," I said.

"No worries. Breakfast is the one time of day people can usually catch me." She took a sip of coffee. "Sometimes I think we need to have someone on staff who's able to translate medical terminology into words average people can comprehend."

"I suppose you'd worry about facts getting miscommunicated."

"That, and budget." She laughed, then took a bite of buttered toast. "So what do you want to understand?"

"I was surprised that Frank's alcohol level was so high. He was on several medications from his surgery—"

"Yes, I noted that he'd had recent bypass surgery."

"He wasn't supposed to be drinking."

She swallowed more coffee. "In my experience, people do a lot of things they aren't supposed to that damage their health."

"I'm just so shocked; I'm not sure what to do with that information. He was really good about following his new diet, taking his meds on time, limiting caffeine ... all of that."

She nodded. "So what can I do for you?"

I'd thought I had a clear question, but now my concern

once again felt like the trivia Wyatt had labeled it. "Do you think drinking caused his death?"

"Not directly. But the temp in the sauna and his condition ..." She forked scrambled eggs into her mouth and took a bite of toast. When she was finished chewing, she spoke again. "The thing that was more of a contributing factor was that his body showed he'd been exposed to excessive heat. His temperature was abnormally high. We estimated his time of death just after midnight based on other factors. His temp should have been approximately eighty-six degrees Fahrenheit. Approximately. But his temp was ninety-two." She took a bite of toast.

"I guess in the sauna that makes sense."

"I assume the maximum setting in your sauna is just over 190, which is the standard in the US. But for someone with his medical profile, and the quantity of alcohol, that would be far too hot. Even many healthy people would struggle at that temperature. I would advise you in the future to instruct your guests how to use it correctly. You should consider not allowing them to use it without you present."

I nodded. "I know." Frank had also known. Besides, we had preset temperatures. The longer she talked, the more ill I felt. I suppressed the desire to argue with her or defend myself. I didn't want to get into more details until I had a chance to sort things out in my mind, to talk to Wyatt. And Louise.

"I'm not condemning you. Mr. Brooks was an adult. A certain amount of common sense is a reasonable expectation."

"Yes." My brain felt as if it were floating inside a bottle of syrup. I thought I should ask more, but I wasn't sure what. I was glad she'd been willing to talk to me without an appointment, but I also felt very ashamed that we hadn't taken better care of Frank. I couldn't understand why he'd made a series of such dangerous choices. But the coroner couldn't help me with that. No one could.

It felt as if I were talking to her about a stranger. Frank was stubborn and willful and didn't like people telling him what to do. But he'd said several times that he'd been given a second chance at life and he wasn't going to blow it. Why, in one night, would he do two things that were decidedly dangerous? I supposed having too much to drink had paved the way to the next foolish, and fatal, decision. "Thanks for answering my questions," I said.

Dr. Blankenship nodded. "You're welcome to email or call if there are more."

"I will. Thank you."

I walked out of the cafeteria slowly, dazed by the activity and clatter around me. The echoing sounds of people eating in the high-ceilinged room made them seem like a pack of animals—feeding time at the zoo.

When I arrived at my office building, I was still numb. The usual calm I felt pulling up to our offices, located in an old Spanish-style building that normally gave me a sense of tranquility, offered no calming mood.

Inside, I chatted mindlessly, hardly knowing what I was saying, or what the others were saying, before I made my way to my second-floor office. I closed the door, lowered the blinds over the window that looked out into the common area, and collapsed into the armchair in the corner. I faced a second window that looked out on an enormous park, making it feel as if the building were at the center of a large, beautifully kept estate.

I opened the app that allowed us to control our sauna remotely and began scrolling through the history. Finally, I located the week of Frank's death. Normally, Wyatt and I liked to use the sauna after the kids were in bed when we could really relax and burn off the stress of the day. Our sauna had a feature that allowed us to preset the temperature so the room was ready for us when we went outside. For a year or more, we'd had it set at 130 degrees Fahrenheit on Tuesday and Thursday evenings.

I'd found Frank's body on a Thursday morning. The night before, the sauna had been at 190 degrees for nearly an hour. I stared at the numbers until the digits seemed to spin before my eyes. We'd never set it that high. Some people did, but not us. We liked to enjoy the heat of the small room, but we didn't want to broil ourselves. Maybe over time, we would have become acclimated and felt the desire for a higher temp, but 190 was incomprehensible, even for me, in a much healthier and younger state than Frank.

That evening, I was forced to wait again before I could tell Wyatt about the awful things I'd discovered. The hours dragged as we ate dinner, played with the boys, and tucked them into bed, all with Louise either right at my elbow or hovering nearby. It was the new normal—I couldn't talk to my husband outside of whispering in bed, when both of us were half falling asleep.

The moment he was settled beside me, I handed my phone to Wyatt without saying anything.

"What's this?"

"The sauna temperature log."

He handed the phone back to me. "Yeah, I wonder if I'll ever want to use it again. I should have thought of that—we need to disable the preset temps. Since we're not using it, we don't need to be paying the gas bill for it."

I nodded. "Right. But this isn't about the preset. This is the temperature reading from the night your dad died."

"Kelly ..."

I ignored the warning tone. He needed to pay attention. To me, it felt negligent not to figure out what had happened. "The temp was set at one-ninety. We never—"

"Kelly! I told you, I don't want to talk about this."

"Okay. But I'm just wondering if he killed himself. And that just doesn't make sense, because he seemed so determined to not only recover from the surgery, but to improve his health."

"I don't know. It doesn't matter."

"It doesn't matter if he killed himself?"

"Why would it? How will it improve my life to answer that question? How will it help my mother or the kids? It won't make anyone feel any better, and it won't bring him back. He's gone. You need to accept that you can't help him anymore."

I stared at the little screen in my hand. It had faded to black, locking the phone. I unlocked it and kept my gaze steadily on those three numbers: 1-9-0. The sauna didn't regulate its own temperature.

The screen dimmed, then went dark, but it seemed as if those numbers had turned from black to blazing white, screaming at me that something was wrong, that his death was not an accident.

After we turned out the lights, I was plagued by strange dreams that had nothing to do with a sauna or death or drinking too much alcohol or heart problems. Instead, I was chasing a venomous snake through a jungle. Suddenly, we were in the parking lot of my high school—me and the snake. It slithered under a car, and I had to get down on my stomach to search under all the cars.

When I woke, the dream lingered longer than most. It was the snake. I could still see the brilliant green scales and the harsh yellow eyes. I'd never seen a snake like it. The boys were more into dinosaurs than reptiles. I wasn't particularly afraid of snakes, so I had no idea why my subconscious had manufactured that story. I didn't want to try to figure it out.

I went downstairs and made a pot of coffee. I walked into

the living room and looked out at our peaceful street. I cracked open the window to hear the songbirds, but their tunes didn't blot out my terrible thoughts—had Louise gotten Frank drunk and turned up the sauna heat while he was in there, half passed out? Had Frank himself done it? Had Wyatt known anything about it? Could he ...? No. Not ever. The thought made me feel light-headed, and I sat down for a moment before returning to the kitchen to gulp coffee, with the hope of sharpening my mind rather than letting it run amok.

I felt as if I were living in a house full of strangers. And that didn't even include Jason.

23

Sitting across from Louise and Wyatt at the breakfast table, I studied the similarities in their expressions, their gestures, even their tastes in food—both liked an orange every day before eating a single bite of anything else. Wyatt even ordered orange slices when we ate out, he was so married to that ritual and burst of flavor to start his day. He ate his orange before he took a sip of coffee.

The fleeting thought that my beloved partner, the man I considered my soul mate, could have done something to cause his father's death, or known something about its disturbing circumstances, sickened me. I hated myself for allowing it to come into my mind. With a force of its own, the thought had risen out of nowhere, as all kinds of thoughts do. But this one ...

Breakfast conversation was dominated by Nick's and Sam's melodic, excited voices. They asked questions and talked about the bedtime stories they'd heard. They made plans for the day and told stories. They mimicked the adults in their lives in the way they touted their opinions and handled their utensils and sipped their beverages.

Wyatt stood and began loading the dishwasher while I went upstairs to finish putting on makeup. When I came down, he was already in the music room. Louise and the boys were in the family room, and Jason was ringing the bell. I left in a flurry of hugs and logistical chatter. It was impossible to make eye contact with Louise, and I felt that my kiss with Wyatt was stiff, that a space had grown between us.

I spent the day staring out my office window. I was relieved I had no speaking engagements and only two brief meetings that didn't require my full attention, since they were for projects I wasn't directly involved with. I was there to consult. In the end, they didn't need me, and I walked numbly back to my office when the meetings were over.

I left work early. It suddenly felt urgent that I talk to Louise about the autopsy report. I knew it wouldn't go well, I knew I might end up with a very upset husband and a livid mother-in-law, but I couldn't let this go. Yes, Frank was dead, but there's something in the human psyche that wants to know the answers. We can't put things to rest, can't find peace, when there are questions, no matter how seemingly unimportant. The fact that Wyatt did not seem to care about the discrepancies in the report of his father's last moments on earth bothered me.

At home, Jason, Louise, Nick, and Sam were in the pool. They were clustered near the steps in the shallow end, working on helping Nick and Sam put their faces in the water, blowing bubbles to make learning to breathe out seem like a game. Originally, I'd thought I would enroll them in swim classes during the summer, but Jason had said he'd be happy to get them comfortable in the water. Formal instruction could come later, because feeling comfortable and seeing water as something fun was the biggest hurdle.

The kitchen smelled of chili simmering in a large pot on

the stove. The aroma made me wildly hungry. I realized I'd only eaten half a small salad at lunch, saving the rest for later, and then forgotten all about it.

I took a spoon out of the drawer, scooped out a bite of chili, blew on it to cool it off, then ate it. The single spoonful took away my craving. I put the spoon into the dishwasher before going upstairs to change into shorts and a T-shirt.

It was nearly five thirty when Jason left. Wyatt wasn't performing that night, but the group had a rehearsal that was expected to go late because they were learning new material.

Our bedtime routine took longer than usual, and once Nick and Sam were settled, I felt more like crawling into bed myself than talking to Louise. But this couldn't wait. I poured a half glass of white wine and went into the family room, where Louise was watching a romantic comedy.

"Do you mind pausing that?" I asked.

She looked at me, her gaze darting immediately to the glass of wine in my hand. "Were you going to offer me a glass of wine?"

"Sure." I went into the kitchen and returned with a glass of wine for her. I sat across from her in the armchair. "Louise, do you mind pausing the movie for a minute? I need to ask you something."

She took a sip of wine. "Can't it wait?"

Raising my voice over the volume of the TV, I said, "I was wondering if you've had a chance to read the autopsy report."

She glared at me, picked up the remote, and paused the movie.

"You received an electronic copy, right?"

"I deleted it."

"Without reading it?"

"Why on earth would I want to know the gory details of my husband's death?"

I heard Wyatt's voice in hers, and it bothered me. "Don't you want to know what they found out about how he died?"

"Why does that matter?"

Was *I* the one who was behaving strangely, wanting to know everything? I was sure my reaction was normal. But I couldn't know for sure if my interest was perverse, because there was no one I felt comfortable posing that question to. I honestly didn't think it was morbid or creepy to want to know the details of how someone you loved had died, especially when the circumstances were so unusual, so sudden. "He had a lot to drink," I said.

She took a sip of wine, as if to assure me that drinking was perfectly normal.

"I heard you tell Chris he'd had a shot of whiskey."

"What?"

"At his funeral. I heard you talking to Chris—"

"You were listening in on a private conversation with my attorney?"

"Don't play games. You listened to my conversation too, if you recall. And I wasn't *listening in*. You were sitting right beside the pool. There were people all around. It wasn't a private conversation at all."

"I don't remember."

"You told Chris that Frank was sneaky, and that he had a shot but didn't want me to know about it."

She laughed.

"You think it's funny?"

"I think Frank was a very funny man sometimes. He acted like a big kid, trying to hide that from you." She laughed again and pointed the remote at the TV. The movie resumed playing.

"Can I just? ... We're talking."

She heaved a deep sigh and hit the pause button again. "What do you want?"

"You said he had one shot. But the autopsy report said his blood alcohol was 0.091%."

"I have no idea what that means."

"It means he had three or four drinks."

"One drink, four drinks. It doesn't matter."

"You said one. And I don't recall seeing a dirty shot glass."

She glared at me. "I probably washed it." She took another sip of wine. "Why are you so concerned about this?"

"I wondered if you knew that he'd had so much to drink. It wasn't good for him, with his medication."

"Are you trying to blame me?"

"I just ... it's bothering me."

"I don't know what to tell you. I think you should let the poor man rest in peace."

"The other thing is that his body temperature was very high. The coroner said—"

"You talked to the coroner? This is none of your business."

"I think it is. And I'm a little surprised you don't care."

"I care that I'm a widow. I care that it was one of the most horrible experiences of my life. I do not care to know every little detail. You should put it out of your head."

"I checked the sauna log, and the settings for that night were ..."

"What, exactly, are you trying to say?"

"Did you adjust them? I mean ..." I scrambled to find words that wouldn't sound like I was accusing my mother-in-law of killing her husband. "If you aren't used to it, you might not know what the right temp is. And if Frank said he wanted a sauna ... maybe you—"

"I know nothing about saunas. Keeping it working correctly is your job. Yours and Wyatt's. Now can I get back to my movie?"

"I just—"

"You just like to stir things up. I know that about you. Or is something weighing on *your* conscience?" She smiled, then pressed the remote. Voices from the TV filled the room. She pressed the remote again, raising the volume until it sounded as if all the actors were shouting at me.

K elly was sitting up in bed when I got home at
twenty after twelve.

I could almost see the adrenaline pulsing
through her, partially because of the wild look in her eyes.
Normally this late, she would have been yawning and
fighting drooping eyelids. Instead, she looked like she'd had
three cups of coffee. She waited until I climbed into bed to
speak. When I asked why she was still awake, she didn't
respond. I didn't push it.

I turned off the light on my side. "'Night." I turned to
kiss her.

"I know you're sick of me talking about this," she said,
"but the more I get brushed off, the more it bothers me."

I groaned. "Kelly, please."

"I talked to your mother."

I sat up. "About what?"

"About the temperature in the sauna. About how much
Frank had to drink."

"Let. It. Go."

"It's important. I don't understand why neither one of you is interested."

"Because it doesn't matter how it happened. He had a heart attack." I couldn't figure out her obsession. My father was dead. Was this a manifestation of her inability to accept the finality of that? She'd lost her own parents when she was young, but from conversations we'd had in the past, she seemed to have a very philosophical, healthy attitude about death.

"Someone changed the temperature. I'm sure a hundred and ninety degrees is fine for a young healthy guy, for a short time. But several shots of whiskey? Heart and blood pressure medication? Invasive surgery? A history of a heart attack? It's negligent, and I'm a little surprised that wasn't noted in the autopsy report."

"*Negligent*? What are you saying? You think he killed himself? You think my mother turned up the heat and cooked him to death?"

She looked like she wanted to laugh, but I guess she wanted to fight more than she wanted to take a step back. "Yes. Someone set the heat too high, and in Frank's condition, that was negligent. The coroner said she—"

"The coroner?"

"I met with the coroner today."

"Are you kidding me?"

"No."

"Why would you do that? What's wrong with you?"

"I want to know what happened. In our house. Under our watch."

"Oh. Okay." I leaned against the headboard and reached for her hand. "I get it." I did get it. My mother had been right. It was very perceptive of her. "You're feeling guilty." I leaned closer and spoke softly, hoping to soothe her. "It was not your fault my dad died. You have to believe that."

As if she hadn't heard me, she launched into an explanation that had clearly taken her some time to develop. "I'm not accusing Louise of killing him. But I wonder, if after all those years of Frank cheating on her, she wanted to punish him. Wounds like that can fester for a long time. She always acted so unfazed by it. Well, maybe she wasn't. Maybe it was repressed and—"

"Stop. I don't want to hear this."

"You have to consider it. You can't stick your head in the ground. What if she has years of repressed anger? Maybe she turned up the sauna temp to make him suffer, just a little bit. She didn't realize what it would do. Maybe she was angry at him right then, for drinking too much? I don't know the details of her feelings, but it makes sense, I think."

I yanked my hand away from hers. I moved toward the edge of the bed, hardly able to be near her. Why was she obsessing over this? Why was she thinking such vicious things about my mother? I'd known they didn't get along. I'd always known there was this weird battle of mother versus wife over where they stood in my life. But this was disgusting. She was accusing my mother of killing my father.

"I'm not saying she meant to kill him. I just mean that she wanted him to feel awful, to suffer like she had, and that was the only way she could think of. Then maybe he had the heart attack, and she was scared. Of course she would be scared, so she pretended she didn't know."

"God, Kelly. I can't believe I'm hearing this. My mother has done nothing but support and care for us. And love us. Yes, she gets possessive of me sometimes. And she has a different style with children than you or me, but what are you doing?"

"I'm trying to find out what happened."

"You're trying to crucify my mother. And you betrayed us by going to the coroner."

"I didn't betray you. I didn't understand the report. I had some questions."

"An email, copying all of us, would have been the right approach. This way, it's obvious you went behind our backs."

"*Our* backs? So now it's you and her against me?"

"No one is against anyone. This isn't a war. Unless you want to make it one."

She leaned against me. "I don't. I just want to know what happened." Her voice was soft and sounded suddenly very weak.

I wrapped my arms around her and pulled her close. I needed to handle this carefully. She was clearly obsessed; it was going to end up hurting our relationship and possibly damaging our children if she didn't stop. This wasn't about my mother at all, or my father's death. It was about Kelly being traumatized by finding his body and what I now realized must be overwhelming guilt at failing to nurse my father back to health.

I placed my hand on the side of her head, pressing her against me. I wanted to do nothing but hold her close. I also wanted to go to sleep. Neither were options right now. I had to find the words to say something she would likely take as an attack, or a judgment of her, but I still needed to say it.

"Hey." I kissed the top of her head. "I know how hard you worked to keep Dad healthy. And my mom knows that too, even if she has trouble expressing it."

"What?" She tried to pull away, but I kept my grip on her shoulders and head tight, forcing her back toward me, wanting her to feel the solidity of our connection.

"I think it would be a good idea for you to talk to someone," I said.

She wrenched herself out of my arms. "What?"

"A therapist."

She laughed, a loud, harsh sound that I was sure could be

heard in my mother's room, although hopefully she was asleep.

"I don't need a therapist."

"I'm sure it's normal to feel guilty like you are, since you were in charge of his care."

"I don't feel guilty. Not at all."

"It's okay to admit it. No one is condemning you for what happened. It was a horrible, tragic accident. That's all. No one touched the temp control; no one—"

"It's in the log. Don't tell me no one touched it."

"Apps have bugs all the time. It doesn't mean anything."

"This is not a bug. All the dates are there; all of our presets show up exactly as they should."

"It was a hiccup. The autopsy confirmed he had a heart attack, just like we thought. This other stuff is nothing but details that won't change anything, ever. I think if you can talk about your feelings, talking about—"

She shoved herself out of bed, dragging the blankets behind her. She stood glaring at me, her hands on her hips.

She looked kind of hot—her hair tangled and her eyes blazing, her cheeks flushed. Her nightgown had slipped to the side, and one strap fell off her shoulder, ripping my attention away from everything we were saying.

After glaring at me for several seconds, she grabbed the strap and yanked it back onto her shoulder. It didn't change how I was feeling. Even though I was tired from rehearsal and the concentration it had required, even though Kelly had to be up in a few hours to get ready for work, I wanted her. It also helped me put her insane comments about my father's death out of my head. Both of us needed each other's bodies. We needed a few minutes of escape, the release from all of this mental clutter. "Come back to bed."

"You're acting like I'm crazy."

"No, I'm not. I just think talking to someone can be helpful."

"Maybe you should *talk to someone*. Louise, too."

She felt the need to add air quotes to that, but I hardly noticed, aware of wanting her even more, but also wanting to help her see how off base she was. So maybe I was acting like she was crazy. I didn't mean she'd lost her mind, that she couldn't function. I just thought she was letting her imagination and guilt get the best of her. I was sure it was a protective device. This was starting to feel out of my league, but there was no way to force her to see a therapist. I would have to hope the guilt would fade. "If you don't want to, that's fine. It was just a suggestion."

She glared at me and folded her arms across her chest, suddenly aware of where my attention was. "Something is not right here, and you should care."

"Let's get some sleep."

"I can't sleep."

That was further proof she was obsessed. But maybe if I simply listened to her, she would eventually work it out of her system. If I could encourage her to talk about her feelings regarding my father ... I sighed. "I'm really tired. And I don't want to argue."

"You're being really condescending."

"How?"

She tugged the covers into place and crawled into bed. She turned her back toward me. I waited for her to say more, but she lay there motionless, her breathing steady. I knew she wasn't asleep, but I was too tired to talk any more about it. Maybe she would get busier at work, busy with the kids, and it would fade on its own.

I switched off the light and lay down, facing her back. I put my hand on her hip. She didn't move, but I fell asleep feeling the heat of her.

25

KELLY

I slipped out of bed before anyone was awake. It was still dark, but I'd woken suddenly at four a.m., fully alert. The thought that woke me was a compulsion I should have experienced the day Frank died. I wondered why it had just now occurred to me.

Barefoot, a T-shirt pulled over my flimsy nightgown, I crept down the stairs. As I filled a glass with water, my unfinished conversation with Wyatt the night before wormed its way to the surface of my mind. While I'd been talking, I'd felt his attention shift from what I was saying to my body. I wondered if he knew I'd seen the desire in his eyes, in the shape of his mouth. It was bad enough he wasn't willing to talk about what I'd learned from the coroner, he was so completely disinterested, his thoughts immediately gravitated toward sex. He wanted my body, but not my opinion.

I took a few sips of water and placed the glass on the counter. I walked through the darkened, silent family room and into the short hallway leading to the room Frank had slept in during those weeks just before and following his surgery.

I turned on the light. Looking around the deserted space was more disturbing than I'd anticipated. I hadn't been in this room for weeks. The only change was that Louise had asked the movers to put Wyatt's desk and computer in the corner when she'd created the music room where his office had been. The desk crowded the room, destroying the tranquil atmosphere I'd created to nurture Frank's recuperation. The dark, powered-down computer reminded me how much our lives had changed. Wyatt used to spend part of nearly every weeknight tapping at that keyboard, his shoulders tense, his face tight with pressure.

Other than that, the room was exactly as it had been when Frank was resting in bed, sitting in the armchair, trudging slowly toward the bathroom. I closed my eyes, and for half a second, I felt his presence—a lingering force, those eyes that often held the glint of lust when I glanced at him before he'd had time to compose his expression. Sometimes, he hadn't tried to compose himself.

That sense of his essence still filling the room was probably a function of my body's muscle and habit memory. My cells were recalling all the times I'd come into this room with a tray of food. My body remembered the first few days after surgery when I'd insisted he get out of bed and settle in the armchair, to be sure he didn't develop sores. He fought me on getting up, but I was firm, and eventually I prevailed, although it had been exhausting. It had also filled me with a fair amount of anger for the way he fought things that were necessary, for taking his sense of helplessness out on me.

I went to the armchair. I sat down and studied the room from a different angle. I would search every corner of it. I wasn't sure what I was looking for, but it had to be done, and I was shocked I'd never thought of it until that moment. Then, as if the heat of Frank's body remained in the armchair, as if his ghost had entered the room, I sensed his presence in a way that made my lungs tight with mild panic. I felt him moving closer, his hand reaching out to touch me.

I bolted out of the chair and lunged toward the door, which offered escape to our backyard. I flung it open and stepped outside, taking a deep breath. I looked up at the sky slowly shedding stars and darkness, filling with a faint light.

I walked along the length of the pool, telling myself it was logical to search the sauna first. I pressed down on the handle to open the door. A stale odor assaulted my nostrils. As far as I knew, no one had been inside since that morning when they'd taken away Frank's lifeless body.

On that morning, the air had been warm. Now, I knew it had been extraordinarily warm because it was set at 190 degrees, then turned off. I tapped the light switch.

The room looked familiar and strange at the same time— a simple wood bench and a large container for the heated rocks, which were mostly for show, since the heat came from gas, not from heated rocks.

I sat on the bench and stared at the partially opened door. There was nothing to be found in here. It was all wood and empty space. Still, I knelt on the floor and ran my fingers along the joint where the walls and floor met. I reached under the bench and swept my hand methodically around. Not satisfied, I grabbed my phone off the bench and turned on the flashlight, pointing it into the dark corners. The room was spotless. The lack of a human body sitting in the hot air meant no dust had gathered since that awful morning.

I sat down again and closed my eyes. My heart was racing, and I realized that despite my focus on searching for something that eluded me, I was having a mild panic attack. As if it were happening again, I recalled Frank lying on the floor, recalled the intense heat that I just now realized had been far hotter than normal. It was such a claustrophobic room, when I thought about it. Why had I ever enjoyed sitting inside, sweating, watching Wyatt sweat, thinking it was helping us remove toxins from our bodies, thinking it was helping me relax and unwind? It was anything but.

With my eyes still closed, images flashed across the backs of my lids as I imagined Frank's final moments. I felt the heat rising, unaware at first that the temperature was making me anxious, that the sweat pouring from my body was growing thicker. I imagined trying to breathe the stifling air, imagined it making even the insides of my lungs feel hot. My heart thudded, making me aware of how little I controlled the organ that kept me alive. It beat harder, straining to keep going.

I opened my eyes and stood quickly. I rushed to the door that had fallen closed. I pushed, and for a moment, it stuck. A shiver of panic ran through me. If I collapsed, would they wake and find me in time? I shoved both hands against the wood. There was a moment of resistance, and then it swung open. I went outside, gasping under the predawn sky, drawing in cool, calming air.

Returning to his bedroom, I crawled around the floor, feeling under the bed and chair for anything, a note Frank had written, maybe, one of the hundreds of sticky notes that used to cover his laptop and stick out of magazines he was reading. He'd hated reading articles online and had continued subscribing to three newspapers and several magazines, forwarding them to our home when he was staying with us. The subscriptions had been canceled now, the remaining issues transferred to Chris. That way, we wouldn't have to be reminded of Frank's absence every single morning when we stepped out the front door and saw the newspapers. As if that had allowed us to stop thinking about him.

I stood and slid my hands between the mattress and box spring. I was starting to feel foolish. There was nothing to be found. The idea had seemed so important when I woke, and now it looked like fruitless desperation. What was I doing? But I couldn't stop. I lifted the chair cushion and checked the drawers in the nightstand. After that, I stood in the center of the room, numb, feeling more foolish by the minute, but unwilling to stop.

In the bathroom, I searched the floor, including behind the toilet. I opened the medicine cabinet and saw Frank's prescriptions. I wasn't sure why we'd never thought to throw them out. I'd cleaned the bathroom before his funeral lunch, but hadn't looked in the cabinet.

I took out the bottles and boxes and lined them up on the counter. I returned to the bedroom and sat in the armchair again. My gaze traveled around the room and landed on the leg of the nightstand. Tucked up behind the leg, wedged under it between the wood and the floor protector cap, was a tiny yellow, oblong tablet. I bolted off the chair and plucked it out of the spot where it had been lodged.

In the bathroom, I began opening bottles and boxes, trying to find the matching pills. The yellow tablets were in the bottle labeled with the generic name of a blood pressure medication.

So he'd missed a dose. Had that made him more susceptible to a heart attack? I had no idea if missing a single dose mattered, and no idea if blood pressure was directly related to a heart attack. Between that and the alcohol and the heat ... I collapsed back into the chair, staring at the pill in the palm of my hand.

It meant nothing. It could have been a pill he'd missed days or even weeks before he died. It didn't give me a shred of information about the sauna and how the heat had gotten so high. That was the important question that needed answering.

Searching felt good for those few moments because it

gave me something to do; it made me believe that finding answers was within the realm of possibility. It was not.

I put the medications back into the cabinet. It seemed important not to throw them away quite yet. I placed the stray pill on the shelf and closed the cabinet door.

I went upstairs and showered and dressed for the day. When I stepped out of the bathroom, Wyatt was still sleeping. The sky was growing light.

Breakfast was done, and I was just about to leave for work when Jason arrived. He had his trunk filled with a set of building blocks he'd borrowed from his cousin. There were six boxes filled with solid pine blocks in all shapes and sizes.

"We can use them as long as we want. His kids have grown out of them."

"We can buy our own blocks," I said.

"These are free." He grinned as if that was all that mattered.

I shrugged. I followed him to his car, and he handed a carton to me. I started toward the house, Jason beside me, carrying one of the other boxes. "Things are going good?" I asked.

"Yep."

"I don't mean life in general. I mean working here. Being with the boys; balancing the childcare with Louise?"

"Absolutely."

"No issues?"

"Do you think there are issues?"

"It's a unique situation. I'm sure you're used to being the only caretaker."

"True."

"I want to be sure you two aren't tripping over each other or having any power struggles. It would be natural if you were. I just want to make sure things are working smoothly. For the boys, but also for you. And for my mother-in-law."

I could feel his eyes on me as we stepped onto the front porch. "No issues. Louise and I get along great."

Something in his tone chilled me. I'd had the idea he was on my side, but now ... he sounded like he wanted me to back off, or that he was warning me not to say anything negative about my mother-in-law.

Had I misread him in the garden that day? Or was I reading into his attitude now? Why was I feeling this very clear chill?

I shouldn't have been thinking in terms of taking sides, but Louise had a way of bringing out the worst in me. And now, after asking about Frank's time in the sauna, the tension had accelerated to a dangerous level. Accusing your mother-in-law of contributing to her husband's death was not an endearing stance to take.

I pushed open the front door. "Glad to hear it."

Louise was standing just inside the door. "Glad to hear what?"

"That Jason is doing well," I said, hoping I sounded easy, knowing I probably did not.

Jason stepped around me and looked back. He gave me a knowing smile that made me feel ill.

26

LOUISE

Seeing Kelly and Jason all chummy as they carried boxes of children's building blocks into the house irritated me. Kelly had practically turned my son against me in her selfish outrage over my help in hiring a nanny. Now, she acted like she'd done all the profile reviewing, all the interviewing, asked all the right questions, and confirmed the background checks. She'd done none of that. Well, I suppose she had. But only after I'd already taken care of it. She repeated the process, because she had to show me that she didn't trust me to be as careful as she was in looking out for my son's precious children.

I cleaned up the breakfast dishes and waited for Kelly to fiddle around before she finally left. It seemed like she was waiting for something to happen. She kept looking at the closed doors of Wyatt's music room, but she didn't go in there. Usually, she would knock. He would come to the door, and they'd have a kiss good-bye. It looked to me like there was trouble in paradise.

Kelly's behavior was getting more concerning to me, and I wondered if Wyatt had the same concerns. Of course, he probably wouldn't tell me if he did, but something was definitely not right between them. He knew what time she left the house in the morning, and he hadn't come out for that ritual kiss. Her attack on me the previous evening, accusing me of killing my husband, still burned in my stomach. I tried to imagine her expressing that viewpoint to my son. It would not go well. My son loved me, and he was not going to let someone, even Kelly, say whatever they wanted about me.

Although maybe she had said something similar to him. He knew how his father flirted and overstepped boundaries, even with his daughter-in-law. Maybe Wyatt was wondering if Kelly had adjusted the temperature in the sauna to a dangerous level.

On some level, I'd always known Kelly was unstable. I was pretty sure that childbirth, especially giving birth to twins, had pushed her over the edge. She'd been colder and more and more sharp with me for the past three or four years. She'd been exactly the opposite with Frank. She doted on him. It was almost flirtatious at times, at least it seemed that way to me—quite sickening.

Things were so bad with her now, I was worried for my son ... for my grandsons. She manipulated them terribly, and I was worried she was going to end up causing permanent damage. I couldn't say how this might happen, but it was a heavy, painful ache in my bones.

But now, I'd figured out a way to expose her true nature to Wyatt. I had a handy assistant, completely devoted to me, who would be willing to help. If he wasn't immediately eager, I knew how to persuade him.

At lunchtime, I told Jason it would be nice to have a chat once the kids were down for their naps. Most days, when I put them to bed after lunch and a few stories, Jason would go for a run. It was our agreement that we each took sole responsibility at different times of the day. What was the point of two caregivers if you didn't get some time off?

He said *sure*. He always said *sure*. He was a very agreeable kid. I liked him, and I knew my plan would be beneficial to him as well.

We sat on the lounge chairs in the shade of the patio. I'd made a pot of tea. Even when it was warm out, I preferred warm tea over iced, which tasted like sugar water to me. Jason seemed to feel the same, unless he was only trying to make himself agreeable.

I poured tea into his cup and then into mine. I offered him the sugar bowl. He took three cubes, as he always did.

"Remember that I mentioned I've seen Kelly looking at you?"

"Not that again."

"It happens quite a lot. You haven't noticed at all?"

"Nope."

"She's very subtle, I guess. Or maybe I'm more aware, because I've had a lot more years to learn about people." I laughed. "And I'm a woman, so I know how women do these things. We have more finesse than men."

Jason laughed, then stopped abruptly. "No doubt."

"She's really attracted to you. Of course, I can see why. You'd have to be blind not to notice how good-looking you are." I glanced to the side. He wasn't blushing. "It doesn't help that she's jealous of the women who come to see Wyatt perform."

"I really am not into talking about this," Jason said.

"I'd like to ask a favor." I took a sip of tea, feeling the warm herbs settle my nerves.

"What's that?"

He sounded suspicious. I guess after the things I'd said, it was to be expected. At least he wasn't so suspicious he turned me down without finding out what I was asking. People are so easy to persuade when they're curious. It's kind of funny. Most people don't have the self-control to say no to a request and not try to find out what it is. "I'd like you to make a pass at Kelly," I said.

"No way. That's ... no effin' way."

"Hear me out."

"What kind of game is this? Kelly's a nice lady. She treats me with a lot of respect. She's a good mom ... She's my employer!"

"She's not what you think, Jason. What kind of good mom, or nice lady, for that matter, indulges lustful looks at the nanny right in front of her children? And once, right in front of her husband?"

"I don't believe that. You're misinterpreting something."

"I've known Kelly for over ten years. I'm not misinterpreting. The problem is, I'm scared she's going to hurt Wyatt. He quit his job, you know. Or he's on leave ... but who knows if they'll have him back. And if he doesn't have a chance to succeed with his music before she sets her eyes on someone else ..."

"If you think her and me—"

"Oh, well, not necessarily. But any man really, even if she's just doing it to get back at Wyatt because she *thinks* he's flirting when she's not around."

"That's not gonna happen. They seem really into each other."

"If that's the case, making a pass won't hurt anyone."

"Still ... no. I don't want to do that."

"What if I made it worth your while?"

"You sound like some guy in a mob movie."

"I would pay you fifty thousand dollars."

He turned suddenly, banging his arm on the table, rattling the teapot and the cups in their saucers. "What the —? Are you insane?"

"This is really important to me. I've watched Kelly for a long time, but especially lately. I couldn't bear to see her destroy Wyatt and my grandchildren. They're my whole world."

Jason stood. "I really don't—"

"Please sit down. If it's not enough, I can offer more. I just sold a very nice home in Marin County. Name your price."

He didn't sit, but he stared at the pool. I could almost feel his thoughts proceeding step by agonizing step, realizing he would not be damaging their marriage. All Kelly had to do was say no. He could make a lot of money. Enough money to not have to work, to put all his energy into school and his band. Life-changing money.

"It's not hurting anyone," I said. "And maybe you're a better judge of character than I am. Maybe she'll reject you. In fact, I hope she does! But if she doesn't, I'd prefer Wyatt to know now, before he's too long out of the workforce."

"It feels wrong."

"But it's not. Put yourself in my shoes. I feel sick every day, watching her look at you with pure lust written on her face. If she's so bold in the house, what is she like at work? What does she do when she goes on these speaking engagements and gets all dressed up and does her makeup and stands there with a roomful of men staring at her? Giving speeches is half-flirting anyway—look at most politicians. She's trying to get her audiences to buy into what she's saying; she has to woo them. Have you ever noticed that?"

"I don't think so ..."

His voice faded. He was still thinking about the fifty thousand dollars.

I tried to decide if I should add a bit more money to the pot. It was completely worth it, but I also wanted to be a good negotiator. "You would be helping ease my mind. And you'd be doing something good for these children."

"I guess she'll probably say no. You're right. But then I might get fired."

"I can write you the check now and date if for the future."

"No. That's okay. I guess I could see how it works out."

"I can't ask for anything more than that. Thank you so much." I sat up and strained to lean across the space between us. I patted his elbow. "Thank you."

He turned to face me. "Yeah. We'll see."

That evening, when my son went into the music room to get his laptop, I followed him. I stood in the doorway. "Are you still enjoying the room?"

"It's great. It really gets my head in the right space. Thanks again for doing this."

"Everything seems to be settling down."

He looked at me. He was probably wondering what Kelly had said to me about Frank, but he didn't want to bring it up if she hadn't mentioned it ... yet. He was always so sensitive to my feelings. It really took my breath away at times, seeing how gentle and tender he was with me.

He picked up his laptop and moved toward where I stood, reaching around me for the light switch.

"Kelly and Jason are really connecting, don't you think?" I asked.

"What do you mean?"

"They seem comfortable with each other."

"I guess."

"You can tell she really likes him."

"Good," he said.

"And he seems quite taken with her."

"That's a weird way to put it."

I laughed. "Well, you know ..."

"I don't know. What are you saying?"

I laughed again. "I'm just saying they're getting along really well. I'm glad to see that after such a rocky start."

"Yes." He turned out the light.

He started back toward the family room.

"I think I'm going to go to bed."

He turned. "Are you feeling okay?"

"Yes. Just tired."

"You're sure?" He moved toward me and placed his hand on my shoulder.

I covered his hand with my own and leaned gently into him. "Thank you for asking."

"We've had a lot of changes. And missing Dad ... I know I don't talk about him much. I hope you know I'm always here, any time, if you want to talk. I should have said that a long time ago."

"It's okay." I smiled up at him. "I know that. You don't have to tell me."

He gave me an awkward, nervous smile that reminded me of when he was sixteen years old. For a moment, I thought I might swoon.

27

KELLY

Things had been so disrupted at home for so long now, I'd learned to function well at work despite that. The day I spoke to the coroner, I'd turned down a speaking engagement that was perfectly suited to my background, telling my colleagues I wasn't up to it. I hadn't given an explanation for my refusal. I'd sensed one or two of them giving me the side-eye for a few days, wondering if I wasn't fully committed.

Now, I was used to being stirred up emotionally, and I was learning to shift my focus onto tangible projects and tasks, reining in thoughts that wanted to swarm around things I couldn't seem to do anything about. I'd gotten nowhere with my concerns about the discrepancies between the autopsy report and what Louise had said about Frank's death.

Someone had turned up the temperature in the sauna, and I was almost certain it was Louise. She did like to punish people. Her usual methods were emotional, but it wasn't a huge leap to this scenario.

I'd studied every single hour of the sauna log, starting with the day Frank and Louise had arrived at our home, through his surgery, and up to the day of the funeral. There were no other times the temp had been adjusted outside of our regular Tuesday and Thursday evening settings. The temp had never once been over 130 degrees. I considered contacting the manufacturer to see if they had the full history, going back to when we'd had it installed. It would have been helpful to confirm our sauna had never been that hot in the entire six years we'd owned it. I knew it hadn't, but written proof would be nice to show Wyatt.

Or not. I already had proof it had been set too high. I had proof Frank had had far more to drink than we'd been told. Wyatt didn't care.

I arrived home and opened the garage door. Wyatt's car was gone, which reminded me that the boys had a doctor's appointment that day. Wyatt had wanted to take them, pleased that this was another one of the great things about leaving the corporate world. He could be more of a hands-on parent with our sons. I loved that he wanted that. Despite the dangerously widening gap between us regarding his mother, I was relieved to know we were still equally invested in the boys' well-being.

I went into the house and found Jason loading the dishes and utensils Louise had used to prepare dinner into the dishwasher. She'd made another one of her casseroles, the ones she boasted that Wyatt couldn't live without.

"You don't have to do that," I said.

"I'm here to help."

"Not with housework. You could have gone home early."

"Louise asked me to stay. She went to the doctor with Wyatt, and—"

"Oh? I didn't realize she went with them."

"Yeah. But she wants me to take Sam and Nick to the park when she gets back, so she can finish fixing dinner. Wyatt's dropping them off and heading out to his gig."

I looked around at the near-spotless kitchen—the bowl filled with greens and veggies for a salad, the aroma coming from the oven. I couldn't imagine what else Louise had to do, but I didn't ask.

"How was work?" he asked. "Are you passionate about your career?"

The question surprised me, or at least his seeming interest beyond the generic question about my day. "Good, actually. I've been kind of distracted, so it felt really nice to get refocused today."

He nodded, giving me a warm, encouraging smile.

It flashed through my mind that he was showing more interest than Wyatt sometimes appeared to. It felt good, and I was ready to tell him the details, but stopped myself even as my lips parted to speak. I needed to save it for Wyatt. Life had been tense. It didn't mean he wasn't interested. Shutting him out, making the nanny my confidant, was not going to help that. Trying to ease back from the moment and my sudden impulse, I opened the fridge. "Do you want a beer?"

"Uh, sure."

I pulled out two bottles, twisted off the caps, and handed a bottle to Jason. I tapped the neck of my bottle against his. "Cheers."

"Cheers." He took several long swallows, as if he'd been dying of thirst before I offered the beer.

I put my bottle on the center island and filled a glass with water. "Should we go sit outside?"

"I ... " He placed his bottle beside mine and nudged it away. "I shouldn't have this. I'm taking the kids to the park."

"I appreciate you being so conscientious." I smiled. "But one beer is probably okay. Wyatt and I sometimes have beer with lunch on the weekends, and we take the kids to the park."

He picked up the beer and took a tentative sip, then put it

back on the counter again, moving away from it as if it were radioactive. I took a few more sips of mine, then drank some water. The beer was doing its trick. I felt a little less wound up. I was ready to figure out a new way to get Wyatt to listen to my concerns. I hadn't decided if I should mention the missed pill, or if that would just confuse the issue. I'd decided that I might need to take a stronger stance, to tell him I believed Louise had intentionally tried to hurt Frank, and we needed to forbid her from spending time around the children when we weren't right there. I wasn't ready to say she'd murdered her husband, but my thoughts were dancing around that idea.

"You look tired," Jason said. "And kind of stressed."

I nodded. His words made me yawn, but I tried to stifle it. I was standing in the corner where the two sides of the counter joined, feeling the hard edge of the tile against my hip bones.

"How come you offered me a beer?" he asked.

I shrugged. "I felt like one. I thought you might also. I'm not going to grab a beer and gulp it in front of you. It's rude."

"Not really. I work for you."

"Yes, but it still seems rude. Just because I'm your employer doesn't mean I'm not going to treat you with respect."

"Yeah." He nodded. "How come you're so tired?"

"I'm not sleeping well." I gave him a defeated smile.

He stepped toward me and brushed the hair off my cheek. The shock of his touch made my body stiffen. At the same time, the touch was so gentle I felt my skin and the nerves around the spot he'd touched respond, craving more. I looked at him and saw what I interpreted as some confusion in his eyes, but also, something else that I couldn't read.

He took another step toward me, placed his hand on the back of my neck and began kissing me. It was sudden, and the thrusting of his tongue so immediate, I gasped. And then, his other hand slithered up beneath my shirt and brushed against my breast. Again, my body responded before my brain. He was so strong. He tasted so good. That thought shocked me into jerking my head to the side. I shoved him away from me. "What the hell was *that*?"

"I thought ..."

I waited. "You thought ... what?"

"I thought you were into me."

I laughed. The sound was more like a shriek. "You're my children's nanny. I'm not *into* you."

He shrugged. "No harm, no foul."

"Wrong." I took a deep breath, my mind racing to see whether I was overreacting. But this was too ... I couldn't fathom what had possessed him. "I'm sorry, Jason. I need to ask you to leave. I feel terrible ... you've been doing an awesome job with Sam and Nick, but this is ... it's way over the line." I turned and poured my beer down the drain, already feeling a prick in my heart, the piercing, all-too-common female affliction of self-doubt—had I done something to encourage him? Sent the wrong message? Offering the beer had definitely been a mistake. I'd wondered what he was thinking, but the bigger question was—what the hell had I been thinking?

"You're firing me? But ..." He shrugged.

"Yes. I'm firing you." I wanted to slap him. At the same time, I was furious with myself. How had I so misjudged him? He came onto me and then shrugged when I told him he was being let go? I'd thought he actually liked and cared about my children. I'd thought he was responsible and ethical and an all-around great guy. Were my instincts that far off base? Did that mean all my instincts were inaccurate? Were the nagging suspicions about Frank's death also off base? Was that why Wyatt was brushing my concerns aside? Maybe I was the one with distorted perceptions.

"I'm really sorry ... Kelly."

"I'll be in touch about your check."

"Sure. Yeah ... I get it." He turned and walked out of the kitchen. A moment later, I heard the front door close.

I collapsed against the counter, turning toward the sink. I yanked the faucet handle, letting the water stream out full force, adjusting it to the coldest setting. I cupped my hands and filled them with water. I splashed it on my face, getting my hair wet in the process. I imagined my makeup was smeared everywhere. I turned off the faucet, felt around for a clean towel and scrubbed my skin dry. I grabbed the other beer bottle, poured the contents down the drain, and dropped the bottle into the recycling container.

As I ran up the stairs, I heard the garage door rumble, announcing that my children and mother-in-law were home. I couldn't face her or my kids. I needed to wash my face properly, if nothing else. And I needed to calm down. My hands shook. My insides felt equally unstable. While Louise did whatever it was she thought had to be done to finish preparing dinner, which was really just a pretext to make leftovers for Wyatt to enjoy when he arrived home after midnight, I would take the kids to the park. I needed to be out of the house, breathe fresh air, and ground myself in my children.

I was glad I hadn't finished the beer. Most of the time, beer made me sleepy. I needed to stay awake until Wyatt came home. He needed to hear about me firing Jason before I told Louise. The trick would be keeping Wyatt from telling my mother-in-law what had happened. I was certain she would consider it ammunition for attacking me, planting seeds in Wyatt's head that I'd encouraged Jason, suggesting I'd wanted it.

It also wouldn't surprise me if she didn't believe it had happened. I felt like the idyllic family and the life I'd dreamed of was starting to crumble, and I couldn't see how to fix it. All my concerns about getting to the bottom of the circumstances around Frank's death now seemed like an insurmountable problem that I had no time for while I began another search for a nanny, while I tried to help my kids understand why the guy they loved had suddenly disappeared. Right after their grandpa had been snatched out of their lives.

28

KELLY

It was almost one in the morning when Wyatt came into the room. He stopped just inside the doorway and looked at me, sitting up in bed, my hands folded in my lap, as they'd been for the past hour. While my mind had whirled around the pieces of my life, sweeping them up like a tornado, and dropping them miles away, my body had remained motionless. I felt like my brain was detached from the rest of me, as if I were outside my flesh and muscles and bones, looking at my still, clasped hands. I wasn't normally someone who found it easy to sit quietly, and that, too, made me feel outside myself. "We need to talk," I said.

"You bet we do." He yanked his black T-shirt over his head and wadded it up in one hand. He strode toward the bathroom. He threw the shirt with such force, I heard it hit the laundry basket. A moment later, the water came on in the shower.

I continued to sit in my slightly numb, immobilized state, reminding myself to focus only on Jason. I couldn't allow myself to start in again on his mother. If I was coldhearted about it, if I followed the thoughts deep inside my mind, I would blurt out that we had a murderer living in our house. A killer was caring for our children, sleeping a few yards away from our unlocked bedroom doors.

Who knew what was really going on in Louise's life? She'd sold her house as fast as someone would who was fleeing the country. Maybe the sale wasn't about rooting herself in our home. Maybe she needed the cash, and she'd needed Frank gone to pull that off. I gritted my teeth, forcing my thoughts back to Jason and his attempt to kiss me, his groping, entitled hands.

As I waited, I slowly absorbed what Wyatt had said—*You bet we do*. What did he mean? Had Louise said something to him? I closed my eyes and tried to focus on breathing slowly, calmly. With my eyes still closed, I felt around on the night-stand for my glass of water, picked it up, and took a tiny sip.

The sound of the shower water stopped, and a few minutes later, Wyatt was standing near the foot of the bed. His wet hair was uncombed. He wore blue sweatpants and no shirt. I wanted him to crawl in beside me, I wanted to feel his body, to remind myself of our physical connection, but he looked like he had no desire whatsoever to join me in bed.

"I thought you loved me. I never imagined you'd betray me." His voice was steady, low, but his mouth twisted in a way that suggested he was fighting physical pain.

"What? I need to—"

"I talked to Jason."

I stared at him. Talked to Jason? What did that mean? Jason had left hours ago.

"He told me what you two did."

"What we did? You mean what *he* did? That he tried to kiss me and—"

Wyatt laughed, a single staccato sound. "Why would you ...? I thought you loved me. I *believed* you loved me."

"What are you talking about? Of course I love you. How can you think I don't?"

"Our nanny? God. What a cliché. It's a twist on the usual cliché, isn't it—the husband screwing the nanny."

"What? No!" I threw off the covers and got out of bed. "I didn't ... who told you that?"

"Jason. He apologized. Then he resigned."

"He didn't resign. I fired him."

He stared at me, hardly seeming to absorb what I'd said.

I walked toward him and put my hands on his waist. He stepped back. I moved closer, and he took several more steps away from me. "Don't touch me."

"Come to bed. Please. This is insane. I didn't have sex with him. I love you. You're my whole life."

He laughed, a short mocking tone.

"Why don't you believe me?"

"Why would he lie about it?"

"I have no idea! But I'm your wife ... I ..."

"Yeah." He walked around me and got into bed, positioning himself as close to the edge on his side as possible.

I climbed in and moved toward him.

"I said don't come near me." He grabbed his pillow and punched it, lowering himself onto it and turning his back to me. "In fact, I'd prefer it if you'd sleep somewhere else. Conveniently, there's a bed downstairs."

"I'm not sleeping downstairs." I had no intention of going to sleep anywhere before Wyatt saw that, for whatever incomprehensible reason, Jason was lying. It made no sense. How had I been so wrong about him? "I did not have sex with Jason. I didn't go near him. He tried to kiss me and grab my breast. I pushed him away. I told him he was fired. That's it. And he left. Hours ago, before your mother brought the kids home."

"You're a pretty good liar, Kelly."

"I'm not lying. I can't believe you—"

"You didn't think you'd get caught. You thought you had him under your thumb. Thankfully, he's a stand-up guy. He couldn't live with the guilt."

"He's not a stand-up guy. He's making up the whole thing. Maybe he's upset I fired him, and he thought he could get you to hire him back, I don't know. I have no idea what he's thinking or what he's up to. But I did not cheat on you, and I never would. Not in a million years, not ever."

"I'm going to try to get some sleep. I'm exhausted."

"How can you sleep when this thing is between us?" My voice shook. I felt tears filling my head, sobs pressing against my throat. I didn't want to get hysterical. Wyatt hated that. He hated dramatic crying, and I hated it too, but the urge was overwhelming, and I wasn't sure I could stop it.

"I've been playing for hours, interacting with crowds of people, and I'm tired. That's how."

"But we're ... how can you fall asleep, thinking such a terrible thing about me?"

He didn't respond.

I put my hand on his back, feeling his warm, smooth skin. He shook me off so violently I almost fell against the nightstand.

I tried the opposite of my instinct. I lowered my voice to a whisper. "I love you, Wyatt. I love you so much. I would never cheat on you. It's never even crossed my mind. No one has ever—"

"That's what I believed. Apparently, I was wrong."

"You aren't wrong. Why would you trust a guy you hardly know over me? That hurts."

"Good night."

"Wyatt, please. We have to talk. I won't be able to sleep at all, knowing what you're imagining, what you'll wake and think about in the morning. Please." Now I was crying. It was impossible to stop. I reached for my water and gulped it down. I wiped my hands across my wet face and took a long, slow breath. "This is insane. I didn't have sex with anyone; I fended off a pass. I'm feeling a little set up here."

"Set up by whom?" He snorted and wrapped the pillow around the back of his head, as if to block my voice.

"Can't you see how strange this is? Waiting for hours for you to come home, outside our house, almost like a stalker? Telling you an outright lie. When would we even have—"

"He's not a stalker. Stop deflecting. What's *strange* is that you cheated on me. That's all I know."

"I'm starting to get angry that you don't believe me, that you won't even talk to me. Is that how little you trust me?"

"Nothing compared to how angry I feel. It wasn't enough for you to accuse my mother of ... and now this? I don't ... I'm going to sleep. Stop talking."

I sat in the dark until almost three thirty. When I finally lay down, I still couldn't sleep. Eventually, I drifted to sleep for an hour or so before the alarm chimed. I woke feeling as angry and frustrated and full of rattled nerves as I had been during all those hours lying alone in the dark.

Wyatt wasn't beside me in bed.

Downstairs, I found Louise at the kitchen table, sipping tea. It was unusual for her to be up so early. She usually waited until just a few minutes before the boys woke. Because she showered at night, she basically rolled out of bed and went into their room to greet them.

I walked past her and went to the music room. The doors were open, the lights off. I returned to the kitchen. "Where's Wyatt?"

"Good morning to you, too." She picked up her cup and took a sip of tea, staring at me over the rim.

I wondered if Wyatt had spoken to her. It seemed possible, since she was up. Had she heard us last night? We weren't shouting, had hardly even raised our voices, but I never was sure how sound carried in our house. Sometimes it was startling the things you could overhear, so I usually spoke to Wyatt in whispers when we were in bed. I wasn't going to ask her if he'd told her what he believed about me. "Did he go out?"

"I believe so."

I went to the garage door and opened it. His car was gone. I felt too humiliated to ask her if she knew where he'd gone. I'd check the find-my-friends app when I went back upstairs. "Can you get the boys up and take care of breakfast?"

"Don't I usually?"

She didn't. She went into their rooms to kiss them, but then drifted downstairs to make one of her endless cups of tea. It wasn't worth it to argue, so I pushed ahead. "You'll need to watch them all day today."

"I'll *need* to?" She gave a short laugh. "I usually do. And Jason will be here."

"I fired him."

Her cup clattered against her saucer. "Why? Why on earth would you fire him? Why would you do that to your children?"

"I don't want to talk about it right now, and to be clear, *everything* I do for my children is for their absolute good."

"Mmhmm." She returned to sipping her tea.

I went upstairs, grabbed my phone, and checked Wyatt's location. He'd gone to a diner where we sometimes went out for breakfast. They opened at seven. I thought about following him there, but I couldn't imagine our conversation going any better than it had the night before. If he'd realized how ridiculous and disturbing Jason's lie was, he wouldn't have gone out. I texted Celia and told her I wasn't coming in to work that day. Then I scrolled through my contacts for Jason's address.

Grabbing my purse, I nearly ran out of the bedroom and down the stairs. I bolted into the kitchen and told Louise I was going out.

"Have a good day."

"Not to work ... I took the day off. I have an errand. I'll be home in an hour or less. If I end up getting held up, I'll text you."

"Bye!" Her voice was filled with false cheer.

As I drove to Jason's apartment, I prayed he'd be home. If he wasn't, I planned to sit in my car and wait, all day if necessary. Into the evening if I had to. He was not going to get away with trying to sabotage my marriage.

His car was parked in front of the building, and luckily for me, he answered the door when I knocked.

"Oh. Hi." He looked past me, as if he expected someone else. "Is everything okay?"

"No. Can I come in?"

"Well ..." He glanced over his shoulder. "It's kind of a mess."

"No worse than the mess you're making of my life." I moved forward, almost shoving him out of the way.

"Whoa. Slow down."

The apartment had a small living area with a futon that was still open, blankets and sheets twisted into a coil and several pillows on top. To the right was a kitchen that was contained within the space of a single counter. I sat on the recliner that faced the futon.

"Is this some kind of absurd revenge for firing you? Telling my husband we had sex?"

"Not really."

"Why would you tell him that?"

He stared at me. He glanced toward the kitchen. "Because I ... it's because I thought you were into me. And ... you know ..."

"Why would you think that? And why are you lying about it?"

"It's because I thought ..." He shifted slightly on the futon. He ran his hand through his hair and left if there, resting on top of his head. "You were ... um ... you were checking me out ... And your husband should know the truth about you being into me."

"That's ridiculous. Two things I want you to do—come over tomorrow morning and say good-bye to the boys, because they're going to be hurt and very confused about your sudden disappearance. And while you're there, you're going to tell Wyatt you lied. I know you're lying, and you know it, too. You're going to make sure he understands that *nothing happened* between us."

"We kissed."

"*We* didn't kiss. You *tried* to kiss me."

"You kind of—"

"You tried to kiss me. End of story. Anything else that you thought you understood was nothing but absolute shock. I thought I knew who you are. I thought you were a decent kid. I was very wrong."

He looked as if he might cry. I stared at him until he looked away. "Did Louise put you up to this?"

He shook his head. "No. No. She said you blame everything on her, that you keep accusing her of awful things."

"Really." I laughed.

Something flickered across his face.

"She *did* put you up to this. Otherwise, it doesn't make any sense."

He shook his head.

It was suddenly very clear. I hadn't entirely misjudged him, I'd just overestimated the strength of his character. "Why would you hit on a forty-year-old woman? I don't think so."

"You're kind of—"

"Stop lying. How much did she pay you? A thousand dollars? Five?" I laughed at the look of horror and guilt on his face. "More?"

He stared at me, shaking his head, but I knew I was right.

Breakfast was long, punctuated by four cups of coffee. While I lingered over my southwest omelet, I caught up on the Reddit threads for musicians that I'd been following. Reading what other musicians were up to helped me avoid thinking about how the woman I loved more than I could say had stomped on my heart. After breakfast, I drove around without a destination in mind. Finally, I returned home. Lovestruck was playing that night, and I wasn't sure how I was going to get my head into the right place to perform. But I was not going to screw up this chance to get my career inching forward by caving to my feelings and making an excuse that I couldn't make it.

At home, my mom and the boys were working in the garden. I talked to the kids for a while, heard the stories of their plants, pulled some weeds with them, and then went upstairs. I closed the drapes and lay on the bed. I remembered how Kelly had freaked out when my mom had taken a nap in that very spot. Maybe her hysteria had been some weird kind of guilt—overreacting to a simple nap because she was having sex with another guy. A young, very good-looking guy. A guy who appeared to be everything I wasn't, except the father of her children. I wondered if they'd done it more than once. Did they do it in our bed? I sat up and got off the bed as fast as I could. I bent over and sniffed the sheets, but there was no unfamiliar odor.

I couldn't stay in the house. I went down to the music room, grabbed a notebook and the sheet music for our newest playlist, told my mom she would be without the car, and took off. At first, I continued my earlier pattern of simply driving around without a destination. Getting on the freeway, I headed north, curious about why that was the direction I'd instinctively chosen. I couldn't come up with an answer. When I reached San Mateo, I knew if I wasn't planning to head to San Francisco, I needed to turn around.

I pulled off the freeway and tried to think. I decided to head over the hills to Half Moon Bay. A walk on the beach would clear my head. I could stop at a restaurant with sweeping views of Monterey Bay and have a lobster roll and review the music. Even without my guitar, it never hurt to get the chords and words implanted more firmly into my mind.

With a weak, distracted focus on my music, I enjoyed two beers and a rich, filling sandwich. I didn't allow my memory to indulge the scenes of Kelly and me at this very restaurant, more times than I could count before the twins were born, and a few times after that. When the second beer was gone, I forced myself to go for a walk instead of succumbing to a third beer, which would mean I couldn't drive home.

It was three o'clock when I pulled into our driveway. Kelly's car was in the garage. She was probably waiting for me, had probably left work early to catch me before I went out again. The minute I entered the bedroom to change my clothes, she would pounce. But I couldn't avoid her indefinitely.

The kids were still napping. My mother told me, with a

slightly irritated tone, that because they'd gotten up late, their schedule had slipped off track. She was sitting in a chair in the living room, fiddling around with her phone. She seemed anxious ... upset, but I couldn't deal with her feelings right then. I sensed her attention move from the phone to me as I headed toward the stairs.

Kelly was in our bedroom, sitting in the chair by the sliding glass doors. The door was partially open, a warm breeze flowing into the room. A smoothie sat on the table beside her. Like my mother, she was fiddling with her phone. It's funny how those things give us something to do at all times, so we never have to be idle. I sometimes wonder if they're slowly rewiring the human brain, the constant influx of data, the endless distraction of the entire world at our fingertips. And I wondered then, what Kelly was actually doing on her phone. Was she exchanging sexy messages with Jason? That was the other thing about phones—they put the owner in an entirely separate world. Others have no clue what's occupying them at any moment in time.

She looked up. She tucked the phone between the cushion and the arm of the chair and stood. "Can we talk?"

I went into the closet and pulled a light green T-shirt out of the drawer. When I landed the gig, I'd bought about seven or eight good-quality T-shirts. The band dressed informally, but until I'd started playing with them, most of my T-shirts had been borderline dust-rag quality. Pulling on a new, thick cotton shirt made me feel I was dressing up.

I decided it might help my mood if I took a shower. Fresh start for the evening and all that, even though I didn't have to be there for another three hours.

Kelly had followed me into the closet. She stood blocking the entrance. "Please talk to me. Or at least listen." She moved closer. "I went to see Jason."

"How nice for you."

She glared at me. "He's coming over tomorrow morning to—"

"No way. I don't want that creep anywhere near our house."

"He needs to say good-bye to the kids."

"No, he doesn't."

"They need it. They're already devastated and very confused about your dad. Having another adult they love whisked out of their lives is disturbing and slightly scary for them."

"Did my mom say they were asking questions about him?"

She ignored the question. "You need to talk to him. He's going to explain that he lied."

"Just like that, he volunteered to come over and tell me he lied? That's a little hard to believe. Either way, it doesn't matter. I don't want him here."

"You have no choice—"

"I have no *choice*?"

"I didn't mean that the way it came out ... but Sam and Nick need closure."

"Then I'll make sure I'm not here. Easy enough."

"Please, Wyatt. Why won't you give me a chance? How can you throw away what we have so easily? I didn't sleep with him. Don't you know me better than that?"

Looking at her eyes, clear and obviously desperate for me to believe her, I hesitated for a moment. Why didn't I believe her? Because it made no sense that this near-stranger would lie to me about something that was of no benefit to him. That was why. At the same time, I was suddenly aware that it was possible my absolute belief in what Jason had said was fueled by the insecurity that had flickered inside me once or twice over the past few weeks. I'd considered the guy a threat, competition, a better version of me—whatever—and that made it easy to believe he actually was a threat. It was too confusing to think about. I shook my head as if I were shaking water out of my ears.

Kelly must have seen me weaken slightly, because she pushed ahead, full force. "The kids need closure, and I'm giving it to them. If you ever loved me, you'll talk to him, and we'll get this cleared up. Just so you know, I'm almost positive your mother paid him to make up that story. She's trying to split—"

"Oh, for God's sake. Stop this attack on my mother. This is the woman who raised me, have you forgotten that? She loves you. She loves our kids."

"Maybe she does, in her own way. But when I asked him if she'd given him money, he got very twitchy."

I laughed at her fantastical comments. "*Twitchy?*" I laughed harder and tried to maneuver past her.

She grabbed the door frame and widened her stance. "Your mother is not who we thought. You need to read the summary of the autopsy report. You need to look at the sauna log and ask yourself why on earth the temperature reading was that high. It wasn't a bug. And you need to talk to Jason."

I grabbed her wrist and moved her hand away from the door frame. She didn't resist me. "I'm not going to listen to any more slander of my mother. I don't know what's going on with you, if this is all guilt and trauma related to your care for my father, or something else, but it has to stop. You and I need some space. By the time I shower, the kids will be up from their nap. I'm taking them and my mom out for an early pizza dinner. While we're gone, you need to move your stuff to the room downstairs."

"What?" She blinked rapidly, trying to keep tears from spilling out of her eyes. "No, please don't do this. I don't understand what's—"

"I said we need some space. I need it. I'm not telling you

to move out of the house ... yet, but I need to figure things out, and I need space, even if you don't."

"Please don't do this."

I tossed the clean T-shirt onto the bed. "We'll be back by five thirty so I can head out. I want your things moved by then. This way, the kids won't see what's happening and be even more upset. Tomorrow, you can figure out how to explain to them why you got rid of the nanny they adore."

She was weeping silently. She walked slowly to the armchair and slumped into it. I grabbed a clean pair of jeans, the T-shirt, and went into the bathroom. When I got out of the shower, she was gone.

Completely broken by Wyatt's lack of trust in me, I went downstairs, curled up on the couch, and waited until I heard my family leave. I wasn't going to explain to my children why I wasn't joining them for pizza. Let Wyatt do that. Of course, Louise might say something to them, suggesting I didn't want to be there, but I'd finally realized I had no control over the things she was saying to them. My sole focus needed to be on removing her from our home before she destroyed it.

Carrying my things downstairs as I'd been instructed would take me ten or fifteen minutes, but I had at least an hour with the entire house to myself. I wasn't going to waste it.

After a solitary, humiliating transfer of my toiletries and some clothes to the first floor, I pushed open the door to Louise's room. I paused inside the doorway and stared at the tightly made bed, the clutter-free dresser, the framed photographs of Wyatt and our children on the walls. I was rarely in this room since she'd started staying with us. Louise dusted, vacuumed, and cleaned the adjoining bathroom herself, saying she didn't want to be a burden. But I suspected she didn't want me in her space.

Unlike my futile, pathetic search of the room where Frank had slept, the room I was now banished to, there was something specific I was after in Louise's room.

This had been our guest room until the day she and Frank had moved in. It was decorated with dusty rose drapes and a matching comforter on the bed, cream and rose throw pillows, and furniture I'd bought at a used store. I'd stripped and painted the furniture with cream-colored gloss. The dresser top held nothing but Louise's framed photograph of her husband. The nightstand had a lamp and a small blue book of prayers. The only objects sitting on the desk were a rectangular container of pens, a trivet where she placed her cup of hot tea, and her thin, sleek laptop.

It had never been clear to me why she felt she needed a laptop. As far as I knew, she only used it to answer email and watch movies in bed.

I opened the top desk drawer and removed Louise's pale blue day planner. It was held closed by a strap that slipped under a band on the cover. The edges of receipts and business cards poked out the top, having been stuck in various sections in a method that seemed intentional, but made no sense to me. I'd watched her working with her day planner many times. I'd also seen her pull it out of her purse at the grocery store on the rare occasions when she used her debit card. She had trouble remembering her six-digit PIN—*Too many numbers to remember*, she'd laughed. *Numbers are swimming in my head all the time—social security, phones, birthdates, anniversaries, passwords, PINs ...*

In the most unsecured fashion imaginable, she kept an index card that contained all her passwords in the front flap of the day planner. I pulled the card out, found the password for her computer, and opened the laptop.

First, I checked her browser history to see if there were any red flags. There were none.

Next, I opened her email and began to look back through her correspondence over the past few months. There were quite a few exchanges with Chris, her friend-slash-attorney. The guy who almost seemed like a henchman. It was a ridiculous thought, but had often come to mind. Whenever Louise needed something done, she asked Chris. He was the one who set up Frank's physical therapy, of all things. He'd also managed the logistics for the funeral and burial. Chris had arranged the sale of her house and hired the packers and movers who put her things into storage. He'd also organized an estate sale to be rid of possessions she didn't think she'd want in her mythical new home, always just beyond the horizon.

Over the years, Chris had helped Louise set up her computer and taught her how to use a cell phone. He'd arranged their family trust, of course, but also the hiring of a gardener when Frank started having heart trouble, and a hundred other things. It was a strange relationship. The fact that he'd essentially hit on Louise immediately after her husband's casket was lowered into the ground had made me even more curious about what kind of role this guy played in her life, in both their lives.

I began reading the emails. Most of them were about little things she wanted his advice or help on. Ridiculously little things—recommendations for everything from florists to exterminators, what to do about an apricot tree that seemed to be diseased ... it was almost funny. It seemed as if she just liked knowing his opinions, and he seemed equally thrilled to provide them.

Then I found it.

I don't know if I'd expected something quite so clear-cut, or what had made me zero in on her exchanges with Chris instead of her emails overall. I think it was her comment at the funeral about his single shot of whiskey. It had embedded itself in my subconscious and created a blister that rubbed constantly and then broke through the surrounding tissue when I read the autopsy report.

Three months before Frank's surgery, Louise had sent an email to Chris with the subject line—*Current Market*.

Had she chosen that subject line to conceal what she was asking, in the unlikely chance that Frank would read her email? I had no way of knowing, but what it contained told me everything. It made me see my suspicions were indeed gut instincts that had proven to be correct, as gut instincts often are. However, those instincts fail often enough that it can be difficult to trust them.

Weeks before Frank had even scheduled his surgery, she'd asked Chris what he thought the market conditions were like for the sale of her home. She'd wanted to know what Chris thought they could get for it, and how quickly it might sell.

Announcing to Wyatt and me that she'd suddenly sold her house had been a game. She'd planned the sale for months. And I was one hundred percent sure this hadn't been a plan she and Frank had developed together. First of all, Frank was not copied on her message or on the reply from Chris. Second of all, Frank had adored that house. It had been custom designed and built when Wyatt was a child. It was Frank's dream home, and in the past, I'd believed it was Louise's as well. Now, the email made it clear that she couldn't wait to be rid of it. Her comments to Chris were cold and clinical, not the words of someone selling a beloved family home made more precious with the memories of a lifetime.

I heard the rumble of the garage door opening.

My fingers shaking, I scrolled to the top of her email, shut down the app, and slammed the laptop closed. I shoved the index card back into her day planner, then pulled it out again, fingers shaking even more violently. I eased it in more carefully to be sure it was straight, as it had been when I found it. I placed the book in the top drawer, closed it carefully, and darted out of the room. I raced to the kids' room and busied myself organizing their shelves.

Since I was *persona non grata* in my own bedroom, their room was the only neutral territory on the second floor.

As I listened to my family and my mother-in-law entering the house, Louise calling out to the boys with an offer of ice cream, and Wyatt telling them to go with Nana because he had to leave, I leaned on the windowsill. I looked out at our backyard and tried to calm my heartbeat.

It was going to take incredible resolve not to tell Wyatt about my discovery. In my mind, there wasn't a shred of doubt that this email proved Louise had been planning a life without Frank. When her plans were complete, she lured him into the sauna, got him drunk, and turned up the heat.

Wyatt was not going to see it that way. He would once again accuse me of being cruel, unfair, suspicious, spiteful, unkind or whatever other new attributes he might see in the fact that I'd snooped through her email.

My heart ached as I thought about what was happening to our marriage. I adored my husband. I needed him, and I missed him. Wyatt was my closest friend and the person at the center of my life. I couldn't imagine life without him. I wanted his mother out of our house. Honestly, I wanted her out of our lives ... but absolutely out of our house so we could return to the relationship we'd had since they day we were married.

I wanted to talk to him and feel the connection of our minds. I wanted to watch TV, half-reclining on the couch, our legs entwined. I wanted meals alone, and with our children. I wanted to feel free and not watched all the time. I wanted to feel safe from a woman who would commit murder to get what she wanted.

I wanted my husband back.

He didn't believe me about Jason because Louise had set him up. Whatever she'd instructed Jason to say, whatever seeds of suspicion Wyatt might have harbored before Jason spoke to him, had been crafted by Louise to hit Wyatt exactly where it hurt. She knew her son inside and out—she was always proclaiming that fact. If someone is going to gaslight you, they can do a pro job of it when they know how you think, when they know your fears and self-doubts and insecurities and buried wounds.

I had no idea what I was going to do with this new information. Nothing, yet. The main thing it had done was to assure me that Louise had murdered her husband. The coldness of it, the planning of it, chilled me so that I shivered. I rubbed my arms. I closed the boys' window, which had been opened partially to take advantage of the late-afternoon breeze.

I went downstairs and joined my family—and the murderer reveling in her disguise as an adoring mother and devoted Nana.

31

LOUISE

I t felt as if a bite of pizza had glued itself to my tongue when Wyatt casually mentioned that Kelly had invited Jason over the following day to say good-bye to the boys.

I knew the boys would be confused when we told them they would never see Jason again, but having him come to the house to announce this himself was a very bad idea. It would make them even more confused. They would cling to him and cry. The dramatic farewell would make Jason uncomfortable. The twins were young. They would forget all about him in a few weeks. In two years, if they were shown a picture of him, they would ask who that guy was.

I chewed and swallowed my pizza but said nothing to Wyatt.

He hadn't spoken to me about Jason's confession to having sex with Kelly. I suppose he thought that belonged only between himself and Kelly. Or maybe there was an explosion brewing. Of course, eating pizza in a public place with the boys would not be the place to talk to me about it.

Besides, he was likely still in shock from hearing the awful, disgusting story.

We asked the server to box the remainder of the pizza, and Wyatt drove us back to the house, where I promised the boys ice cream. I needed them busy while I tried to think about what I was going to do.

As I opened the fridge and pulled out a carton of chocolate ice cream, Wyatt touched my arm. "Can I talk to you for a minute?"

I put the carton back. Nick and Sam started complaining loudly about their ice cream. I didn't know why Kelly and Wyatt, mostly Kelly, allowed them to get away with the constant complaining when their needs or wants weren't immediately indulged. It drove me crazy, but I said nothing. It's best for a grandmother to bite her tongue as much as possible. After all, it's the parents who decide how their children will be shaped, and they are the ones who will live with the consequences of those decisions.

I followed Wyatt into the music room, where he began putting his guitar into the case. "This is a little awkward, and please don't ask any questions, but I just wanted to let you know that Kelly is going to be sleeping in the room where Dad stayed. Just for a few days, probably. We need some space."

"Oh, Wyatt. I'm sorry. I hope—"

"I said I don't want any questions."

"I wasn't going to ask a question, I was just going to say ..."

He held up his right hand to stop me from speaking further and snapped the case closed.

I nodded. "I understand. I hope you work it out."

It was interesting that he didn't assure me they would. Things must be pretty bad if he couldn't even bring himself to lie about it to keep me from getting too inquisitive.

After I'd given the boys their ice cream, I took them

upstairs to wash up and read stories before bed. Kelly didn't come into their room, and I didn't go looking for her. She knew it was their bedtime. I assumed she was in the downstairs room already.

When the boys were settled, I tiptoed around the corner and saw the downstairs bedroom door was closed. I went into the kitchen and took a box of brownie mix out of the cabinet. I still had some of the marijuana that I'd asked Chris to buy for me when I was trying to make Jason feel welcome and accepted. Using the same recipe as before, I doubled the amount of marijuana and made a small batch of brownies. While they cooled, I went up to my room and changed into jeans, a warm shirt, and athletic shoes.

When I came down again, the brownies were still warm, but I cut them and scooped them out of the pan anyway. I didn't have a lot of time. I put them on a sturdy paper plate covered with foil. I took my phone out of my purse and ordered an Uber, marveling, as I often did, at what a self-sufficient, twenty-first-century woman I was.

I didn't text Jason that I was coming until I was seated in the back of the car, the brownies on my lap. I told him I was coming over to give him his check. When I arrived, he was standing in the open doorway of his apartment. He looked down at me without speaking as I climbed the stairs to the second floor.

Inside, I asked him if he had anything to make cocktails. He had vodka, and I said that a vodka tonic would be nice.

"Are you planning to stay?" he asked.

"I thought we could chat for a while. I really like you, Jason, and I'm very sorry you won't be in my life anymore. But it was unavoidable. Still, I'll really miss talking to you. We had some great conversations, didn't we?"

He stared at me with a rather blank expression. I wasn't sure if he was trying to recall even a single great conversation, or if he was so surprised I enjoyed our talks that it took a moment to respond. Finally, he nodded.

I handed the brownies to him. "Why don't you have one of these?"

"Okay. Sure. The last ones you made were incredible."

I smiled. "Thank you."

He lifted the plastic and took out a small wedge of brownie. He took a bite, then went to make my drink.

I sat in the recliner, which was the only other place to sit besides the futon, which he'd already opened for sleep.

When he handed me my cocktail, I took a sip. "Very good."

He held up the beer he'd brought back for himself. "Cheers."

"Cheers." I smiled. "You're a great guy. You meant a lot to the kids."

"Yeah, I feel kind of bad about that. They must be confused and a little hurt."

"Children forget. They'll be fine."

"Do they? Forget?" He sipped his beer and took another bite of the brownie. He chewed it slowly, appearing to savor the texture and the rich chocolate. "This is awesome. You should go into edible sales for a living. Yours are really balanced. I know I can eat the whole thing without freaking out. Other edibles, you have to go slowly, testing how it's hitting you. Which, to be honest, I did with your first batch. Just to be sure." He laughed. "Sorry."

"Not a problem," I said. "I totally understand why you'd want to be careful." I took my checkbook out of my purse and placed it on the end table. I laid my pen beside it and smiled at him.

He looked embarrassed. He shoved the rest of the brownie into his mouth, chewed with great care, his lips turning dark with chocolate.

"Are you excited?" I asked.

"About what?"

"About the chance to devote all your time to your music." I laughed softly. "It's like I'm your benefactor, maybe your muse, almost, even though I'm not giving creative inspiration. I guess more of a patron, but that's almost like a muse."

"You've never heard me play." He gulped some beer and placed the bottle on the floor. He leaned back on his elbows, legs spread wide, his bare feet planted on the carpet.

"But I support the arts. And the money will help you pursue your creative vision, whatever it is."

"Yeah." He closed his eyes and tipped his head back for a moment, then sat up. "It feels more like a payoff."

"Please don't think of it that way. I really want to support you. It's hard to get started in a creative field. I'm glad I can help."

"But you're not really helping me, are you? I fucked over your daughter-in-law and maybe your son, and you're paying me for doing that."

I sighed. "Please try to be more positive."

"She came to see me."

I decided not to be coy. He wasn't stupid. "Kelly?"

"Yeah. She sort of guessed that you paid me to tell Wyatt that story."

"Really? How would she guess?"

He shrugged.

"She's just trying to blame me, like always."

"But in this case, it's true."

"Did you tell her?"

"No."

I smiled.

"But I'm going over there tomorrow," he said. "To say good-bye to Sam and Nick."

"That's thoughtful."

"She might ask again about you paying me. I think she didn't just invite me to see the kids. I think she wants me to tell Wyatt I made it up."

"But you won't."

He shook his head.

I asked him about his music and the classes he was taking when the fall quarter started in a few weeks.

After a while, he looked uncomfortable. He squirmed on the futon. "Wow. I'm feeling a little ..." He leaned forward and picked up his beer. He took a long swallow, then another. He put the bottle on the carpet. It tipped over, and beer seeped out, but he didn't seem to notice.

"Should we go sit at the table?" I asked.

"I dunno ... I'm feeling really ... buzzed." He scratched his arm vigorously.

"Are you okay?"

"I'm not sure."

"Let's get you some water." I took my cocktail to the sink, poured the contents down the drain, and washed and dried the glass before returning to the futon, where Jason lay with his eyes closed.

"How much was in these brownies?" he said, his voice a faint, slurred mumble.

"Same as before."

"It's kicking my ass."

"Here." I grabbed his hand and began pulling.

He forced himself up, which was a good thing, because I didn't have the strength to lift him. I worried I'd miscalculated, that I should have made sure he was seated at the table earlier. A few more minutes and I wouldn't be able to manage him at all.

He swayed slightly. "I just wanna lie down."

"It's better to sit at the table. Just in case."

He gave me a puzzled look, but didn't resist or ask why

sitting at a table was better.

I helped him settle in a chair and nudged it closer to the table.

He folded his arms on the table and bent over, resting his forehead on his wrists.

I sat across from him. I talked about the twins. I talked about my life. I talked about the movies I'd watched recently. I asked about his dreams of becoming a globally known musician.

It wasn't long before I heard him moan slightly, shifting his position. He grunted. I stood and rubbed his shoulder gently. "Are you okay?"

There was no answer.

I went to work quickly. I took a pair of plastic gloves out of my purse. I re-wiped the glass I'd used and put it away. I found a cabinet in the bathroom with extra towels, including two beach towels. I lined them along the windowsills in the living room area and the kitchenette. I tossed one by the front door.

I moved the brownies to one of Jason's plates, then folded the paper plate and foil and shoved it into a plastic bag I'd brought with me, burying it inside my purse.

I looked around the room to see what else I'd touched, wiped up a few places, even though I was pretty sure I'd kept my hands to myself. I searched the recliner for loose hairs but found none.

Finally, I went to the stove, I opened the oven door, turned the gas on, and walked quickly to the front door. If he hadn't had a gas oven, I would have had to return to the house to get one of the propane tanks Wyatt used for his outdoor grill. I was deeply grateful for this small mercy of a gas oven.

Standing by the door, surveying the scene I'd set, I realized there was no way to close any gaps near the bottom of the door and leave the apartment. One minor mistake, although I didn't really think it was. Jason was out for the night. By the time he came out of his weed-induced stupor, the gas would have disoriented him enough that he wouldn't be able to save himself. Sleep would overtake him.

The odor of gas was already strong. I grabbed the beach towel, raced to the bathroom, and shoved it back into the cabinet. I went out the front door, pressed the lock in the doorknob, and pulled it closed. I didn't look around, not wanting to appear furtive if anyone did see me. But there was no one around. I walked down the stairs with purpose and along the street toward a cluster of restaurants I'd mapped out earlier. When I was three blocks away from Jason's apartment, outside a coffee shop, I ordered another Uber.

My breath came rapidly. I felt edgy and slightly scared, but not as scared as I'd been when Wyatt had told me Jason was coming to the house. As much as Jason seemed to be on my side, I couldn't trust him to keep our agreement between us. Also, I'd saved fifty thousand dollars, which was nice.

Before I knew it, Wyatt would ask Kelly for a separation. The divorce was sure to be ugly, especially the fight for custody of my precious grandsons. I knew the boys would be damaged for a while, but they would recover. They had a grandmother who loved them dearly and a father who was utterly devoted to them. Not like my son's father at all. And children do forget. I know this for a fact, because Wyatt forgot about the women Frank brought into our house. It wasn't just the one affair. It was a parade.

Wyatt had seen them once—Frank and some girl he picked up at the airport, naked in my bed. I remembered every detail, even now, but Wyatt had no recollection whatsoever. I'd asked him leading questions several times over the years, and I knew the memory had been wiped from his mind, as cleanly as a computer can be wiped clean.

32

KELLY

W hen I woke up, my face was wet with tears. For half a second, I wasn't sure where I was. I had no idea why I was crying. Had it been a heart-wrenching dream? My mind was blank. Then I turned over and felt the edge of the narrow bed on my left, where Wyatt should have been.

It was still dark outside, and I was in the room where Frank had slept for all those weeks.

I felt the flow of tears increase as the memory of my failure to convince my husband to trust me returned with the force of an avalanche. The recollection of him telling me to leave our bed hit me like a punch to my solar plexus. Except for business trips, we'd never slept apart.

Every morning of my life, since the day I married him, he'd been there to hold onto. Finding him in the half-sleep of dawn, a lingering kiss to start the day, knowing we had the world because we had each other. At night, he held me until we drifted to sleep. Now, I was alone. He didn't want me. When I'd looked into his eyes, I'd felt he couldn't bear to even meet my gaze.

A smooth, charming kid, with one fantastical lie, had split our marriage as cleanly as if he'd taken an ax to it.

Then I remembered Jason was coming over. It wasn't so awful—only a single night. This could be fixed. It *would* be fixed. I crept out of bed and showered and dressed, knowing I wouldn't be able to sleep anymore. When I finished, it was almost five thirty, and the sky was growing light. I'd paid extra attention to my makeup, even though it was a Saturday. I blew my hair dry and left it down, which also wasn't typical for the weekend.

In the kitchen, I thought I smelled the aroma of something baking, but the oven was empty and cold to the touch. The cookie jar was empty.

I made coffee, filled my mug, and took it out to the backyard. I sat in the lounge chair with my phone and scrolled through the news and social media. I didn't know how I could bear waiting until ten, when Jason had said he would stop by. I sipped my coffee and tried to let my mind relax into thinking about nothing.

Getting the kids up, helping them dress—which was mostly them helping me dress them—and then making waffles for breakfast caused the time to move faster. Wyatt was still sleeping, which he usually was on the weekends now, after a late-night performance.

Louise had come down, made a cup of tea, and gone back up to her room without speaking more than a quiet and unenthusiastic good morning to me. She looked exhausted.

At nine thirty, I woke Wyatt to remind him Jason was coming over. I heard him grunt as I stood outside the bedroom door, where I'd had to endure the humiliation of knocking on a locked door. A moment later, I heard him get out of bed. I waited. Finally, I heard the shower, so I went back downstairs.

By ten thirty, I was jumpy and short-tempered from too much coffee. Jason hadn't shown up yet. The kids were whining, because I'd told them he was coming. I'd also told them he wouldn't be caring for them anymore, but they'd acted as if they didn't believe me.

I'd sent Jason a text about ten minutes earlier. I didn't want to pester him too soon, recognizing that he probably believed he owed us nothing. At the same time, it had sounded as if he was sincere about wanting to say good-bye to Sam and Nick. I couldn't understand why he was so late. The delay was making the situation worse.

Wyatt had had his orange and a single cup of coffee. He'd given me a grudging thank you for the waffles I made for everyone.

Jason hadn't responded to the text. I called him, but the call rang out and went to voicemail. I left a message, then checked my texts again to see if he'd responded. I went into my room, just to get away from Louise, who had appeared in the kitchen, peppering Wyatt with all kinds of questions about his performance the night before. He was so talkative with her, after answering my questions in monosyllables, I couldn't take it.

I collapsed on the chair in the corner and sent another text to Jason. Again, there was no answer.

It was eleven forty-five. I opened Facebook. If my life hadn't been coming apart, I would have felt a little guilty that I'd never followed up with visiting Jason's page. I hadn't glanced through his posts, or even liked the page to give him a boost. All I'd done was accept his request and move on to whatever had been at the top of my mind that day.

I went to his profile, just in case he'd checked in. Maybe he'd forgotten about his promise to me and was out with friends, using the check-in feature or tagged by others.

What I saw made me gasp. The phone wobbled in my hand and almost crashed to the ground. I managed to juggle it back into place.

The post was from a woman named Lily, announcing she was Jason's sister.

Hi everyone. I have the worst news of my whole, entire life. For whatever unbelievable, heartbreaking reason, my smart, funny, talented brother took his own life last night. I was the one to find him, and it was the worst day of my life, forever. I went to his apartment to bring him some lasagna my mom had made for him. I was so excited to see him.

He didn't open the door, so I texted him, and then I called, but he didn't answer.

When I went inside, his apartment smelled awful. At first I thought he was asleep. I shook him and screamed at him. Then I touched his face. It was so cold. SO cold! I called 911, but I knew it didn't matter. It was the most awful horrible thing in my whole life.

He didn't leave a note to say why. I don't understand. He was always staying in touch, texting all the time. Why wouldn't he stay in touch for the most important thing ever? His last day on earth? Why?! AND he had a new girlfriend. He was crazy about her. I can't believe he would do this. It's so, so awful. The only thing he left us was an endless river of tears and pain and questions.

If he said anything to you, anything that will make us understand WHY he would do this, please message me. Or call me. There were some homemade brownies on the table. If you're the person who made them, please message me. Maybe you were the last person to talk to him. Maybe he said something to you?

I loved him so very, very much. No words.

There were already over one hundred comments and over three hundred hearts and hugging hearts and crying faces attached to the post. I looked at the time stamp. Nine ten.

I stared at the words, wanting it to be the wrong Jason. Wanting it to go away. Wanting him to be standing on our front porch, ringing the bell.

In any other situation, I might have felt tears spilling out of my eyes, devastated that someone had killed himself. But all I felt was rage. Why would he do this? How could he do this to me? To us? Clearly, he felt terribly guilty for the colossal lie he'd told Wyatt, but rather than correct it, he just killed himself?

A part of me felt like a terrible mother. I'd misjudged this person in every way imaginable. First his outrageous, bald-faced lie, and now this. He was clearly mentally unstable, and I'd never noticed the slightest hint of that. I looked at the Facebook page again, skimming the posted comments of shock and disbelief. But those comments said nothing about who he really was. People were always shocked and disbelieving when someone died, especially by their own intention. I'd never personally known anyone who had killed themselves, but I imagined that was how it would be. It certainly was in this case.

I tossed my phone onto the bed and burst into tears, covering my face with my hands, broken to pieces as I thought about what this meant for Wyatt and me.

After a while, I heard the voices of Louise, my children, and Wyatt in the garden. I went outside and stood across the yard, watching them. It seemed as if they were carrying on their lives without me.

Slowly, I walked around the pool toward them, stopping a few feet from where the boys squatted in the dirt, weeding and watering.

Wyatt looked up and saw my face. "What's wrong?"

"Jason." My breath caught in my throat. I spoke in a low voice. "He ... he killed himself." Normally, I would choose my words more carefully around Sam and Nick, but it didn't seem right in this case. It was one of the awful parts of life that you were forced to explain to your children—dismantling the innocent joy of childhood stone by stone. We couldn't pretend it hadn't happened. They didn't need to know how it had happened, that he'd chosen to walk out of their lives for good, but they needed to know he was never coming back.

They stopped digging and looked at me, then Wyatt.

"Did something bad happen?" Sam asked.

I nodded.

Louise finally stopped plucking the ripe cherry tomatoes and turned to look at me.

I knelt on the lawn and held out my arms toward my children. They came to me. They leaned into me, as if they knew, as if some instinct told them I needed them desperately. Murmuring into their soft, sweet-smelling hair, I said, "Jason has gone to another place, a place where he can never feel hurt again. Like grandpa. He couldn't stay in his body anymore and went to a place where he can be happy all the time."

Although I knew they didn't understand a word I'd said, they knew he was gone from their lives, that they'd never see him again. They began crying, their tears soaking my shirt and making my skin slick, their cries wrenching my heart even further.

"Oh my God." Louise let out a little shriek and began sobbing. She turned to Wyatt and fell against him. He put his arms around her. The wailing coming from her throat drowned the cries of our children. It also made me furious.

That afternoon, when the boys were down for their naps, Louise came into the living room. She asked me if I wanted a cup of tea.

I'd been reading a book, wishing I could divert myself as

easily as I had our children after they heard the terrible news. Wyatt had been in the music room and hadn't said more than a few words to me since hearing about Jason's suicide. I longed to know what he thought, but he didn't seem interested in discussing it.

Did his death give Wyatt second thoughts about Jason's so-called *confession*? Did Wyatt wonder what Jason might have said if we'd had a chance to talk things out? Had he easily put it out of his head, losing himself in his music?

I told Louise a cup of tea would be nice, but as I spoke, I felt as if I were acting in a play. I could hardly bear to look at her, and I had no idea why she was suddenly concerned with my comfort.

A few minutes later, she returned with a cup of tea. She placed it on the table beside me. She settled in the chair that was the farthest from where I sat. She didn't bother with false questions about how I was feeling. "It's horrifying when someone takes their own life."

I nodded.

"They leave so much damage behind. Imagine how his sister will feel for the rest of her life. His mother ... his friends." She gave me a lurid smile. "It should cause you to think about your own life."

"Mine, specifically, or people in general?"

"Take it however you choose, but what I meant to say is that when someone feels they're losing everything, they often take their lives."

"Was Jason losing everything?"

"He must have been devastated about being fired. And that's what others will think. Even if they don't have the details, assumptions will be made."

"I don't know about that."

"Well, you need to be careful, Kelly. If you died suddenly,

and it was obvious you'd done it yourself—" Her voice was cold, completely lacking emotion.

"I would never do that."

"Other people don't know that. Everyone is aware—it's impossible to know what's inside another person."

"What are you trying to say?"

"People will assume Jason had secrets that troubled him more than he could bear."

"I have no secrets."

"So you say. But people assume ... You should be careful. You need to stop talking about Frank's death. Wyatt might get the wrong idea. And then if you died ..." She gave me a hard stare, full of malice.

"I have no idea what you're getting at, but everyone who knows me knows I would never kill myself. Never."

"But when it happens, they tell themselves they hadn't truly known you after all." She stood and walked out of the room.

I didn't thank her for the tea.

Later, when I went into the kitchen to wash my teacup, I found she'd left tea bags sitting on the countertop in a pool of cold tea. I opened the cabinet and pulled out the trash can. Half-buried below an empty milk carton and some soggy paper towels, I saw the bright green top of the can of spray oil we used for baking.

The homemade brownies on Jason's table flashed across my mind. I pulled out the can. I don't know what I expected. It was empty. But no one had done any baking recently. I shook it, as if that would tell me something.

The thought that Louise might have brought brownies to Jason, that she'd paid him to lie about having sex, that he was tragically but conveniently dead before he could reveal that fact chilled me. I dropped the can back into the trash with a thud. I shoved the trash container under the sink and gripped the counter to steady myself. The chill increased, spreading through my body as Louise's words, which had confused me earlier, now terrified me. They felt threatening in a way I'd never experienced. My fingers were too stiff to manage washing the teacup without breaking it.

33

WYATT

fter the shock of Jason's suicide, I decided to take
Nick and Sam to the park. Alone. There was something very grounding about my children. Possibly
it was the fact they mostly lived in the present. I'd seen that
present-moment awareness fading as they grew older, and I
mourned the day it would be gone forever.

When we're small, we relish the very fact we're alive.
Then we spend our adult lives trying to recapture that sense
of pleasure unaffected by assumptions and unpleasant
memories or concerns and fears for the future. Why was it so
hard to feel utter joy by simply running, feeling our bodies
moving with grace, or gliding down the slick surface of a slide
over and over again?

When we left the house, Kelly was shut away in her
temporary room, and my mother was resting in hers. My
mother had wept as she told me how devastated she was by
Jason's death. She was doubly horrified, she'd said, by the fact
that Kelly had fired him.

"I don't necessarily blame Kelly for *driving* him to kill
himself," she'd told me. "But I can't help wondering if losing

a job he loved, being cut off from Nick and Sam, was the straw that broke the camel's back. He truly adored our two boys. And I can see why. They are absolutely lovable, even when they're acting up."

As upset as I was with Kelly, I had a different take on the suicide than my mother. I now wondered if Kelly was telling the truth. Had Jason made up the story about having sex with my wife? Had he felt guilty for that and decided that rather than face me and tell me what he'd done, he opted for the easy way out? Or was there something much darker going on in his life? If it was a lie, as Kelly had insisted from the moment she opened her mouth, what would cause someone to tell a story like that? Or, the opposite—maybe this proved it was true, and he was either lost without Kelly or trying to punish her in some way?

These questions weighed on me. I needed to clear my head. Walking to the park, listening to my children talk about whatever crossed their line of vision, following them around as they raced from one part of the playground to another, would do more to get me ready for the evening's performance than any more practice time could do.

It was hot, and my tendency was to walk slowly, the heat softening my muscles, draining my energy, but the boys propelled their scooters as fast as they could manage, oblivious to the oppressive heat. I walked quickly to keep up, half running at times.

I put their scooters beside a bench that was shaded by a redwood tree and settled myself down to watch them.

The playground was crowded on a Saturday afternoon despite the heat. The screams of children were refreshing and satisfying. I watched as Sam and Nick climbed the platforms leading to the tallest of the slides. The slide itself was encased inside a tube. It was always unnerving when I lost sight of them, waiting what seemed like a moment or two longer than

I should have before they shot out the opening, laughing and chasing each other around to climb up again.

A woman I'd been introduced to once, but whose name I'd forgotten, sat beside me. She opened the sipper on her water bottle and drank some. "Wyatt, right? Nick and Sam's dad?"

I knew she lived only a few blocks away. She had a five-year-old girl and a three-year-old boy. Kelly ran into her often, and they'd had several playdates at parks in the area before Kelly returned to work. "Yes. Sorry, I've forgotten your name."

"Molly."

"Right. Sorry about that."

"No worries." She flashed a smile at me and took another swallow of water. "Do you wonder why they never seem to feel the heat?"

"Yeah. It's some sort of extra chemical support in their bodies, maybe. I don't know."

"I'm dying just from walking over here," Molly said.

We talked about our kids, and she told me she'd had quite a few good conversations with my mother. "She's really easy to talk to. And she doesn't seem like a grandma. Her parenting advice seems really current. I feel like she's just a few years older than me."

I nodded. I looked at her water bottle, wondering why I hadn't thought to bring one of my own. I glanced up at Nick and Sam, who were playing with Molly's kids, all of them standing on the top platform. Nick was organizing a complicated game of make-believe, even managing to get the five-year-old to let him be in charge.

"How's Kelly feeling?" Molly asked.

"Good." I wasn't in the mood to talk about Kelly. With the rift between us, with what she'd done, which was still utterly impossible to sort out, I didn't know how I could control my voice or keep my emotions from bursting through.

"I don't mean to pry, but were you able to convince her to see a therapist?"

"What?" I jerked around to face her.

"I'm sorry. I didn't mean to intrude. Louise was so open about it, and I thought you were all really admirable for not trying to hide from the truth."

"I'm sorry, I don't know what you're talking about."

"Sorry."

What had my mother said to her?

Molly took another sip of water. She stood and called out to her son to let go of his sister's wrist.

"What did my mother tell you?" I asked.

"I really didn't mean to interfere. I realize I misunderstood."

"What did she say?"

"Just that Kelly was having a really hard time. That she was feeling really insecure in her parenting, and that she was probably having delayed postpartum depression. That she couldn't deal with the kids. It made me so sad, because she seemed so in control and so confident the last time I'd seen her. She struck me as a really competent, loving mom."

I had no idea what to say. I didn't want to discuss my wife's mental health with a woman I considered a total stranger. Just because I'd met her once, and she and Kelly—and apparently my mother—had discussed child-rearing, did not mean we were friends by any definition of the word. I couldn't imagine why my mother had told her these things. It seemed a betrayal. At the same time, maybe my mother felt she had no one she could talk to about her concerns. Maybe she'd thought Molly might be able to help.

Molly took a few steps away from the bench, where I was

still seated, slightly numb with the shock of hearing details about my family from someone I didn't know.

"Sorry to be poking my nose in your business. I really am. Louise was just so open about it, I assumed ..."

"It's okay. Not your fault," I said.

"I think she was concerned about Kelly's instability, how it would affect the boys. That's why she wanted to talk to me about it. Again, sorry." She moved farther away from me.

"No need to apologize. I was just caught off guard."

"I hope Kelly is doing better," Molly said. "Give her my best." She turned and walked toward where the kids were playing. When she reached the platform where they were clustered together, she stopped and stared up at them. She didn't call out or seem to be paying much attention to them. It was clear she'd just wanted to escape from me, my ignorance, and my damaged family. I expected that at any minute, she would haul her children away to play somewhere else, somewhere they wouldn't be affected by my children with the mentally unbalanced mother.

As I walked home, Molly's words played back in my mind. I was irritated by the encounter. An afternoon that I'd thought would clear my head for the evening's performance had done the opposite. That, and I felt I'd hardly paid attention to my sons. I wondered if Molly knew more than she'd said. I wondered if my mother's concerns ran deeper than *she'd* said. I wondered what I was dealing with, and I viewed Jason's claim with fresh eyes. Wasn't aberrant sexual behavior a symptom of mental instability? I was pretty sure I'd read that or heard it ... somewhere. Or was that just a stereotype and an unfair, puritanical view of something almost completely outside a person's control? Those with cancer or other serious diseases weren't judged the way people with mental health issues were. Trying to sort it out made my head ache.

At home, my mother took the boys into the family room to watch the half hour of TV they were allowed in the late afternoons.

I found Kelly behind the closed door of the temporary bedroom. "You don't have to shut yourself away in here," I said.

"Don't I?"

I sighed. "Mind if I come in?"

She shrugged.

I closed the door behind me and sat on the edge of the bed. Suddenly, I missed her terribly. "How are you doing?" I asked.

She let out a short burst of laughter. "You mean aside from my husband not trusting me and my mother-in-law murdering your father in the most horrific way imaginable, and paying our nanny to tell lies about me, and possibly even killing our nanny and making it look like suicide? I'm doing great." She glared at me, her eyes glassy with furious tears.

It was a little unsettling, that look of rage and absolute certainty in her eyes.

I stood. "Why do you keep attacking her like this? She's going to move to her own place, eventually. Making all these ugly accusations, assuming things that shouldn't even enter your head ... if you expect me to believe Jason was lying, why are you trying to do the same—telling such disgusting stories about her?"

"Because it's the truth. And if you would look at it without always considering her viewpoint first, always making excuses because she had some upsetting experiences with your father, and believing her without question, you might see things a lot differently. You might realize the truth."

"How can you possibly think she killed Jason? He committed suicide. His sister said so. And just for the sake of argument, how would she even do that?"

"I don't know. But she managed to kill your father and get us all to think it was a horrible accident. It looks like she's getting away with that, so—"

"The coroner said it was an accident!" My voice was raised, and I hated myself for nearly shouting, but I couldn't help it.

"That's why she's so clever."

"I don't understand what's wrong with you."

"Because you can't see clearly. She's manipulated you."

"That's not true."

She closed her eyes. She put her hands over her face.

I studied her now that she wasn't glaring at me. Her hair was tangled and uncombed, even though that morning it had looked as if she were heading off to work. Before she'd covered her face with her hands, her eyes looked dark with shadows. She had smudges of black under her lower lashes. Her skin was pale except for bright red spots on her cheeks that bled out from beneath her fingers.

It seemed as if my mother was right. Kelly was having a lot of trouble, and maybe it was more than I could manage, but that still didn't tell me what to do about it. I couldn't force her to see a therapist.

I'd never felt so helpless.

34

KELLY

It had been four days since Jason's death, and with each day, I was more certain Louise had had something to do with it—whether she'd pushed him over the edge emotionally or threatened him or actually turned on the gas, she'd contributed. Wyatt argued it was the shock and my own guilt that had me believing such *nonsense*.

We hadn't talked any more about Jason's accusation. I was pretty sure Wyatt believed that it was our supposed affair that had driven Jason to it. I was absolutely sure that whatever Wyatt believed, Louise had planted it in his mind. How does a man fight the insidious manipulation, the near-brain-washing carried on by a mother whom he'd felt protective of all his life, a man who'd been expected to offer comfort in the face of a painful marriage? I had no idea, and the internet didn't seem to offer any suggestions, either.

That evening, I had a predinner talk to a girls' high school volleyball team. I didn't have a background in sports, but they'd thought I was the best fit because the coach wanted the girls to learn about achieving balance in your life—giving the appropriate amount of energy to your sports goals, but not letting your schoolwork and eventual career plans fall by the wayside.

When I arrived home, Wyatt's car was gone, which I'd expected. His gig started at six, and he usually left by five to arrive in time for warm-up.

The house was eerily silent. I left my purse on the kitchen table and walked through the empty family room. The doors to the music room were open, and the early evening sun made it glow as if the room's creative energy had taken a physical form. Tearing myself away from that beautiful light, I went upstairs. The boys' room was empty. I checked the master bedroom, on the slim chance they were sleeping there.

Instead, I found an unmade bed, the pillow from my side tossed on the floor, Wyatt's side a tangle of blankets.

When I'd passed by, Louise's bedroom door was closed, so on my return trip, I knocked once and opened it without waiting for an answer. The room was empty.

My heart began to beat faster. I told myself to calm down. Wyatt had the car. Unless Louise had called an Uber, which would have been nearly impossible with the need for two car seats, my children had to be within walking distance of the house. I didn't like that she hadn't texted me to tell me they were going out. She'd known what time I was coming home.

I returned to the kitchen, took my phone out of my purse, and sent her a text. I waited a minute or so without receiving an answer. I got a glass of water, and while I drank it, I sent a text to Wyatt asking if Louise had mentioned any plans to go out. He also didn't respond, which wasn't surprising.

I drank more water and took a few slow, deep breaths. Even though it was close to sunset, it was possible Louise had taken them to the park. She'd never arranged playdates, so I didn't think she would be at the home of any of Nick and Sam's friends who lived within walking distance.

I ran upstairs and changed into jeans and athletic shoes. I grabbed my keys and phone and headed toward the park. I nearly ran, passing houses with the lights already on, reminding me it was unlikely someone would still be at the park with small children at this hour. Especially Louise. With my lungs getting tight, gasping slightly, more from mild panic than my easy half-jog, I slowed to a walk. I pulled out my phone and texted Louise again. Maybe my earlier message hadn't communicated my concern. I shoved the phone back into my pocket, but as I picked up running again, there was no answering buzz against my hip bone.

At the park, the playground was empty except for a group of teenagers sitting on the swings, talking and laughing, twirling the chains into coils, then lifting their feet off the ground and letting the chains unwind, flinging them in frantic, dizzying circles.

I walked around the building that housed the restrooms, checking the picnic area in a grove of pine trees on the opposite side, which made no sense, but I did it anyway. They weren't there.

I pulled out my phone and stared at the blank screen. Wyatt would be playing, of course, so sending another message was pointless. I could call the restaurant and ask them to interrupt the band, call Wyatt away for an emergency. But was it an emergency? Not being able to find my children felt like an extreme emergency; my heart was beating so hard it seemed to slam against my ribs in an effort to escape. But Wyatt would downplay my panic, accuse me of thinking the worst of his mother.

How can you even think she'd do anything to endanger the boys?

Don't be ridiculous, she would never leave with them.

I increased my speed and rounded the corner to our street. Our house looked tranquil but dark alongside the others, since I hadn't turned on any lights before leaving. I ran up the front path, unlocked the door, and flung it open.

"Nick? Sam?" I slammed the door closed. "Hello? Where are you?"

I flicked every light switch I passed, calling their names repeatedly, then stopping to hear whether there was a response. I ran up the stairs to check their room, knowing they weren't there. Knowing the house was empty.

I returned to the first floor and collapsed onto the family room couch. I pulled out my phone and stared at the screen, trying to think what to do. Maybe Louise had missed the text messages. I tapped the icon to launch a video call.

The line rang. Then, as I waited for the call to connect, I became aware of a buzzing on the other side of the room. I stood, holding my phone out in preparation for Louise to answer, then lowered it slowly as I realized the buzzing was coming from the small set of shelves that held baskets of toys. Louise's purse sat on the floor beside the pine shelves. Her phone wasn't visible, but the buzzing was louder as I moved closer.

I ended the call and shoved my phone into my pocket. I leaned on the top shelf and pressed my fingers into my forehead, as if the force would enable me to think more clearly. Where on earth could they be?

For the most part, I felt calmer now, knowing she hadn't gone far. She *couldn't* go far without her purse. The fear dissipated slightly. I turned slowly, looking at the room, trying to imagine what she might have done. Dinner was well over. The boys should have been finished with their baths and be listening to stories, ready for sleep.

I realized I hadn't eaten dinner, but the thought of pausing to do that now was out of the question. I looked out at the backyard, staring at the darkening water of the swimming pool, the shadows of the vegetable garden to my right, silent, the boys' watering cans and tiny spades put away.

Across the water from me, gazing back at the house as if the buildings might come to life and move toward me, were the changing room and the sauna.

She wouldn't have taken the boys into the sauna … would she? I flung open the sliding glass door and jogged past the pool to the small building. I grabbed the handle on the sauna door, and it opened easily, swinging toward me hard, despite the weight that I'd have thought would slow it down. I stumbled back, wondering how hard I'd yanked it.

"Surprise!" Sam and Nick jumped off the bench, laughing and shrieking with pleasure at my stunned expression. "We tricked you!"

Tricked indeed. It wasn't really what they meant, they meant to say they'd surprised me, but they didn't understand the nuanced difference. Their grandmother certainly did.

She smiled at me from the semidarkness.

The lights were presumably off so no telltale glow would seep out and give them away. She held a flashlight in her lap, the globe pointing up at her chin, casting an oval of light on her face.

"What the hell were you thinking?" My voice was a near shriek. Sam clapped his hands over his ears and winced.

"Shh," Louise said. "You're scaring the children."

"How dare you come in here and hide, after …" I broke down, sobbing. My voice rose in pitch until I was almost howling. I wanted to grab her by the neck and choke her until she gagged and turned blue. Images flashed through my mind—Nick and Sam lying on their backs, eyes closed, hands folded across their ribs as if laid out in coffins. Louise sitting beside them, stroking their cold skin.

I fell to my knees, crying harder from the relief of finding them, from the sickening images that shocked me with their clarity.

"Calm down," Louise said.

"Why would you do this to me?"

"We were playing hide-and-seek. The boys wanted to surprise you, and now you're scaring them half to death."

The word *death* started me sobbing again. I was aware of sounding hysterically out of control, but she'd known what I would feel, finding them in this room. She knew I would be panicking, already distraught from not being able to find them inside the house. The memory of Frank's empty room that morning and then finding his body.

"This is not an appropriate place to play hide-and-seek, and you know it. The boys are not allowed in the sauna, ever." I flung my arms around them and pulled them close to my body. I wanted to lift them up, but I wasn't strong enough to get to my feet while holding them, and I couldn't bear to let them go, to lose the feel of their lively little bodies.

Louise stood. She brushed her hands down her jeans, smoothing away imaginary wrinkles. "You're losing it."

"No, I'm not. You're deliberately trying to upset me. You're trying to destroy my family."

The boys were crying softly. I knew she was right about one thing—I was scaring them. But her stoic face, her refusal to acknowledge what she'd done to me made me so angry I could hardly breathe. It scared me, knowing what could have happened. What if she'd touched the controls, what if she didn't really know how it worked and she ...

But, of course, she knew how it worked.

I eased my grip on Nick and Sam and pushed myself to my feet. "It's bedtime, boys." I took their hands and turned toward the door.

"I'll tuck them in," Louise said.

"Absolutely not."

I half-dragged them out of the sauna, knowing I was still scaring them.

"Why didn't you like our hiding place?" Sam asked.

"You know you aren't supposed to play in the sauna."

"Nana said it was okay," Sam said.

"Nana was wrong. Very, very wrong. She did a bad thing."

"Why?" Nick asked.

"She tried to scare Mommy."

"You said hide-and-seek wasn't scary. You can always find the people."

I'd played the game often because they loved it. I'd believed it helped them develop a healthy understanding that separation was temporary, the knowledge that people returned, learning that someone out of sight could be seen once again. The game made them laugh hysterically, and they loved the challenge, finding ever more difficult places as they got older.

She'd not only set out to terrify me in a very carefully plotted scenario, she'd ruined something special I'd built with my children. She'd destroyed happy memories and turned the game into something I would never again enjoy in the same carefree way. And she'd put a barrier between me and my sons, because they couldn't begin to understand why I was upset, and I couldn't tell them.

I walked quickly back to the house. Sam and Nick scrambled to keep up with me. When we reached their bedroom, I closed the door and locked it. Thankfully, they didn't notice me turning the lock. I read them extra stories and sang more songs than usual and hoped that when I finally kissed their cheeks, they would have forgotten my hysteria and forgotten the game. I would never forget.

35

KELLY

A fter the boys were settled, I stepped out of their room, pulling the door closed behind me.

Light came from beneath Louise's bedroom door. I went downstairs and saw that her favorite teacup was missing. That meant she was down for the night. Carrying her cup of tea upstairs was always her last act of the day.

I went into the spare room, gathered up my things, and in three trips, carried it all back upstairs. Nothing on earth was going to keep me sleeping downstairs while that woman waited right across the hall from my sons.

I left my bedroom door open. I placed the baby monitor on the nightstand, never gladder that we'd left the little cameras in place even though Sam and Nick were getting a little old for us to be watching them sleep. Often, it was more of an exercise in watching them slip out of their beds and find toys to bring back with them. It could be very entertaining, although it struck me that Wyatt and I hadn't sat side by side in bed, watching them sneak around in the dark, for ages. Tears filled my eyes. I scurried around, putting my clothes away, arranging makeup in the bathroom drawer, and straightening the room that had become cluttered with Wyatt as the sole occupant.

When it was all in order, I settled into bed, still wearing my clothes. I lay on my back, moved the monitor to my belly, and stared at the ceiling.

A moment later, I heard a creak, maybe the sound of a door opening. I shoved the monitor aside and bolted out of bed. The landing area was empty, Louise's light still on. Had she gone back downstairs? I'd moved awfully fast when I heard the creak. I couldn't believe she'd made it down the stairs far enough for me to miss seeing her.

I returned to the bed and picked up the monitor. The boys were settled now. Louise was not in their room. I stood there for several minutes, gazing at the black-and-white images of their sleeping forms. It felt almost like watching a terrifying film in which a monster lurked out of sight, ready to tear apart the supposedly safe cocoon at any minute.

Sleeping anywhere in the house was impossible. It was only nine thirty, and I was exhausted from my earlier experience and my vigilance over the monitor screen. But I knew I couldn't sleep. I went to the doorway again and stood there for a long time, staring at the empty space.

Finally, the line of light below Louise's door blinked out.

I moved numbly around my bedroom, stuffing clothes into a duffel bag. I crept to the boys' room and carefully opened their door. I went in and closed it behind me. Hardly breathing in my effort to be quiet, I opened their drawers and added some of their clothes to the bag. I moved to their beds and began picking up stuffed animals and their favorite blankets that they didn't actually use for covers, but always had to be an arm's reach away.

When the bag was full, including some books and other small toys, I zipped it closed.

I woke Sam first, shaking him gently, whispering in his ear, "Get up, sweetie. We're going on an adventure."

His eyes flashed open ,and he grinned. He sat up. "What 'venture?"

"Wait there."

I woke his brother, promising the same thing. When they were both awake, I told them that Nana had so much fun with the surprise, we would surprise her. I told them to be as quiet as tiny mice as we left their room, crept across the landing, and down the stairs.

I wasn't worried that Louise would hear the garage opening or the car. Once she fell asleep, she was out unless there was a loud disturbance, like the night of Sam's nightmare about his grandfather. Even if she did hear the garage door, I couldn't care less. It would be too late to argue with me or threaten me.

With the boys buckled into their car seats, I threw the duffel bag into the back and tossed my largest shoulder bag, filled with snacks, onto the seat beside me.

My heart rate slowed once I was out of our neighborhood. I chose a quaint but elegant motel that was often used by guests visiting Stanford University. It was expensive, but I truly wanted the boys to see this as a treat. Hiding out in a utilitarian motel room as if we were running from the police wasn't the impression that I wanted my children to have.

Once we were checked into a room on the second floor with a lovely king-sized bed, I settled the boys with their blankets and animals. The clerk had asked if I needed cots, and I'd declined, knowing the adventure would be more thrilling for them if they got to sleep in the large bed, snuggled beside me.

"Is Daddy coming for our adventure?" Nick asked as he nibbled from a box of raisins.

"Not right now."

"Is Nana coming with us?" Sam asked.

I shook my head and tried to steady my voice. "Not this time."

"Why not?" Sam asked.

"You can watch one episode of *Bluey*." I pulled the show up on my tablet, placed it between them, and moved toward the bathroom.

I used the toilet, washed my face, and brushed my teeth. I sat in the armchair facing the bed, watching my children smile and giggle, their spongy little brains cataloguing clues about how the world worked, according to a group of humanized Australian cattle dogs.

Tuning out the sounds of the animated show, I considered the widening gap between Wyatt and me. Sitting there in that moment, I couldn't recall when or even how this space had split open between us. I tried to figure out whether I'd done anything hurtful, anything to push him away aside from trying to tell him what I believed about his mother. I couldn't pretend I wasn't suspicious of her. Part of it was the simple knowledge that her stories and the autopsy report and Jason's *suicide* didn't add up. Part of it was a growing sense that the woman would do whatever she believed was needed to make sure she was the most beloved woman in her son's life. I was absolutely certain she would continue to use my children and might possibly endanger their lives.

I imagined how her husband's betrayals must have hurt her, how it must have caused her to look at everything they'd done before she'd discovered it with a bitter regret. I wondered what it would be like to let that kind of pain fester silently, transforming itself deep inside you until it turned you into a monster.

There had to be a way to make Wyatt see. I felt as if someone had placed a blindfold over his eyes, blocking not only his vision, but even the most minuscule sliver of light. Of course, it was a terrible thing to accuse someone you loved of murder. Still, I didn't understand why he thought she was essentially perfect and that most of the conflict was my fault, for being too demanding, too perfectionistic, too territorial ...

I closed my eyes for a moment and leaned my head back against the chair. Part of me wanted to cry, terrified by what was happening to my relationship with my husband. The other part of me was furious at Louise for trying to destroy her son's family. I wondered whether leaving the house, taking our children, would make any difference at all.

After two episodes of the adorable show, I put away the tablet. I read them a story and tucked the blanket around them. I turned out all the lights, finding my way around with the help of nicely placed, softly glowing nightlights in the wall sockets. I returned to the armchair, watching the faint movement of my sons' bodies as they breathed, their faces no doubt tranquil, utterly unconcerned about their future.

I picked up my phone and sent a text message to Wyatt—

The boys and I are at a hotel. We'll return when your mother is out of the house for good. If you want to know why, ask her.

The text messages from Kelly confused me. The first one, sent just before seven o'clock, asked if I knew where my mother had taken Nick and Sam. Then, hours later, she'd sent a cryptic message that said she and the boys had gone to a hotel. Why on earth would she do that? What had happened between the sending of that first message and her leaving the house with the kids, long after their bedtime. A *hotel*? Why? And what did my mother know about it?

I drove home distracted, wired from the show, and now jumpy and worried about what was going on with my family.

I pulled into the empty garage and turned off the engine. Before opening the car door, I sent Kelly a text, asking for the name of the hotel. I also wanted to ask her what was going on, but the tone in her last message, clear even in printed words, suggested she wasn't going to say a word about it until I heard my mother's side of the story. That was unusual. Kelly usually liked me to hear her version first. Everyone does when there's conflict.

She didn't respond to my message. After a few seconds of impatient waiting, I went inside.

The house was dark, no sounds beyond a few creaks in the floor that greeted me as I made my way through the kitchen and family room and into the front hallway. The blinds were still open in the music room, which made it clear that Kelly had not followed her usual evening routine.

I jogged up the stairs and knocked on my mother's door. I heard a grunt, then the sound of her shifting in bed. I knocked again—louder and longer.

"Who is it?" Her voice sounded feeble, and I was suddenly conscious of her age. She looked relatively young, and it was easy to think she had the vitality of a woman in her forties, not her late sixties. She was slowing down, her eyesight and hearing starting to dim.

"It's me, Mom."

"Is something wrong?"

"Can I come in?"

"Of course."

I opened the door.

"You don't have to ask my permission," she said. "You don't even have to knock." She laughed. "Although you might scare me if you walked in while I was sleeping."

I stepped inside just as she turned on the bedside lamp.

"What's wrong, honey?"

I shoved my hands in my pockets. "Kelly took Sam and Nick to a hotel."

"What?" She sat up suddenly.

She wore a semi-sheer blue nightgown, with thin, fragile-looking ribbons for straps. I looked away, not wanting to see glimpses of her body that she seemed unaware she was exposing. From the corner of my eye, I saw her swing her legs over the side of the bed and grab her robe off the foot of it.

"They checked into a hotel. She said you could explain why."

She let out a violent laugh. "What hotel?"

"I don't know."

"You mean you have no idea where your children are? And their mother is—"

"What happened?"

"I have some serious concerns about her. I don't think you're doing enough to help her. Or to protect the boys."

"What are you talking about? What made Kelly so upset?"

"It was nothing, as always. The boys wanted to play hide-and-seek before she came home."

"Yeah. They always do."

"Exactly. They used to want to do it when you were working outside the house. Remember?"

I nodded. "Get to the point."

"She couldn't find our hiding spot right away, and when she did, she had a complete meltdown. She fell on the ground! She accused me of *doing something* to her, whatever that means, and trying to destroy *her* family. You need to address this. No more keeping the peace. Her antics terrified the boys, and I'm concerned for them. You need to figure out how to ..." She paused, softening her expression. "I'm a little surprised they were willing to go anywhere with her after the way she behaved. Maybe they weren't willing ... I think she kidnapped them."

"Don't be dramatic. She didn't kidnap her own children."

"It happens all the time."

"Playing hide-and-seek probably isn't a great idea right now, since things have been ..." I didn't want to say more. It was obvious to my mother that Kelly had been sleeping downstairs. There was a good chance my mother knew about the affair with Jason. I was a little surprised she hadn't said anything, but I didn't want to talk to her about it, so I appreciated her discretion.

"Kelly is deteriorating," she said. "I've done nothing but try to help, walking on eggshells around her, and all I get in return are hateful accusations. Never a thank you, never, God forbid, an *I love you*." Her eyes filled with tears.

"It's been a difficult time. We've all been through a lot of changes and—"

"You need to call her and tell her to bring those boys home. Now."

She was right about needing to call her. And right about our kids, but what Kelly had done was so unusual, I didn't want to upset her further. I hated this—always in the middle, always trying to broker peace. It had been the story of my life, not just between my wife and my mother, but I'd found myself in these situations at work, and even a few weeks earlier when there was a disagreement among band members. I was the new guy, the outsider, but I was the one helping the others understand differing points of view.

Without saying more, I walked out of the room and into my own. I called Kelly. The call went immediately to voicemail. I sent her another text message. I opened the app to find her location, but she'd disabled it—the phone strained and churned, finally coming up with a message that she couldn't be found. Seeing it displayed on the screen made my stomach feel hollow. It seemed so final. I felt a clench in my heart and stood, walking quickly back across the landing to ease it away.

My mother was standing in the doorway to her bedroom.

My phone buzzed, and I looked down.

Kelly: Did you ask her?

I typed a reply:

She said you got upset about hide-and-seek?

Kelly: That figures. Another half-truth.

Wyatt: What happened?

I felt my mother's gaze on me, hard and angry.

Kelly: Ask her where they hid.

I looked up. "Where were you hiding? When you were playing with the boys?"

"Kelly's being ridiculous. And so are you. It's very possible those kids are in danger right now."

"Mom, where did you hide?"

She sighed. "We hid in the sauna."

I stared at her, trying to read her expression. When I spoke, my voice was rough. "Are you kidding me?"

She shrugged.

I messaged Kelly.

I'm sorry. I get it now. I'll talk to her and get back to you.

I stepped closer to my mother and looked down at her. She stood like a defiant teenager, hands on her hips, glaring back at me.

"That's sick," I said. "Why would you do that? Deliberately upsetting her like that? Making her think ..."

"She's too fragile. Why do I always have to worry about *upsetting* Kelly? The boys wanted a good hiding place, and I thought of the sauna."

"Of course it scared her."

"When they were excited about hiding there, I realized it could be a good thing. Her sons and I could help her get over the trauma of finding your father in there. If she saw the kids hiding ... having fun ..."

"I find that hard to believe."

"Well, it's the truth. So now that it's out in the open, you need to tell her to bring those kids home. This is not good for them. They're probably terrified."

"I'm not going to do that right now."

"Stop coddling her and making excuses. She kidnapped them!"

"She didn't kidnap them."

She stared at me for several seconds. She turned and went into her room. I went downstairs and took a beer out of the fridge. I opened the sliding door and stepped outside, desperate for fresh air. I sat in a lounge chair and sipped my beer, trying to relax, trying to sort out my feelings about Kelly. The whole time I'd been talking to my mother, I hadn't given a single thought to Kelly cheating on me. Did that mean, in my gut, I believed her? Just like I knew that accusing her of kidnapping was exaggerating what was happening here. It was not even close.

I took a sip of beer and let my mind drift, thinking about the kids. I knew they weren't scared. Kelly would have spun it to them in a way that made them feel comfortable. She was good at that.

My beer was almost empty when I heard the doorbell. My first, nonsensical thought was, *Kelly and the boys are home.* Then I realized I would have heard the garage door, and she certainly would not have rung the bell. I got up and went inside, starting toward the front door. I glanced up. My mother stood at the top of the stairs.

"A strange time for someone to be at the door," I said. "Are you expecting anyone?"

"I ... it's probably the police."

"The police? Why—"

The bell rang again. I yanked open the door. A police officer, his middle thick and intimidating with weapons and communication tools, stood on the front porch. He was tall, lanky, and had an impressive mustache. I tried to take my eyes off the thick, light brown facial hair and put them on his eyes. "Can I help you?"

"Mr. Brooks?"

"Yes."

"I understand your wife has taken your children without your permission."

"No. She has my permission. They're fine."

He narrowed his eyes at me, staring directly into mine, making me feel that if I broke his gaze, I would look furtive. "Louise Brooks called emergency services. She reported—"

"Yes. That's my mother. She was upset. We had a misunderstanding. That's all."

As if I hadn't spoken, he kept going. "She reported your children missing. She said your wife snuck out of the house with them and hasn't let you know their whereabouts."

"My mother was upset. My kids are fine. I just talked to my wife."

"Do you know where she is?"

"She's fine."

"Are you worried about the safety of your children? Three-year-old boys, correct?"

"Yes, the boys are three. I'm not worried about them. Not at all. Like I said, my mother made a mistake. She overreacted to a miscommunication. She shouldn't have called you. I'm sorry for the trouble."

"Are you sure?"

I nodded.

He pulled a card out of his shirt pocket and handed it to me. "We take reports of missing children very seriously, as well as spousal kidnapping."

"She didn't kidnap them. We're not separated."

I heard a noise from the stairs, but forced myself to keep my attention on the officer. "Everything is absolutely fine."

"Keep my card. If you have any concerns at all, please call me. There's also a twenty-four-hour hotline listed on the card."

I nodded and stuffed the card into my pocket. "I won't need it, but thanks."

The officer gave a single nod. "Have a good evening."

I waited until he was halfway down the front path before I closed the door carefully, not wanting him to think I was trying too hard to get rid of him, that I was hiding anything. The minute I turned away from the door, my mother hurried down the stairs.

"I don't think that was a good idea," she said.

"Kelly did not *kidnap* our children and you know it. You scared her to death with that stunt in the sauna. If I have to spell it out for you—that was the first time she's opened the sauna door since Dad died. You knew she would remember that moment, and you knew her first instinct would be panic that the sauna had overheated again and the boys were dead."

"That never, ever crossed my mind. I don't know how you can even imagine something so awful."

I didn't think I was far from the truth, but I was suddenly exhausted. "I'm going to bed." I went into the kitchen, poured the rest of the beer down the drain, locked the sliding glass door, and returned to the entryway. She was still there, looking slightly lost, like a child herself.

"Good night, Mom." I walked past her and climbed the stairs. When I closed my bedroom door, the light above the staircase was still on.

It took a long time to fall asleep, but finally exhaustion took over.

When I woke a few hours later, my heart swelled and beat slightly faster. Beside me, I felt the incredible, surprising, reassuring warmth of Kelly's body. I felt a surge of confused emotion and the prick of tears. I blinked them away and turned toward her.

She was curled on her side, her back facing me, as she usually was. I put my arm around her waist and pulled her close, pressing my chest and hips against her. And then, like an electrical shock, I was fully awake, my whole nervous system shaking. It wasn't Kelly. I was holding my mother's body, behaving as if we were moving tentatively toward making love.

I flung myself away from her, banging my forearm on the nightstand. I got up. "What the hell are you doing?" I switched on the light.

She gazed at me, her eyes full of love, moist with tears and something that looked disgustingly close to desire. "Always remember, Wyatt, I loved you first. I will always love you more than any other woman on earth."

I walked out of the room and went downstairs. I poured a shot of whiskey and drank the entire thing with a single flick of my wrist. Then I poured another and stared at my phone lying facedown on the counter. I wanted to tell Kelly about this, but even allowing the memory of my mother's warm flesh to brush against the edges of my mind made me feel ill.

I looked up. She stood in the doorway, barefoot, her robe hanging open around that revealing nightgown.

I spoke quickly, in a loud, jarring voice. "You can't stay here anymore, Mom. In the morning, I'll check you into a hotel. And then we'll start looking at condos in the area unless you prefer to find a small house or—"

"You're kicking me *out*?"

"Yes."

She started to whimper. "Dumping me on the streets to rot like an unwanted old addict?"

"I'm not *dumping* you on the *streets*. Stop spinning dramatic stories out of every little thing."

"This is not a little thing. Even if you don't love me, you need me. Who's going to watch your children? She needs me just as much."

"You won't be seeing the boys for a while. I'm sorry. Until Kelly and I can work things out, we need to be a family. Just the four of us. And what you did ... maybe more than I ... you can't see them. Not right now."

She was quiet for several minutes. "You've stuck your head in the sand when it comes to Kelly. I don't know why you can't see that she has serious problems. Look what she did with Jason. And—"

"Stop. It's none of your business. You can't be involved in our lives like this anymore."

She blinked at me, as if she'd checked out and wasn't really grasping what I was saying. A moment later, still not speaking, she turned and walked out of the room.

After that, the house was silent. I picked up my phone and went upstairs to call Kelly, waves of nausea washing through my stomach as I recalled what had just happened. Would I ever escape the memory of that brief but never-ending moment when I realized I was holding my mother as if she were my wife?

37

KELLY

The buzzing of my phone while Wyatt was texting me must have disturbed Sam's sleep. A few minutes later, he was murmuring, then whimpering slightly. Then he began crying. I went to the bed and turned on the light. I shook him gently, placing my hand on his head, bending down to kiss his cheek.

His eyes opened, tears pooling around his eyelids.

"You had a bad dream, Sammy. It's okay now. You're at the hotel with Mommy and Nick? Remember our adventure?"

"I'm sorry we hid in the *sah-nah*, Mommy." He reached up and took my face in his hands.

It melted my heart when either one of them turned my face toward them with their tiny hands. "It wasn't your fault, sweetie."

"We made you cry."

"You didn't make me cry, honey. Nana made me cry, by hiding in the sauna."

"Why?"

"It's hard to explain. It's for grown-ups."

"Nana said it was safe. She said the only time people burn

up in the *sah-nah* like Poppa did is when they're bad. And we're not bad. So it was okay."

A painful spasm shot through my stomach. "That's not how it is."

"Nana said—"

"Nana is wrong. Very wrong. Nana says and does a lot of wrong things."

"Why?"

"I honestly don't know. Sometimes people are sad inside, and they want to hurt other people with their words because they think it will make them feel better."

"Why?"

I kissed him again. "We can talk about it tomorrow. You need to go back to sleep."

"I'm still sorry, Mommy. I don't like when you cry."

I kissed his forehead. "Thank you. But sometimes I do cry, and it's never your fault. Okay? You need to remember that." I rearranged the blankets around him, marveled that Nick was still asleep, and turned off the light.

After changing into a nightshirt, brushing my hair, and cleaning my teeth, I pulled up the covers and slipped into bed beside my sons. I moved toward them and placed one arm gently over them.

I fell asleep quickly. I was in the midst of a confusing dream when my phone began vibrating. A call this time, not the short burst of a message.

I slipped out of bed and saw Wyatt's face on the screen. I took the phone into the bathroom, closed the door, and answered in a whisper. "Why are you calling so late?"

"I'm sorry."

"Okay."

"For everything. For not believing you, first of all. And for not recognizing my mother's issues."

"Thank you."

"I hope you can forgive me, eventually. But I mostly called because I wanted to tell you—she's checking into a hotel first thing in the morning. And I'm going to help her find a condo."

This didn't go all the way to the bottom of the issues with Louise. He was still gliding past the fact that she'd contributed to her husband's death and, very likely, Jason's. Still, it was a big step away from the direction we'd been headed. "What changed?"

"It's a long story. I'll tell you when I see you."

"Okay, I guess so."

"Will you come home now?"

"I don't know. You woke me, and I'm still trying to—"

"She called the police."

"Why?"

"She told them you kidnapped the kids."

I laughed. It wasn't at all funny, but it was so bizarre and so like her. Besides, there was nothing else to do. I was beyond crying.

"It's not funny," he said. "It was a little scary, actually. Trying to explain to this cop ... I don't know. It made me see that she's doing things that aren't normal. That she's not thinking right."

"What did you tell them?"

"That it was a misunderstanding."

"Did they believe you?" My mind leapt to Nick and Sam just a few feet away, blissfully secure in their sleep. I imagined a knock on the hotel room door, a threatening-looking cop wanting to snatch my babies out of their nest, ripping them from my arms.

"I think so. For the most part. He gave me his card and told me to call if anything happened."

"What did he think was going to happen?"

"I don't know. He was probably just following the

process."

I leaned against the sink and closed my eyes for a moment. It had seemed over-the-top paranoid not to tell Wyatt where we were staying, to turn off the tracking on my phone, but now I was very glad I'd done all of that. "What about your father?"

"What about him?"

"Do you believe me about that, too? That she turned up the heat? That she pushed him to drink too much and left him alone in the sauna when it was at such a dangerous temperature? Then turned the temperature down again so we wouldn't know? She must have known he was dead ... so ..."

"I don't know. I can't think about that right now. It's too much ... because she ... I found ..."

"She murdered your father. She's extremely disturbed." I shivered. I pressed my hand against my belly, my fingers cold even through my nightshirt.

A choking sound came from Wyatt, as if he were being strangled or were about to cry.

"I know it's hard to take in," I said. "But it's pretty clear—"

Another sharp, pained gasp came from Wyatt. "I can't ... I can't ..."

"Are you okay?"

He was quiet for a long time. I wasn't even sure I heard him breathing. "Are you there?" My question was met with silence. "Wyatt? What's going on?"

He coughed. "It's really hard to say it out loud. I wanted to tell you in person, but ..."

"What *happened*?"

"She ..."

"Tell me." I waited. I couldn't imagine what he might be trying to say. Why was he taking so long? If the kids hadn't been snuggled up four feet from where I stood, I would have been in the throes of gut-wrenching fear, the way he was dragging this on.

"She got into bed with me, and—"

"Oh my God. Oh my *GOD!*"

I thought of Louise lying in our bed, telling me she was napping, chastising me for overreacting. I thought of all the times she'd touched Wyatt and kissed him with what I'd thought was too much affection. The way she cooed that she was his muse and leaned on him and wanted to have whispered, secret conversations with him. For once, I had no idea what to say. It made my skin crawl, and like him, I wasn't sure I wanted to talk about it.

"So ... anyway," he said slowly. "Give me time to think about stuff."

A violent shudder ran through me as I thought of Louise in our bed, touching my husband like that ...

At the same time, it was surprisingly gratifying to know that my instincts had been correct. All of them. It was satisfying to prove that I wasn't the neurotic person Wyatt had believed I was over the past few months. It had been difficult holding my ground against that. When someone is constantly telling you that you're the one with the problem, if you're a person who's self-aware, you don't want to keep dismissing suggestions that you need to take a closer look at yourself. Especially when those suggestions come from someone you've trusted and respected for nearly all of your adult life.

"Are you coming home now?" he asked.

"Sam and Nick are asleep. It's better if we come home in the morning." I wanted him to say he would call the police to report our certainty that Louise had turned up the temperature in the sauna, but the proof was thin, I could see that. Even though I knew it was the truth, they would want more. If that was enough, they would have already started investigating. The coroner would have called Frank's death suspicious. "What did she say when you told her she has to leave?"

"She was upset."

"How upset?"

"She said I was throwing her out on the street." His voice broke slightly as he spoke.

Now that he believed me, I could afford to be kind, or at least gentle with him, if not with Louise, so I said nothing. He needed time to fully absorb how terribly and wrongfully he'd mistrusted me, and to see who she really was. "What else did she say?"

"Not much. She accepted it. I think she knew she went too far."

"Maybe."

"I'll let you get some sleep," he whispered. "I love you. And I miss you more than you can imagine."

"Why don't you come here?" I said. "I'll text you the address."

"Really?"

"Yes."

We said good-bye, and I sent the text. I called the front desk and told them to expect my husband in about fifteen or twenty minutes.

All my sleepiness was gone. My mind spun, so happy that we were turning in the right direction, but also working back over all the things he'd told me—about Louise calling the police, snuggling up to him in our bed, agreeing to move out. It was a lot. It was too much.

I rearranged the pillows behind me, trying to move carefully so I didn't disturb Nick and Sam, who shifted their positions every so often, bumping against each other, but not enough to wake. I stared at my phone, waiting for him to give me an ETA. I tried taking slow, deep breaths. I tried visualizing waves on a beach to calm myself. Nothing worked.

Images of Louise in our bed, reaching for my husband, flashed through my mind. Recollections of things she'd said repeated in circles, but I strained to remember the specific threads of conversations.

Was she really so willing to move out of our house? After all the things she'd done to try to make my family belong solely to her? After selling the home she'd lived in for over thirty years so she could entrench herself in our lives? Now, she was agreeable and content to leave her beloved son, her grandchildren?

My phone was still dark. I unlocked the screen to double-check. No reply, not even a thumbs up. I turned on the location services. The app showed him still at our house. It had been at least thirty minutes. Maybe he'd fallen asleep. I sent three messages in a row, just fun emojis, hoping the insistent vibrations would wake him. Still, he didn't reply. I couldn't believe he would have lain down again. He would have packed immediately and been on his way in five minutes. I tapped his face to call. The phone went directly to voicemail.

I left a message, then stared at my phone, waiting for a response.

After twenty minutes, he hadn't replied, and my anxiety had increased with each advance of the clock glaring at me from the screen, minutes ticking past.

I could imagine Louise crying to Wyatt that she'd made a mistake crawling into our bed, that she'd been tired and upset. That she was grieving and still wasn't always thinking straight.

She would never leave willingly. Never. And the other thing about Louise—she never showed her cards. She would not accept being separated from her son, but she wasn't necessarily going to let him know that right away. She would come up with a plan.

The woman who had turned up the sauna to a deadly

temperature, sending her husband to his grave, the woman who hired a nanny and bribed him to say he'd had sex with me—the nanny who then conveniently and oddly killed himself—that woman was alone in that house with my husband. I couldn't imagine she would ever want to hurt her precious son ... but what if she thought she was losing him forever? Maybe she just didn't want me to have him.

I opened the number pad to call the police, my finger hesitating over the first nine. Louise had set me up as a woman who spirited her children out of the house, who was unstable and untrustworthy. The police had been to our home, had seen Wyatt and Louise on good terms. Would they believe me, much less recognize the urgency?

I turned on the light and yanked off my nightshirt. I dressed, then woke Nick and Sam. The hotel room was ours until noon; I didn't need to pack. I lured them with little bags of gummy animals I'd brought with me and hurried them out to the car. When they were buckled in, I turned on a playlist of their favorite songs and drove home. At that hour, the streets were clear. Less than fifteen minutes passed before I was pulling into our driveway, but my hands had been shaking, and my heart had jittered inside my rib cage the entire time.

38

LOUISE

After my beloved son, the only human being left on the earth who truly loved me, who had *ever* loved me, cut me out of his heart and his life, I drifted up the stairs like a ghost. My feet barely touched the carpet. I didn't grip the handrail, not caring if I fell all the way to the tile floor below. When Wyatt told me he didn't want me, that I wouldn't be seeing my grandsons, his eyes were cold, almost lifeless. He was looking through me as if he didn't even see me. I'd felt like a ghost.

I walked across the landing to his room and lay in the center of the bed. I closed my eyes. I folded my hands and placed them on my rib cage. He didn't want me.

Or was I wrong about that? He'd clearly had a conversation with *her* that I wasn't privy to. *She* was the one who wanted me out of the house. She was the one who wanted me cut off from the boy who had loved me with all his heart. The charming boy who had cried when I walked out of a room, who clung to me with warm, strong arms when I tried to leave him at preschool. That boy adored me. He'd loved me without reservation from the moment he first opened his eyes and gazed into mine. He'd loved me and leaned on me when his father hurt him. He'd sent me messages and emails when he was away. He'd called me every day as he drove home from work, for years.

He was a kind and devoted and loyal man.

She, on the other hand ...

Telling me I needed to go to a hotel had not been Wyatt's desire at all. Kelly was the one who seemed to think families should be split up and run away, hiding out in hotel rooms. She'd stolen my grandchildren, and no one cared. I didn't even know where they were. They might be in San Francisco. They might not even be in a hotel. They might be driving to Southern California, planning to escape over the border to Mexico, where I'd never see them again. Then she would demand that Wyatt join them there. I'd be alone, cut off from Wyatt for the rest of my life. She wanted to destroy me. Honestly, I didn't think she would truly feel happy until I was dead.

Even though he'd shoved me out of his bed, almost seeming repulsed by my body, I knew he loved me. His love had been pure and strong every moment of his sweet life. Any disgust he felt had been planted and fed by *her*.

Lying there, my beautiful gown draped around my legs, feeling the bedding that was still warm from Wyatt's and my bodies, the image of Juliet on her bier came to mind. I recalled the movie made in the 1960s. I saw Juliet, so young, exquisite, having swallowed the potion meant to fool everyone into thinking she'd died. She'd been so beautiful when Romeo found her. But then came that tragic moment when he drank the tiny bottle of poison, ending his life so he could be with her in death. Forever.

I sat up and slid off the bed. I went to my room and closed the door, locking it just in case. I opened my bottle of sleeping pills. I took a small dish that I'd bought to hold a candle but never used out of the desk drawer. I poured all the tablets into the dish and started crushing them one by one. It was a mindless, almost calming task, trying to break them apart without small chunks spraying off and disappearing into the carpet fibers. I turned the broken tablets into ever smaller bits and then to a fine powder, using the handle of my sterling silver hairbrush.

Kelly's plan was to force Wyatt into shutting me away in a dingy apartment. I would sit there alone, day after day. I would lie alone in a narrow bed night after night. I would have nothing to comfort me but pictures of my grandchildren. I would never see my beloved Wyatt, never touch his beautiful hands or shoulders. I would be forgotten and left to decay. One day, I would be found dead, the rooms stinking of rotting flesh because it had been months since anyone had been in the apartment. Only a neighbor, noticing I never went out for groceries anymore, calling the police for a welfare check, would realize I might be gone.

The thought of ending my life that way, especially when that cold, hateful, selfish husband of mine had been allowed to leave the earth from the home where his son had welcomed and cared for him. Frank got to enjoy nice whiskey and a relaxing sauna. I know the last few minutes were probably difficult for him—those long, brutal moments when I used all my strength to hold the sauna door closed, knowing his weakened arms would eventually be no match for mine, which were strong from swimming laps in Wyatt's pool. All those days when I'd soothed myself by gliding up and down the length of the swimming pool, in a silent world of my own, where my thoughts were free to dream of a better life.

My husband had had sex with every wiggling butt that walked past him. He'd flirted and lured them; he'd told them whatever they wanted to hear, just as he'd told me what I wanted to hear for so many years.

I'm sure Ms. Kelly, with her modern ideas and self-assurance and persuasive speeches about how to exert your power, would not have put up with that kind of never-ending betrayal and pain. Although she probably also thought that could never happen to her, because she was *so amazing,* of course. She would ask why I hadn't left Frank, why I'd let him humiliate and hurt me for all those years. But she had no clue what it was like to build your life around a man and your child. It wasn't so easy to walk away and acquire money of your own when you'd never done anything that might allow you to earn an income. Only when Frank was dead had I finally had access to money that belonged solely to me.

I'd hinted, once, that I might leave him. I told Frank if he didn't stop, I would take Wyatt and start my life over without him. He laughed in my face. Then he grabbed me and pulled me onto his lap. He shoved his hand up my shirt and wormed his fingers into my bra and pinched my nipple—hard, until I cried and begged him to stop.

Then he laughed harder. "You aren't taking my son anywhere. If you even think about leaving, you'll never see him again. You can't threaten me. You belong to me. And so does that boy. So don't ever talk like that again. I can have who I want. Men have needs that women will never understand, so stop complaining and accept it, like other women do. That's your job. That's the order of the world. Women were made to be helpers; men were made to sow their seed."

Kelly was so smug about figuring out I'd wanted to be rid of Frank. She had no clue; she'd never known even a sliver of that kind of hurt and hatred and how it festers for years, for decades. For your entire life.

I used a makeup brush to gently brush the powder from my newly filled prescription into a small plastic box I used for carrying painkillers when I was out of the house for the day, especially sitting in the hot sun at the park, which often gave me a splitting headache. I went out to the landing and glanced toward Wyatt's bedroom. The door was closed, but as I moved closer, I heard him thumping around.

I was careful as I turned away from his door and crept down the stairs. I closed the door between the entryway and family room and went into the kitchen. I made several cups of strong green tea, poured it into an insulated cup, and screwed the lid on tight. I placed it on the center island. Wyatt had left a bottle of whiskey on the opposite counter. I placed it near the insulated cup along with an expensive cocktail glass.

I opened the garage door and stepped into the warm, musty space. I tightened the belt of my robe to be sure it didn't catch on anything as I made my way to the workbench. I picked up a roll of duct tape, heavy-duty scissors, and some wire cutters. Then I went back into the house.

In the music room, I searched the closet until I found the small packets that held Wyatt's spare guitar strings. I found a basket in the pantry and piled the tools and beverages, the highball glass, and a nice teacup and saucer into it.

Carrying the basket over my arm, I went back upstairs. I stopped outside the bedroom door and pressed my ear against the wood, listening.

S eeing Wyatt's car in the garage gave me a feeling of security I hadn't experienced in a while, certainly not over the past few days. I nestled my car beside his and turned off the engine. Fortunately, Nick and Sam hadn't fallen back to sleep during the ride home. Their body clocks were probably completely shattered by all the activity that evening.

I unbuckled them and ushered them into the silently waiting house. The kitchen and family room were dark. Clearly no one was on the first floor, since I didn't see a shred of light beyond the overhead kitchen light I'd just flicked on. I trembled to think where Louise and Wyatt might be. For a brief moment, I'd considered leaving my sons secured in their car seats while I conducted a frantic, terrified search for my husband. But I couldn't do that to them.

I shouted Wyatt's name, but there was no response.

Moving as quickly as I could without scaring them, trying to hold my own fear in check, I tugged Nick and Sam toward the family room. I brought up more animated shows on my iPad and settled them on the couch with a blanket tucked around their legs. My hands still shook. I was gasping at the speed of seconds ticking past, not knowing what Louise might be doing. I shoved away the whisper fluttering behind my forehead, hissing that Wyatt might already be dead, that I should have called the police despite the risk of being detained myself. I never should have allowed Louise to be alone with Wyatt for a second longer than necessary. I shoved their sippy cups, still half-full with juice, into my sons' hands. "Don't leave the couch. No matter what happens. Even if Nana says it's okay."

They stared at me, clearly confused.

I raced up the stairs. Louise's bedroom door was open, her bed empty.

Stumbling across the landing, I saw the door to my room was also open. I nearly fell into the room.

Louise sat on my side of the bed. She was holding a teacup, about to take a sip. When she saw me, she let out a small cry.

Beside her, Wyatt lay on his back, groaning as if he was in pain.

At first, I hadn't realized what I was seeing because the blankets covered him, and the room was dark except for the lamp on the nightstand beside Louise.

My husband had a large gray strip of duct tape across his mouth. He moved awkwardly, twitching as if he was trying to break free, but was physically restrained by the blankets. I lunged at the bed and yanked off the covers. His wrists and ankles were bound with some kind of wire that was cutting into him, causing angry red marks like burns on his skin, a few drops of blood oozing out where the wire had cut more deeply.

I screamed at Louise, something incoherent that even I couldn't decipher—the cry of an animal backed into a corner. I knelt beside the bed and reached for the strip of tape.

Before I was able to peel back the tape, Louise flung the contents of her teacup directly at my face. I screamed, stinging pain slicing the tender skin of my eyelids and cheeks. Blinded, I tried to wipe away the liquid, pressing my fingers and palms against my skin, trying to cool it. I wiped at my eyes, desperate to see.

Louise scrambled out of bed and fumbled around on the nightstand. Through a blur of tears, I peeled the tape off Wyatt's face. I felt his pain as his tears spilled out of his eyes, running down his cheeks, soaking the tips of my fingers.

"Are you okay?" he asked.

Unable to truly see clearly what I was doing, I picked at the bindings on his wrists, trying to work the knots apart as I nodded that I would be okay.

"Guitar string," he rasped.

"Why are you ... how did she—"

"I was putting a few things in my backpack. She came into the room and hit me on the back of the head with something hard. Not sure what. I collapsed, and I must have passed out for a few seconds. When I woke, my hands were tied, and she slapped the tape over my mouth. While she sat on my legs and tied my feet, she said that once I calmed down and stopped fighting her, we would have our drinks. The entire contents from her bottle of sleeping pills was dissolved in my whiskey and her tea. We would leave the world together." He laughed with a bitter edge to his voice.

I turned, suddenly aware we were alone. "Where did she go?" A sob spilled out of me. I screamed louder than I ever had in my life—"Nick! Sam! I'm coming!"

I scrambled to my feet and rushed toward the door. I raced across the landing, tripping on the sash from her robe that she'd dropped on the carpet. I picked myself up and lunged toward the stairs, nearly falling again as I flew down them, skipping steps here and there, hoping I remained upright, but unable to stop from flinging myself forward.

I lurched around the corner and into the family room. The blanket that I'd wrapped around my sons' legs was coiled like an empty nest on the couch, their stuffed bears tossed on the floor. I screamed, the sobs tearing at my chest, making it difficult to breathe.

Still wailing, choked by tears that filled my throat, refusing to come out of my eyes, as if they were frozen with terror, I wrenched open the sliding glass door and ran across the yard to the sauna. I yanked on the handle, but the door was locked from the inside.

"Louise!" I pounded my fists on the heavy door, so solid there was no answering echo, just a solid thud. "Open the door. Louise! Right now. Open the door." I moved back and kicked the door. Pain shot through my foot and up my leg. I hadn't even made a mark on the smooth, finished wood.

I whirled around, wildly searching the dark backyard, as if some magical being might emerge from behind a tree, coming to my aid. There was nothing but the still, dark water of the pool, the peacefully growing vegetables and trees, the sound of crickets in the warm air.

I tore across the pavement surrounding the pool and onto the lawn, cutting through the vegetable garden, not caring what I trampled in my blind terror. My feet sank into moist earth, slowing my progress. When I reached the back door to the garage, I realized that, of course, it was locked. Sobbing again and gasping for air, I ran to the sliding door, into the house, and through the kitchen to the garage. I grabbed the axe that Wyatt had used only once, trying to remove the stump of a dead tree.

Unsnapping the leather case as I went, I rushed back outside, not moving as quickly now to be sure I didn't have a horrible accident. At the door of the sauna, I raised the axe and heaved the blade into the door. It wedged into the wood. It took all my strength to pull it out. I finally dislodged it, raised it above my head a second time and slammed it into the well-sealed planks. There wasn't a single sound coming from inside, but I knew the room was nearly soundproof with its thick walls and the insulation required to retain heat.

After five assaults with the axe blade, I was sweating and breathing hard, my heart pounding as if it were trying to break through my ribs in time with the blows from the axe. The door had splintered, but I was so far from gaining entrance, I began whimpering. It would take forever.

I thought of my phone—if she'd turned up the heat, I could disable it, but would it cool fast enough? And I had no idea where my purse was and no time to look.

My hands and arms were weak, as if my muscles had collapsed entirely. Still, I continued swinging the axe. The door was slowly beginning to come apart. Then I heard Wyatt's voice behind me, calm and so utterly soothing, speaking my name. He took the axe from me and began hacking the door. Finally, the splintered wood began to fall away, and then there was an opening, and then it was larger, and I was able to reach inside and turn the lock.

The door swung open.

Louise sat on the bench. Alone.

An insulated canister sat beside her on the bench. She held a cup and saucer as if she were enjoying high tea with the Queen of England. The Mad Hatter was a more fitting image.

I lunged at her, screaming, knocking the teacup to the floor, where it shattered. "Where are Nick and Sam?" For half a second, I wondered if any of our neighbors had heard all the chaos, the violent cracks of an iron blade going into planks of oak, my screaming and wailing. I didn't care, and I was angry at myself for having such a trivial thought when I had no idea what had happened to my babies.

They weren't babies, of course, but they were so small, so sweet-smelling, their skin soft and unblemished, their eyes innocent and filled with trust, their words laced with joy.

Louise looked at the floor. "That was my favorite cup."

"Where are they?" Wyatt's voice was colder than I'd ever heard come from his lips.

I grabbed her hair, yanking her face toward mine, trying not to stare down at the sheer nightgown exposing every detail of her body. "Where are they?"

"Calm down, Kelly. Why do you always overreact? They're playing hide-and-seek, of course. They love that game."

As if our hearts were linked, Wyatt and I turned simultaneously and ran to the house. He slammed the sliding glass door to the side and went inside, calling for Nick and Sam. We searched under tables and behind furniture, calling their names, telling them the game was over. Of course, they were trained not to respond to that. They knew you never revealed your hiding place. You kept silent. You made your breathing as quiet as possible. You didn't move a muscle.

As we moved through the first floor, continuing to call out despite knowing they wouldn't answer, I wondered if Louise was playing yet another game. Was it possible she'd had enough time to take them somewhere? I didn't think so. I'd only been blinded for a moment or two, had only turned my attention away from her to Wyatt's restraints for a few seconds longer. She couldn't have taken them out in the car, returned, and locked herself in the sauna during that brief time. Unless it had been longer than I'd realized, unless my sense of time was so distorted by the events of the evening.

I was sickened by the knowledge I'd left my children unattended long enough for her to get to them.

fter what seemed like endless hours, but was only a
minute or two, Kelly and I found Sam and Nick in
my mother's bedroom closet. They were huddled
on the floor, holding their juice cups. Kelly grabbed the cups
and flung them into the room, terrified that my mother might
have put some of her sleeping pills into the juice.

She swept Nick into her arms, and I did the same with
Sam. We leaned against each other, kissing our children's
faces. Kelly sobbed with relief, and I felt the terror gradually
subside from my lungs as well. Unsure what all the emotion
was about, the boys strained to pull themselves away from
our frantic embraces and smothering lips.

When Kelly and I had calmed ourselves, we took the boys
to their bedroom and tucked them into their beds. I kissed
them both on the forehead and left to deal with my mother.

The atmosphere in our backyard felt like something out
of a horror movie—the quiet water of the swimming pool,
the perfectly tended plants and trees, the lush vegetable
garden, and then that yawning cavity in the beautiful wood
door to the sauna. I'd turned on the outdoor lights when I'd

come outside to find Kelly slamming the axe into the sauna door. I didn't have to ask what she was thinking.

Now, the lights gave it a friendly glow. I walked slowly toward the sauna.

My mother was still sitting inside, the flimsy nylon of the nightgown clinging to her body, making her look almost naked. I wished I had a blanket, a towel, but there was nothing available, and I wasn't going back into the house before speaking to her.

She gave me a sad look and leaned back against the wall, wedging the insulated canister between her legs, which were trembling. "So ... you managed to tear yourself away from her long enough to say good-bye to me."

"I don't know what to say." I honestly didn't. She was out of her mind, truly and medically, and I wasn't sure whether trying to have a conversation even made sense.

"It's alright. You don't have to offer an emotional farewell." She raised the canister to her lips, her hand shaking. The lid tapped against her teeth as she took several sips. "I've taken all my sleeping pills. Or most of them; I didn't want to take so much I'd throw it up. I studied how to do it properly, so you can relax."

My insides were frozen. I didn't know if she was telling the truth or wanted to upset me, to enjoy watching me rush to rescue her. "Is that the truth?"

"I suppose you could call the paramedics, but what's the point? My life is over. I've lost you. I realize that. And I'm sure you'll keep the boys away from me. Even if you want them to know their grandmother, she won't let you." She gave me a sad, almost compassionate smile.

"I don't understand—"

"You'll probably never know, or maybe you will, time will tell ... the feeling of having the person you've joined your life with, the person you love with all your heart, throw you aside and give their body to someone else. It makes you feel ugly. Unwanted. Humiliated beyond anything I can describe. It makes you feel like you're not desirable, that your body and your entire *being* are just not ... that you're repulsive." Tears filled her eyes. She took another sip of tea. "This is almost gone. In less than an hour, I expect I will be too."

"Why? Why would you destroy the people who do ... who *did* ... who still love you?"

"She knew I'd killed him. I thought she might tell you, that you'd believe her, that I'd lose you. I don't want to spend my life in a cold, violent prison, eating revolting food."

"You could have divorced him."

"That's so very easy to say. So easy. I would have been destitute if I'd left your father. And that's another aspect you fail to understand. I loved him. I loved him all my life, even when he did what he did. I humiliated myself because I couldn't stop loving him."

I moved toward her. She hugged the tea canister to her chest. Around the opening were flecks of white, wet chunks of tablets that hadn't fully dissolved.

She laughed. "If you cared whether I lived, you would have called for help by now. I know you, and I know what's in your heart. Always."

"You don't."

She gave me a condescending smile. "I just have one request. If I could be so selfish and demanding as to ask for a single act of love, a single act of acknowledging that I gave you everything I had to give ..."

"That's not fair."

She held up her hand to stop me from talking. "I'd like to ask that you keep my memory pure for Nick and Sam. It won't change anything to tell them the details of their grandfather's death ... or Jason's. It won't make their lives any better to know about the things that happened here tonight. If you would do that for me ... let them love me, so that two people on this earth have kind thoughts toward me. I know I'll become nothing more than a face in a photograph for them by the time they're grown, but just for now ..." She swallowed the rest of the tea, made a face at the sour taste of the undissolved pieces, and placed the insulated canister beside her.

I knew I'd already decided, the minute I came face-to-face with her, what I was going to do. I'd decided by doing nothing. She was right, as she almost always was. If I'd planned to call for help, I would have done it immediately. I could see she was getting tired, her eyelids drooping, her shoulders slumping forward slightly. I went into the house and got a blanket.

Returning to the sauna, I stepped inside and looked at my mother, her eyes closed now. I went to her and took hold of her upper body. I turned her carefully and lowered her to the bench, lying her on her side. I placed the blanket over her. I realized I should have brought a pillow, but it was almost too late for that. She didn't need it.

I kissed her hairline. I took a step back, considered the alternatives in a flash of thought that included the loss of my wife, my sons further traumatized, the failure to protect my family, my mother in prison ...

I took another step back, then went out of the sauna. I pushed what was left of the door closed. I stood for a moment, my mind empty, then turned and walked toward the house.

Inside, I'd thought it would be an effort to climb the stairs, but I found myself walking up quickly, eagerly, as if I hadn't been whacked on the back of the head, bound with wire, and then wielded an axe.

I stopped at the boys' room and went inside. They were already asleep, their faces peaceful. I imagined they were dreaming of a positive outcome to a magnificent game of hide-and-seek. I kissed them both, letting my lips linger on their cheeks, feeling their trusting warmth.

Stepping into the landing area, I moved toward my mother's room and pulled the door closed. Then I walked slowly into the bedroom I shared with my wife. I faced the bed.

She sat cross-legged, her back straight, her hair falling around her shoulders. She looked more beautiful than I'd ever seen her, possibly more than on our wedding day or the moment she'd given birth to our twins.

"Did you call the police?" She leaned forward, her eyes bright with the trauma she'd been through in the past few hours.

I shook my head.

"Why not? What's wrong with you? After all the—"

"She took her sleeping pills."

"So?"

"All of them. The stuff she'd crushed up for my drink and hers."

She stared at me.

Moments earlier, as I'd made my way across the yard, into the house, and up the stairs, I'd thought about what I would say to Kelly. The journey seemed as if it took hours, but at the same time, barely gave me enough space to think about what I'd done, what I would be asking Kelly to do. I'd foolishly hoped I wouldn't have to provide a lot of details, but I should have known it would be impossible for her to comprehend if I didn't. "She'd already taken enough to kill herself. So I let her."

"You ...?"

"Yes. I let her die."

"Why?"

"Because of what she's done."

"That's a job for the police and the courts, not you."

"Why? Do you want to put our family through an arrest, a murder trial? To let Nick and Sam find out about it?"

"Someday, they will."

"But we can control how they hear it, instead of the media shoving it down their throats. We can prevent the worst thing in their lives from being stored forever on the internet."

"Do you realize it will look like you killed her?"

Her concern over what it would look like to others made me realize she was already starting to shift her position, starting to see my point of view and hopefully agree it was the best way to go.

"It sounds worse than it is," I said. "She's the one who swallowed the entire bottle of sleeping pills. I didn't force her, like she planned to do with me."

"That's not what the police, what other people, will think."

"I'm not going to call the police."

"Until she's dead?" She shivered, then gripped her upper arms.

"Not ever."

"Ever?" she whispered. "What are you going to—"

"I'll bury her in our garden. No one has to find out. Everyone knew she'd just lost her husband. They knew she hadn't really expressed any grief. It's easy to believe she would do that. And that is what actually happened, in a way."

"When they don't find her body, they'll come here looking for her."

"I don't think so. Her car is gone ..."

"They'll track the sale. It will be clear she sold it weeks ago."

"Okay. Well ... we can come up with something. No one's going to think we killed her."

"Because normal people don't do that!"

Her voice was shrill. The sound of it ran up my spine like

an insect with venom in its feet that delivered a sharp, burning sensation.

"This is a terrible idea." She reached for her cell phone sitting on the nightstand beside the monitor that showed the twins in their beds, their faces innocent and untroubled.

I went to the bed and sat on the edge, placing my hand over hers, pressing the phone into the bedding. "There's not any clear-cut evidence she killed my dad. Or Jason. How would you feel if she was arrested and then released? She would be free to think of ways to get back into our lives, to punish you."

She stared at me, her eyes blank.

"I'll bury her in the garden. We'll think of something to tell people, to tell the boys."

"I don't want to lie to our children."

"There's a way to tell them without lying. They're young, and they don't need a lot of information. They'll be devastated. They really did love her. But I can't think of another way that wouldn't be worse."

She was quiet for a very long time. She closed her eyes, leaned her head back, and still I kept my hand cupped over hers, wanting her to feel from the pressure and warmth of me that this was the best choice. The only choice. After a while, her hand relaxed slightly. She released her grip on the phone and let her fingers settle into the blankets. "Maybe it could work. At the funeral, she was talking to Chris about how there was only one man for her. I thought she was referring to your father, and so did Chris. I realize now, she probably meant you ... but Chris might support that idea, that she was overcome with grief and drowned herself or something. Jumped off a bridge, a cliff."

"It's not like they're going to launch a massive long-term search for someone in this situation. They'll ask around, talk to her old neighbors and friends. But when they don't find her body, it will become an inactive case."

"And we'll have it hanging over our heads the rest of our lives," she said.

We were both quiet for a long time.

Then she sighed—a long, loud exhalation. "I don't know. It feels ... the kids ..." Her eyes filled with tears.

I moved toward her and put my arms around her. "She almost destroyed us. It feels right to me." I felt her relax into me. "She's probably gone now," I said.

EPILOGUE
KELLY

Two months later

I was still aware of something missing every time I looked out the glass doors from the family room and saw the empty space where the sauna used to be. Wyatt had taken it down himself, renting a truck to haul away the pipes and debris. When our neighbors asked about it, which only two of them did, we told them that after Wyatt's father died in there, we couldn't enjoy it anymore. They said it was a shame, because it had been a beautiful structure, although one of them also mentioned she didn't like the claustrophobic feeling of saunas. I agreed. I knew I would never step inside one again.

Two days after she died, we reported Louise missing. We said she'd told us she was renting a car, driving back to her old neighborhood to see friends whom she'd felt had disappeared from her life. We told the police we were concerned because she'd never shown any real emotion after her husband's shocking, untimely death. We thought she might be in denial. We feared she'd *done something.* They nodded sympathetically.

Wyatt added to this by recalling how she'd had a fit of panic because she believed the boys had been kidnapped simply because I took them out for a fun movie night in a hotel.

Without any real prompting from us, Chris ended up telling the police how devoted Louise had been to Frank, how *she'd wept that her heart belonged only to Frank.* He couldn't imagine how she was coping without him. And that sale of her house—*yes, they'd discussed it before Frank's surgery, but it had been simple exploratory questions. To suddenly instruct him to get rid of it, do something that significant only weeks after her husband's death, was alarming.* We all should have realized at the time—it was a clear sign of unrelenting, unbearable grief.

Feeling like criminals, we turned off Louise's cell phone the day she died. We looked at each other and whispered reminders that this was the woman who had tried to destroy our family, who was ready, and even eager, to kill my husband.

Just before we reported her missing, we drove to Marin County, turned the phone on, and dropped it into a drain a few blocks from her former home.

We reminded Nick and Sam how much Nana loved them. We told stories of their hide-and-seek escapades and talked about how she loved them so much, she'd played that game on her very last night with them. We told them Nana kept going outside to sit in the sauna because that was where Grandpa had died, and she missed him terribly. We said we thought she might have gone to be with him. They wanted to know where that was, and we told them it was a place you couldn't see, but that everyone was happy there. Always.

That story wouldn't last forever. Possibly for another year, maybe less. But eventually they would be able to understand that in the throes of grief, people sometimes took their lives, and that was what Nana did.

Because that was indeed what she'd done. We knew that for a fact.

IT WAS A WARM FALL EVENING. Wyatt and I sat on the back patio. The edges of the overhang were strung with fairy lights that sparkled on the surface of the pool.

We each had a glass of wine, but after clicking our glasses together as background music to saying *I love you*, the wine had remained untouched.

"Are we good?" Wyatt asked, reaching for my hand.

"We're good."

"I'm sorry I didn't trust you, that I had even a single minute of believing you would cheat on me."

I squeezed his hand. "Enough. You've apologized enough."

"Time to move forward?"

"Yes. We both let terrible thoughts take control." I thought about how I'd considered, even though it was only for a few breaths, that Wyatt had killed his father. The thing we'd done with his mother was merciful. I truly believed that. I also knew that even so, it was a difficult thing he would have to live with. It would always be part of him. Everyone has those damaged pieces in their lives—unhappy and unpleasant experiences they must make peace with. I was confident we could learn to let the past die out of our hearts.

"It's kind of strange," I said. "Louise wanted to split us apart, and even though she almost succeeded, she ended up bringing us closer than ever."

"We have to carry this for the rest of our lives."

"Yes."

"And we'll be in this house forever. Until we die," he said.

"We will, but I don't feel trapped."

"Neither do I."

I turned to him and smiled, hoping he saw in my face, in the darkness broken only by those tiny lights, how much I loved him. I picked up my glass and took a sip of wine. I looked past the pool to the strip of grass and the garden beyond that.

The vegetable garden was gone. I didn't have the stomach for it, knowing Louise's body was buried deep in the earth, at the bottom of a hole it had taken us two entire nights to dig. But the exertion felt good. It worked a lot of things out of our bodies, into the soil. Working together helped us come to terms with what we'd done. The garden area was now filled with rosebushes, enough that we would eventually forget the exact place where she lay.

I knew Wyatt believed he had been merciful to his mother.

And I knew that I'd given her what she'd always wanted —she would sleep just below Wyatt's bedroom window, lying beside him for the rest of his life.

A NOTE FROM THE AUTHOR

Thank you so much for choosing to read *Always Remember*. I hope you enjoyed reading the book as much as I loved writing it.

I want to take a moment to give an enormous thank you to Brian Lynch and Garret Ryan at Inkubator Books. Their belief in my writing, their unique, passionate approach to developing and shaping a story, as well as their investment in getting the word out to readers has changed my writing career in amazing ways. Thank you to the brilliant Line Langebek for her insight into character and story, and her editing process that shaped this into a richer story. Her desire to dig out the dark side of characters' lives made her feel like a kindred spirit! I also owe a huge thank you to Jodi Compton for her exquisite editing and Pauline Nolet for her careful attention to the little things.

Reviews are so important to us authors. If you could spend a moment to write an honest review on Amazon, no matter how short, I would be extremely grateful. They really do help get the word out.

Best wishes,

Cathryn

www.cathryngrant.com

ALSO BY CATHRYN GRANT

INKUBATOR TITLES

THE GUEST
(A Psychological Thriller)

THE GOOD NEIGHBOR
(A Psychological Thriller)

THE GOOD MOTHER
(A Psychological Thriller)

ONLY YOU
(A Psychological Thriller)

THE ASSISTANT
(A Psychological Thriller)

THE OTHER COUPLE
(A Psychological Thriller)

ALWAYS REMEMBER
(A Psychological Thriller)

CATHRYN'S OTHER TITLES

She's Listening
(A Psychological Thriller)

THE ALEXANDRA MALLORY PSYCHOLOGICAL SUSPENSE SERIES

The Woman In the Mirror ◆ *The Woman In the Water*

The Woman In the Painting ◆ *The Woman In the Window*

The Woman In the Bar ◆ *The Woman In the Bedroom*
The Woman In the Dark ◆ *The Woman In the Cellar*
The Woman In the Photograph ◆ *The Woman In the Storm*
The Woman In the Taxi

SUBURBAN NOIR NOVELS

Buried by Debt

The Suburban Abyss ◆ *The Hallelujah Horror Show*

Getting Ahead ◆ *Faceless* ◆ *An Affair With God*

THE HAUNTED SHIP TRILOGY

Alone On the Beach ◆ *Slipping Away From the Beach*

Haunting the Beach

NOVELLAS

Madison Keith Ghost Story Series ◆ *Chances Are*

SHORT FICTION

Reduction in Force ◆ *Maternal Instinct*

Flash Fiction For the Cocktail Hour

The 12 Days of Xmas

NONFICTION

Writing is Murder: Motive, Means, and Opportunity

Published by Inkubator Books
www.inkubatorbooks.com

Copyright © 2021 by Cathryn Grant

Cathryn Grant has asserted her right to be identified as the
author of this work.

ALWAYS REMEMBER is a work of fiction. People, places,
events, and situations are the product of the author's
imagination. Any resemblance to actual persons, living or
dead is entirely coincidental.

No part of this book may be reproduced, stored in any
retrieval system, or transmitted by any means without the
prior written permission of the publisher.